Gables of Legacy

VOLUME THREE

The SILVER LININGS

OTHER BOOKS AND BOOKS ON CASSETTE
BY ANITA STANSFIELD:

First Love and Forever

First Love, Second Chances

Now and Forever

By Love and Grace

A Promise of Forever

Home for Christmas

Return to Love

To Love Again

When Forever Comes

A Christmas Melody

For Love Alone

The Gable Faces East

Gables Against the Sky

The Three Gifts of Christmas

Towers of Brierley

A Star in Winter

Where the Heart Leads

When Hearts Meet

Someone to Hold

Reflections

Gables of Legacy Vol. 1: The Guardian

Gables of Legacy Vol. 2: A Guiding Star

TALK ON CASSETTE

Find Your Gifts, Follow Your Dreams

Gables of Legacy

VOLUME THREE

The SILVER LININGS

a novel

ANITA STANSFIELD

Covenant Communications, Inc.

Cover image, map © Photodisc, Inc./Getty Images; Cover image, lace photo by Leon Woodward.

Cover design copyrighted 2003 by Covenant Communications, Inc.

Published by Covenant Communications, Inc.
American Fork, Utah

Printed in the United States of America
First Printing: February 2003

10 09 08 07 06 05 04 03   10 9 8 7 6 5 4 3 2 1

ISBN 1-59156-168-X

Library of Congress Cataloging-in-Publication Data

Stansfield, Anita, 1961-
Silver linings : a novel / Anita Stansfield.
p. cm. -- (Gables of legacy ; v. 3)
ISBN 1-59156-168-X (alk. paper)
1. Mormon women--Fiction. I. Title

PS3569.T33354 S55 2003
813'.54--dc21   2002041282

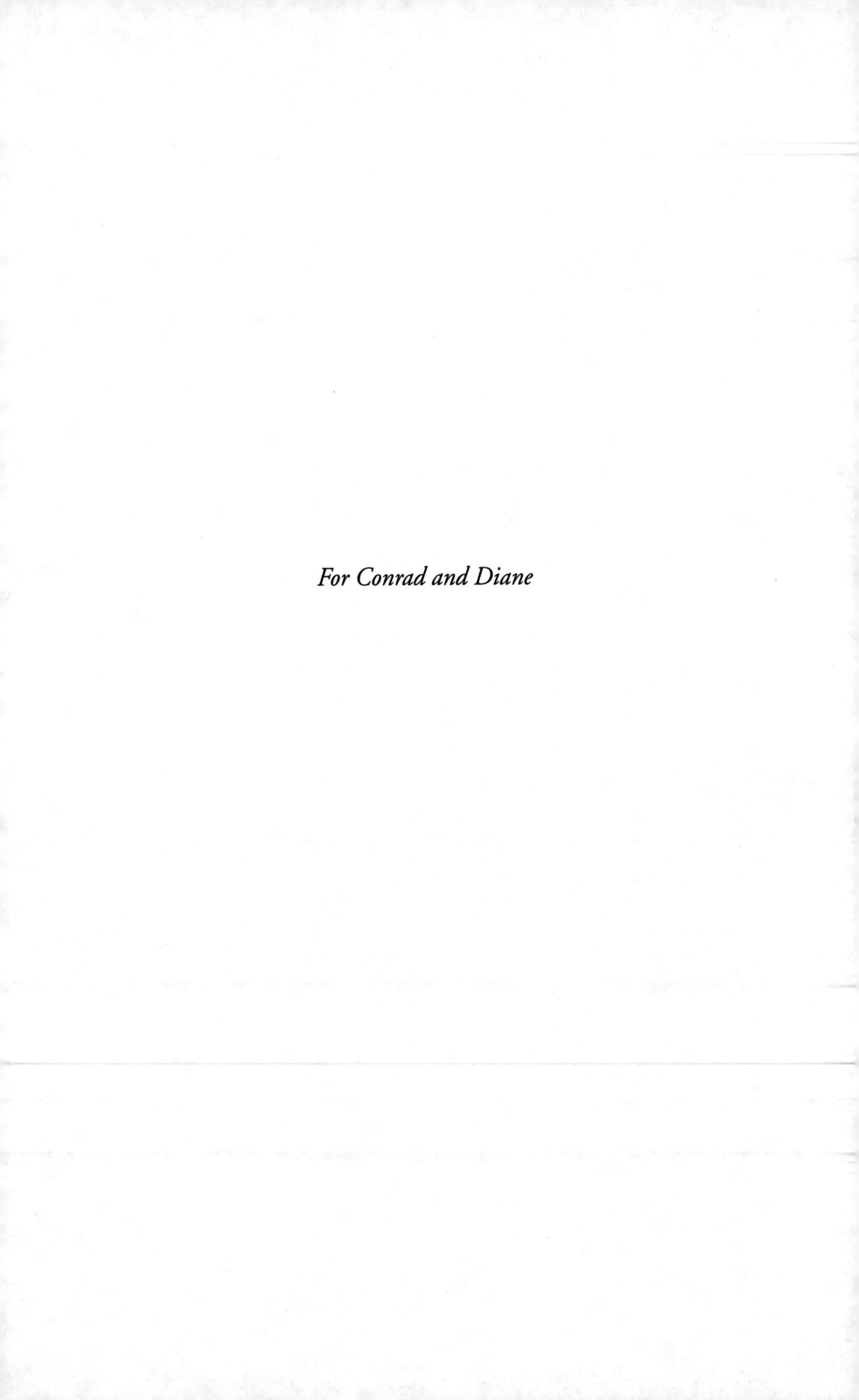

For Conrad and Diane

Chapter One

Tamra Banks stood on the side veranda of the fine Victorian home where she had lived the past several months, and looked out over the vast beauty of land and outbuildings that belonged to the Hamilton family. She felt certain there was nowhere more beautiful in all the world, especially in the early evening light. Deep in her heart she felt an abiding kinship with this place, as if she'd been born with an implanted homing beacon that had eventually led her here. And here she would stay.

In ten days she would be marrying Jess Michael Hamilton the fourth, and together they would begin yet another generation of this great family she was privileged enough to become a part of. Tamra felt an instinctive closeness to Jess's family members, both living and dead—though with some more than others. She had read every existing journal of his ancestors at least once, and she knew the stories well of how this land had first been homesteaded, and how the business of breeding and training horses had first begun. Tamra knew of the struggles that Jess's great-great-grandparents had gone through to preserve this land and acquire the fortune that eventually enabled them to build a boys' home and take in lost souls. The boys' home was an ongoing family legacy, which Tamra had been privileged to participate in through her work there, and her dreams for the future included taking a bigger part, with Jess at her side.

Considering her abuse-ridden childhood and the personal challenges she'd endured to become a member of the Church, she had to count herself one of the lost souls that the Hamilton family had taken in. But she was among the privileged few who would actually become a part of the family. And for that she was deeply grateful. She knew beyond any doubt that marrying Jess Hamilton was the right thing to do. And she knew Jess felt the same way. The months they had known each other had been filled with great joy and notable trauma. Together they had worked to free Jess from the lingering pain of his rebellious youth, and the accident that had killed his closest friend and his brother and sister-in-law. His pain had become so intense that he'd actually attempted to take his own life. But he had eventually risen above his depression and accepted the healing power of the Atonement.

Together they had confronted the residue of Tamra's troubled childhood, bridging chasms that had existed throughout her entire lifetime. With great milestones behind them, they had enjoyed a delightful Christmas celebration just yesterday with Jess's parents and his little niece, Evelyn, who had been orphaned in her infancy, due to the accident that Jess had barely survived. Tamra had quickly grown to love three-year-old Evelyn, as well as Jess's parents, Michael and Emily. And nothing could make her happier than sharing her life with all of them beneath the roof of this beautiful home, surrounded on every side by the magnificence of Australia.

Tamra was startled from her musings when she heard the door behind her open, then close.

"So, there you are," Jess said, putting his hands on her shoulders. "I thought you were lost."

"No." Tamra laughed softly and leaned back against his chest. "I've never been less lost in my life. In fact, I've just been thinking how thoroughly blessed I am." She turned to face Jess, looking into his blue-green eyes and touching the thick, dark hair that waved back off his face. Facing him eye to eye, she wasn't surprised to glance down and see his bare feet. He considered shoes a necessary evil and wore them only when he absolutely had to. And since he barely had two inches height advantage next to her five-foot-ten, not wearing shoes generally put Tamra on equal ground. But he seemed to like it that way. In fact, he was the only man she'd ever dated who seemed comfortable with her height, and he often encouraged her to wear heels in spite of the added inches.

Jess returned the gesture and brushed his fingers through the curly, red ponytail hanging down her back. "I'm the one who is blessed," he said, and kissed her quickly. "And the best part is that this is only the beginning; we have the rest of our lives to feel this way."

Tamra laughed softly and wrapped her arms around him. "My thoughts exactly."

A moment later, Jess's father opened the door and stepped outside. It was impossible to look at Michael and not see an older version of Jess; the resemblance was striking. He was lean and handsome, with gray mildly interspersed into his medium brown, short-cropped hair. The only other hints of his age were the lines in his face that were etched by the life he'd spent working in the sun. But there was an anxiousness in his expression that made Tamra mildly uneasy when he pushed the cordless phone toward her, saying, "Phone call for you."

"Really?" she said, taking the phone from him. Phone calls were rare for her, since most of the people she knew were far enough away that written communication was more practical.

"It's your father," Michael said and went back into the house.

Tamra felt her heart quicken. Was it the very fact that her father had called that made her nervous? Or was it the way Michael had made the announcement? Perhaps both.

Tamra had only gotten to know her father a matter of a few weeks earlier when she'd learned that her mother had purposely kept her out of his life, making her believe that he was a horrible man. But meeting him had proved otherwise. She had quickly grown to love her father and his wife of several years. Brady and Claudia had even initiated an early Christmas celebration while she and Jess had been in Tamra's hometown of Minneapolis in November. They had grown close through the experience, and had kept in touch through letters and e-mail ever since. But why would he call?

"Hello," she said into the phone.

"Ah, it's good to hear your voice," he said.

"And yours," she said, although she detected a hint of sadness in it.

"I wish I didn't have bad news," he said, and her heart quickened further.

Would he tell her that they wouldn't be able to make it to Australia for the wedding celebrations? Or worse . . . "Is it Grandma?" Tamra asked, hearing the panic in her own voice. Until last month she'd not even known she had a living grandmother. Rayna Banks had been living in a care center due to a stroke that had left her unable to speak, among other things. But Tamra had been able to follow her father's example of speaking openly to Rayna, and it quickly became evident that she understood all that was being said. Tamra warmed to her grandmother's strong spirit, and had quickly grown to love her. And now, she felt a deep dread that her first opportunity to get to know her grandmother may have been her last.

"Yes, Tamra," he said, "it is. I'm afraid that . . ." His voice cracked, and tears crept into Tamra's eyes. "She died in her sleep last night, honey. I thought you should know right away."

Tamra sank into a chair and pressed a hand over her mouth in an effort to hold back her emotion. Jess sat beside her and put a hand on her shoulder. His concern was evident as he waited to hear the news.

"Are you there?" Brady asked.

"Yes," Tamra said, unable to conceal the tears in her voice. Then it occurred to her that if the news were this difficult for her, how would her father be taking it? He had been caring for his mother for many years, and she knew well the great love and respect he had for her.

"Are you okay?" Tamra asked in a voice more steady.

"I will be, I'm sure," he said as if he didn't believe it. "But . . . it's rough. What can I say? I know she was old and tired, but . . . we're sure going to miss her."

"Yes, we will," Tamra said. "I'm just grateful I had the chance to know her."

Jess sighed as it became evident what the news was. He squeezed Tamra's hand, then kissed it.

"We're all grateful for that," Brady said. "She loved to look at the pictures I took when you were here. There's one with the two of you together that she wanted next to her bed. You were a great light in her life . . . as you are in mine."

"The feeling is mutual, Dad."

They talked a few more minutes before Jess whispered, "Ask him when the funeral is."

Tamra stopped talking midsentence and whispered back, "We can't possibly—"

"Just ask him," Jess insisted.

"Uh . . . Dad," Tamra said. "Do you know yet when the funeral is?"

"Not yet," he said, sounding surprised. "We have a meeting at the mortuary in an hour. I could call back, but I just assumed you wouldn't be able to make it, so I didn't think it would matter."

"Well, Jess wants to know," Tamra said, sharing her father's surprise. They had a wedding in ten days; flying to the States and back seemed a ridiculous prospect—in spite of how badly she yearned to be there.

"I'll call back then," Brady said, and they exchanged good-byes.

Tamra hung up the phone and looked hard at Jess. "What difference does it make? We can't possibly go to a funeral in Minneapolis when—"

"When what? The wedding is pretty much put together. Announcements have been mailed. Everything's arranged. Mother told me last night that there's little left to be done. Is that not true?"

Tamra thought about it. "Yes, I suppose so, but . . ."

While she struggled to come up with another protest, he added, "There are times when being well off has its advantages. I assure you we can afford to go to Minneapolis. It's your grandmother, Tamra. And you should be there for your dad." He sighed and leaned back in his chair. "I just feel like we should go. What do you feel?"

"I *want* to go, but . . ."

"But what?"

"I don't want to leave and put the burden of the wedding on your parents. We should be—"

"I already told you; it's under control. Everything's ordered and arranged. They can live without us. We can fly out, go to the funeral, fly back, and get past the jet lag before the big day arrives."

Tamra could hardly admit how grateful she was for his suggestion. The idea of the long flights was not appealing. But she truly wanted to be there. She was still contemplating the matter when he took hold of her hand and led her into the house. They found his parents in the lounge room with Evelyn. Emily was rebraiding Evelyn's reddish-gold hair, which rarely stayed in place for long. Michael was reading a book. They both looked up with concern in their faces when Jess and Tamra appeared in the doorway.

"Was it bad news?" Michael asked.

"My grandmother passed away," Tamra said.

"Oh, I'm so sorry," Emily said and rose to embrace Tamra. Jess's mother was as lovely as she was kind. Her ash-blonde hair was pulled back in a loose ponytail, and she wore only a hint of makeup. Like Michael, she was in good health, and only the mild lines in her face revealed the years of life she'd lived. Looking into Tamra's eyes she added, "Are you all right?"

"Of course," Tamra said, her chin quivering only slightly. "I'm just grateful I got to know her. I'm more concerned for my father and stepmother." They sat down and Emily returned to fixing Evelyn's hair, putting a little elastic around the bottom of the braid. "I have the gospel," Tamra said. "It's much easier to find peace with death when you understand the big picture."

"Well, perhaps this could be an opportunity to share some of your beliefs with your father," Michael suggested.

"Perhaps," Tamra said.

Once Evelyn's hair was finished, she rushed across the room to sit on Tamra's lap. Tamra held the child close and pressed a kiss into her soft, fine hair.

"All the more reason that we should go to the funeral," Jess said.

"Oh, you should," Emily said. "Everything's under control for the wedding. You've got plenty of time to go and get back."

Tamra noted Jess's smug gaze; if she hadn't known it was impossible, she might have accused them of conspiring. "Are you sure?" Tamra had to ask.

"Absolutely," Michael said. "These things are once-in-a-lifetime opportunities. I'd say if it's possible to attend, you should be there. Perhaps you'll have a chance to meet more of your relatives."

"Perhaps," Tamra said again. "I hadn't considered that."

A moment later, Jess said to his father, "What are you doing here, anyway?" Michael looked momentarily startled. "It's nice to see you and all, but aren't you usually attending to bishop's business about this time?"

Tamra wondered if she'd imagined a shadow passing across Michael's eyes, however briefly. He smiled casually and said, "Even bishops take a little time off once in a while."

"You okay?" Jess asked, making Tamra wonder if he'd sensed the same feelings, however subtle.

"Just a little under the weather," Michael said. "I'm certain my counselors will manage fine without me for one evening."

"Okay, well . . ." Jess rose to his feet, "I think I'll go call a travel agent."

"Wait," Tamra said. "Shouldn't you talk to my father first and find out when—"

"We know it will be in the next few days," Jess said. "The way I see it, the sooner we get out there, the better."

"Okay," Tamra said and rose as well. "In that case, I'll start packing." She took Evelyn's hand, saying, "You want to come help me?"

Evelyn nodded eagerly then said to her grandmother, "I go help Mama."

Tamra had been surprised on the first day she'd arrived at the station when Evelyn had called her "Mama." Tamra learned that Evelyn called many grown women that, apparently because of the absence of an actual mother in her life. For the same reason Evelyn had called Jess "Daddy." With time, though, she had stopped using the expression with anyone else. Tamra believed that little Evelyn had somehow instinctively known that she and Jess would be the ones to raise her, even though nothing had yet been said to anyone else.

Tamra watched Evelyn skipping up the hall just ahead of her and couldn't help but smile. She dearly loved the child, and enjoyed every moment with her. It seemed the most natural thing in the world to raise Evelyn as her own. Once the honeymoon was over, they would proceed with the technicalities.

Evelyn enjoyed helping Tamra put her things into a suitcase, naming each item as she did. When Tamra was as packed as she could be beyond things she would need in the meantime, she took Evelyn to the bathroom to bathe her.

"It's almost bedtime," Tamra said, removing Evelyn's shoes and socks. "If we hurry and get your bath done, Daddy will read you a story."

Sadie appeared in the doorway, asking, "Do you want me to do that?"

"No, I've got it under control," Tamra said. "Thank you anyway."

Sadie teased Evelyn a bit while Tamra ran the bath water. Sadie was more like a member of the family than an employee, but she did well at helping out wherever she was needed around the house. She was a slightly thick, rumpled woman, in her late fifties. Her gray hair was cut short and full of tight curls that clung close to her head, and she wore thick-rimmed glasses that framed her smiling eyes. Tamra had gotten to know her well upon her arrival here less than a year ago, and enjoyed helping Sadie with household chores that were hard on her arthritis.

Sadie left once Evelyn was in the tub. While the child splashed and played, a thought came forcefully to Tamra's mind. She nearly had a now-clean Evelyn in her pajamas when Jess appeared in the nursery, and she quickly told him what she was thinking.

"I believe we need to tell your parents our intentions concerning Evelyn—before we leave."

Jess looked a bit stunned, but he said, "Okay. But why?"

"I just . . . feel like we need to."

"Okay," he said again, "then we'd better do it as soon as Evelyn's put to bed. We'll be leaving early."

Tamra sat in the rocker while Jess knelt beside Evelyn's little bed and read her a story, using dramatic voices and making funny noises. Tamra loved watching them together this way. Jess's love for the child was evident, and a stark contrast to the time when he could hardly bear to look at her. Consumed with the loss of his brother and sister-in-law, Evelyn had once been little more to Jess than a painful reminder of their absence. But he had finally found peace with their deaths, and Evelyn had become a bright spot in his life. He helped Evelyn say her prayer and tucked her into bed, then he and Tamra went downstairs to find his parents, carrying the nursery monitor with them so they could hear Evelyn if she needed something.

"Good, you're still here," Jess said as they stepped into the lounge room. Emily was now reading a book and Michael the newspaper.

"What can we do for you?" Emily asked.

"Well," Jess said, sitting on one of the sofas with Tamra close beside him, "we'll be leaving early in the morning. Everything's arranged. But there's something we wanted to talk to you about before we go."

"Okay," Michael said, sitting up a little straighter.

Jess cast Tamra a long glance, making it evident that he didn't know where to begin. While Tamra felt certain she could manage, Jess was their son, and Evelyn was his brother's daughter. It was his place to tell them. She gave him a nod of encouragement, and he turned to face his parents again.

"You remember after I left here in October . . . and I did a lot of soul searching, fasting, and praying, and . . . that's when I finally was able to heal and come to terms with the pain of the accident and . . . everything."

"Of course we remember," Emily said. "It was a miracle. We had all been fasting and praying for you."

"Yes, I know," Jess said humbly. "And yes . . . it was. A miracle, that is. And when I came home, I walked in the house and saw Evelyn, and I picked her up, and that's when—"

"I remember that," Michael said. "It was the first time you'd ever held her at all, I believe. I'm assuming she had always been a reminder that her parents were gone."

"That's true," Jess said. "But when I had a change of heart, *everything* changed. When I saw Evelyn, I realized that very moment that she was a gift, that she had been left behind to remind us of James and Krista." Tears came to Emily's eyes. Jess smiled at her and continued. "The thing is . . . I also knew that James and Krista wanted *me* . . . and Tamra, of course . . . to raise her."

Michael and Emily didn't appear as surprised as Tamra had expected. They both smiled as Jess continued with vehemence. "I can't tell you how I know; I just *know*. I feel it with all my heart and soul. Tamra and I have talked about it, and she feels the same way. So . . . as soon as we're married, we want to make it official as quickly as possible. Of course, little will change technically, since we'll all be living here together anyway. But . . . well, we just wanted you to know how we feel, and we hope that it will be all right with you. You've been her guardians since you returned from your mission and . . ."

"I think it's perfect," Michael said.

"And if you must know, I think we felt it coming," Emily said. "Your father and I have even speculated over the possibility. It *does* feel right."

Jess took a deep breath, then laughed softly. Tamra tightened her hold on his hand.

"Okay," Jess said, "well, that's what we wanted to tell you. And I guess we should get some sleep. We're leaving pretty early."

"You're taking our plane to Sydney?" Michael asked. Tamra recalled flying home from Sydney with Jess piloting one of the family's planes. She'd thoroughly enjoyed the experience and had to admit that she appreciated this particular part of the family legacy. She knew from reading family journals that the family had purchased its first plane years before World War II. Having a plane became a great convenience, as isolated as they were. Eventually a piece of land had been cleared for a runway, so the planes didn't have to be brought down in the field, and a hangar had been built, less than ten minutes' drive from the house.

"That's the plan," Jess said. "And we're flying out from Sydney tomorrow evening."

"I'll drive you out to the hangar in the morning," Michael said before they left the room.

Jess left Tamra at the door of her room with a quick kiss and a reminder to set her alarm.

It was still dark the following morning when Jess and Tamra crept into Evelyn's room, guided by the light from the hall. Each of them placed a kiss on her little brow. "You know," Jess whispered, "with that red in her hair, people might actually think she belongs to you." He looked into her eyes and added, "She's almost as beautiful as you are."

"You're too kind," Tamra said and kissed his nose. She touched Evelyn's soft curls and they crept back into the hall.

* * *

Through the series of long flights, Tamra became preoccupied with the reality that her grandmother was gone. She found one bright spot in the matter—at least now she could do the temple work for this woman once the waiting period had passed. Following her mission, Tamra had become deeply involved in genealogy, and she'd seen that the work was done for all her ancestors as far back as she'd been able to find names. And now she could add Rayna Banks to family members on the other side of the veil who were endowed members of the Church. Tamra found peace in imagining her grandmother beyond the restrictions of this earth. Her crippled body had been set aside, and she was free from the physical struggles she'd dealt with since a stroke had taken so much from her. Tamra hadn't known her grandmother before the stroke, but she'd seen pictures, and it was easy to imagine how she might be now.

Jess and Tamra arrived in Minneapolis late. They quickly got two rooms in the same motel they'd stayed in on their previous visit. After sleeping late with the hope of wearing off some jet lag, they shared brunch at a nearby restaurant, and then went to Brady and Claudia's home. Brady answered the door and immediately drew Tamra into a firm embrace, making her feel that her presence alone was a great boon to him. Already, the miles they'd traveled felt worth it. Sensing that her father was too emotional to speak, Tamra drew back to look at him. A wan smile crept through his grieving countenance. It hadn't been so many weeks since they'd seen each other, but the change in his eyes was evident. The loss of his mother was hurting him deeply.

Apparently embarrassed by his emotional state, Brady pushed a hand through his hair and motioned them inside. Tamra got her height and red hair from her father, and she knew he'd gotten the red hair from his mother. In that moment, Tamra found it a touching symbol of the good that her grandmother had passed on.

Tamra's father then offered Jess a firm handshake and led them into the front room. Claudia appeared and Tamra embraced her as well.

"How are you, dear?" Claudia asked, smiling brightly as she always did. Her blonde hair hung past her shoulders, with more fluff than curl. While her skin looked like an older woman's, as if it had aged prematurely from a life spent in the sun, Claudia had a brilliantly youthful aura about her, enhanced by the sparkle in her eyes.

"A little tired, but fine," Tamra said as they were all seated. "How are you?"

"We're coming along," Claudia said, reaching for her husband's hand. "It's been especially hard for your father."

"How was your flight?" Brady asked.

"Good," Jess said. "Just long . . . but I think we're getting used to it."

An uneasy silence settled over the room until Tamra said, "What can we do to help? We didn't come to just sit around and chat. Tell us what we can do."

"Well, actually . . ." Claudia drawled, casting a cautious glance toward Brady, "we're supposed to have an outline for the program to the funeral home in a couple of hours, and we just don't know exactly how to go about it. Neither of us has ever been in charge of such a thing before. We'll be fortunate if the rest of her children show up for the funeral."

She made the statement with no sign of anger, but Tamra knew that her father had a brother and sister who lived out of state, and neither had ever helped care for their mother in the least. But Brady and Claudia had never resented caring for Rayna; if anything they had considered it a privilege, and the love amongst them had been evident. However, planning a funeral was a monumental task to take on alone.

"Let's take a look at what you have so far," Tamra said.

Brady lifted his head, some hope showing in his expression. Claudia rose, saying, "It's all in here."

They gathered around the dining table, where a notepad and pencil had been left. Brady slid the notepad across the table toward Tamra. On it was written her grandmother's full name, and the dates of her birth and death. She exchanged a quick glance with Jess, wanting to tell him how grateful she was for his insistence that they come.

"Okay," Tamra said, "do you have anyone in mind to officiate at the service or . . ." Brady and Claudia looked equally baffled. "A religious leader who can—"

"You know religion's not been a part of our lives," Brady said. "I know that Mom believed in God, and she believed in keeping the Ten Commandments, but . . . as far as religion itself . . . it was just never there."

Not wanting to overstep her bounds, Tamra said, "Is it something you want to be a part of the service?"

"Well," Brady drawled, "it would be appropriate I'm sure, but I wouldn't know where to begin or—"

"What I'm trying to ask, Dad, is . . . well, I'm certain I could make arrangements for a bishop to oversee the service, but I don't want to step on any toes or offend anyone."

"Oh, you wouldn't!" Claudia insisted. "I think that would be fine." She turned to her husband. "Do you have a problem with that?"

He hesitated and Tamra added, "I'm not talking about something overwhelming. But I do feel it would be a good thing."

Brady nodded and Tamra wondered if his hesitation was for religion in general, or more because his brain was clouded with the death of his mother.

"Okay, then," Tamra said, sensing that she needed to be direct here, "I can make some calls in a few minutes, but we need to have some general idea of what you want. Is there someone you want to speak? Any particular songs or—"

"'Amazing Grace,'" Brady said. "She loved that song."

"Do you know someone who would sing it or—"

"No, actually," he said sadly. "She just . . . loved that song."

"Anyone you want to speak?" Tamra asked.

"Well," Claudia said, "there's a woman who worked with Rayna at the care center; we asked her if she'd say a few words, and she said she'd love to. I thought Brady should talk about his mother, but . . . he's reluctant."

Brady's expression made this evident, but Tamra was taken completely off guard when he said, "I was hoping you could speak."

"Me?" Tamra chuckled uncomfortably. "I only met her last month. I don't—"

"Yes, but . . ." Brady took her hand across the table, "you felt a strong connection with her; I know you did. You don't have to say much." His eyes pleaded. "It would really mean so much to me if you would."

Tamra sighed. What could she do? "All right," she said, "I'll come up with something. Why don't I see if I can find a bishop and we'll go from there."

Claudia took Tamra to the den where there was a phone and a phone book. After a quick prayer, Tamra was glad to be left alone, not wanting her calls to be overheard. Ten minutes later she was frustrated, having made no progress, when Jess came into the room and closed the door behind him.

"Any luck?" he asked.

"No. The only people I know who are active in the Church live on the other side of the city, and we should probably work with someone more local. But we're not going to find anybody at the meetinghouses this time of day."

After a minute of silence, Jess said, "Hey, do you think anyone at the care center would have a suggestion? As missionaries we were assigned to regularly visit a care center. Perhaps there's someone who—"

"That's a great idea," Tamra said and found the number for the care center where Rayna had been living. A few minutes later she had a number for some missionaries, who happened to be home for lunch. They gave her the number of the bishop for that area, and Tamra spoke with his wife, who gave her the bishop's work number. Bishop Williams eagerly agreed to be a part of the funeral. He gave Tamra the number of the Relief Society president and one of the counselors, just in case she couldn't be reached. Tamra found the president at home, and following a ten-minute conversation, she emerged from the den to announce, "A couple of ladies are coming over who will help us put it all together."

"Oh, how nice," Claudia said. Brady looked indifferent. Tamra's heart went out to him; she sensed his grief was deep, but she didn't know what to say. If religion had never been a part of his life, he likely had no comprehension of the full spectrum of an eternal plan. But Tamra needed the right opportunity to share her feelings with him. For now, she just sat beside him and took his hand. His smile let her know that her silent concern was appreciated.

Sisters Morris and Clayton arrived right on time. Tamra couldn't help being pleased at the way they showed compassion toward Brady and Claudia, and asked all the right questions. They offered suggestions and options for a program, and Brady was eager to let them take the assignment of getting someone to sing "Amazing Grace," and to arrange for some appropriate hymns. They also offered to see that all of the flowers were transported from the funeral home, to the cemetery, and then to Brady and Claudia's home. And they insisted on putting on a luncheon after the funeral at a church building near the care center. Brady and Claudia were obviously impressed, even amazed—especially when they realized these ladies were not expecting to be compensated for their efforts. Together they arranged a program, and Sister Morris offered to fax it from her home to the mortuary to save them a trip.

After the sisters left, Claudia asked Tamra, "Are all members of your Church so kind and giving?"

"Well," Tamra chuckled, "we have all kinds of people, just like any other religion. Some are better at being compassionate and warm than others, but . . . most of them are pretty good at it."

Brady seemed a little more relaxed as they all went out to eat, then they returned to the house just a short while before Bishop Williams came by with one of his counselors. He too offered sympathy, then he kindly explained the procedure and purpose of the family prayer and dedication of the grave. When he assured Brady that his mother had gone on to a better place, Brady eagerly asked, "How do you know?"

The bishop and his counselor answered Brady's and Claudia's questions for nearly an hour. After the two men left, Brady and Claudia continued to ask Jess and Tamra more questions. Finally, they all had to admit they were tired; Jess and Tamra reluctantly left for the night.

Driving toward their motel, Tamra couldn't hold back a little laugh. "That was incredible," she said. "I think we covered the entire plan of salvation at least twice."

"Yeah," Jess chuckled softly, "I think it's a good thing we came."

"Me too," Tamra said, squeezing his hand. "Thank you."

"My pleasure."

Tamra had barely crawled into bed when the phone rang. She picked it up and heard her father say, "Those things you said awhile ago . . . Will you talk about that when you speak at the funeral? Just a bit about that life after death stuff and . . . I like what you said about this world just being a step in an eternal progression, and that she's just . . . gone home. Will you do that?"

"I would be happy to, Dad," she said.

He sighed deeply, as if he'd feared she would decline. "I thank God you came back into my life when you did, Tamra Sue—and I thank God you came here today. I don't know what I'd do without you."

"I'm glad to be here, Dad. And I thank God that we're together as well. You're a good man, and I'm proud to know you're my father."

Tamra sensed his tender emotions as he told her goodnight, and she fell asleep feeling a deep hope for her father. She couldn't imagine how much joy it would give her to see him embrace the gospel. But she had to tread carefully and let him dictate the pace.

On their way to her father's home the next morning, Tamra told Jess about the phone call with her father. Again she admitted, "I'm so glad we came. Who knows what kind of opportunities we might have missed if we hadn't?"

"My thoughts exactly," he said and squeezed her hand.

Chapter Two

The viewing and funeral all came together smoothly. A warm spirit encompassed the service, and Tamra got through her talk with little difficulty. She was disappointed that she didn't see her brother there, since Brady had told her he'd called to let Mel know of his grandmother's death. She wasn't surprised at Mel's reluctance to be involved with this side of the family, since he had strong ties with their mother, who had spent her life bad-mouthing Brady Banks. But Tamra had made great progress with her mother, and she was determined to be grateful for the bridges that had been built, however small they might be, and not to be concerned for the lack of closeness they shared. She figured they should stop to see her mother and brother before they left town, but she would worry about that later.

Tamra was touched to hear Jess dedicate the grave. Afterward, as Brady shook his hand and thanked him for such a beautiful prayer, Jess admitted humbly, "It was a great honor, I can assure you."

At the luncheon, Tamra had the opportunity to meet her father's siblings and some of their family members. They seemed like decent people, though somewhat hard, and not terribly warm. It was evident that her father was the cream of the crop.

Tamra wasn't surprised at how nice the luncheon was, or at how gracious the ladies were who served the food. But Brady and Claudia were obviously impressed. While they ate, Tamra briefly explained the Relief Society and how it functioned. She couldn't help being pleased with their ongoing interest.

Bishop Williams stopped to chat with them for a few minutes before leaving, and Brady thanked him profusely for all he had done.

"It was a pleasure," Bishop Williams said. "And if there's ever anything else we can do, you have my phone number."

After he'd walked away, Brady said, "He's really a nice guy, but I expected him to wear one of those fancy robes or something."

Jess and Tamra couldn't help chuckling. "I believe that's a different church," Tamra explained. "A white shirt and tie are pretty standard for our priesthood holders."

"Does he get paid for what he does for the Church?" Claudia asked.

"No, it's all volunteer time," Jess said. "Bishop Williams told me he's the CEO of a large firm."

"Really?" Claudia said. "And none of your Church leaders get paid for their church work?"

"Nope," Jess said. "In fact, my father is a bishop."

Brady chuckled. "I'll look forward to meeting him."

"Are you still planning to come for the wedding?" Tamra asked, fearing what the answer might be considering all that had happened. She knew her father had missed time at work, and the last few days had been a strain for them.

"We wouldn't miss it," Claudia said. "Our plans haven't changed."

Tamra was delighted, and she noticed that her father didn't seem nearly as tense and upset as he had when they'd first arrived. She had to hope that some of the things he'd learned about life after death had eased his concerns and given him some measure of peace. And beyond that, she hoped that eventually he would want to further pursue his interest in the gospel.

It wasn't difficult to say good-bye to Brady and Claudia, knowing they would see each other again soon. But Tamra found herself apprehensive about the quick stop they planned to make at the bar her mother owned. Their visits in the past had been tense at best, and more likely upsetting. But since then Tamra had written her mother to offer forgiveness for the ill feelings she'd harbored, and her mother had, in turn, sent a lovely card and gift for Christmas. She couldn't leave town without stopping to at least thank her for the gift and see how they were doing.

Entering the bar at the least busy time of day, Tamra found her mother and brother exactly where she'd expected. Mel stood like the proverbial bartender, polishing glasses and visiting with his mother, Myrna, while she did a crossword puzzle and smoked a cigarette. Tamra's nerves eased somewhat when her mother's expression was void of the usual cynicism. She actually suspected that her mother was glad to see her.

"You came for the funeral?" her mother asked.

"That's right," Tamra said, offering her mother a quick embrace, however awkward. She then added to her brother, "I was hoping to see you there."

"Had to work," he said, but she felt a subtle warmth from him that had been absent in the past. Perhaps the Christmas gift she'd given him had softened him up a bit.

Tamra turned her attention back to her mother, "I just wanted to thank you for the card and gift you sent. It really meant a lot."

"Glad you liked it," Myrna said, glancing at the floor. Looking up she added, "We got the wedding announcement; nice picture."

"Wish you could be there," Jess said, then silence descended.

"So how was the funeral?" Myrna asked.

"It was nice," Tamra said. They chatted for just a few minutes and exchanged casual good-byes, but Tamra left feeling better about her relationship with her mother than she'd ever felt in her life. They could never be anything but congenial; however, it was a far cry from what it had been in the past.

The flights home were long, and Tamra found it difficult to sleep much. But she felt deeply grateful for the opportunities that had come through this visit. And now they were going home—with her wedding only a few days off once they arrived. She thought of her grandmother on the other side of the veil, and imagined her there with all of the people she loved that Tamra had done temple work for. *She's gone home,* Tamra thought, then she drifted to sleep with Jess's hand in hers.

* * *

Tamra was relieved beyond words to arrive home at last. She felt exhausted and wondered how she would ever catch up on her rest in order to feel at her best for the wedding. Michael and Emily drove out to the hangar to pick them up, bringing Evelyn along. It was so good to see the child, and Tamra marveled at how much she'd missed her.

That evening at supper, Michael said, "There's something we need to talk about with the two of you . . . a little later."

"What's wrong with now?" Jess asked.

Emily said gently, "It would be better to wait until Evelyn goes to bed, I think."

Tamra felt a concern that she knew Jess shared when he glanced in her direction, his brow furrowed. After Evelyn got her bedtime story and was tucked in, they found Michael and Emily in the lounge room.

"So, what's up?" Jess asked, sitting on the sofa with Tamra beside him.

"Well," Michael said in a tone that implied bad news, "the timing is rather ironic, but . . ."

When he hesitated, Emily said, "Amee called a couple of days ago, Jess, and . . ."

When she hesitated, Jess demanded, "Is everything all right? Is she—"

"She's fine," Michael said. "Her family is fine; it's nothing like that."

"Then what's the problem?" Jess asked, his confusion evident.

"The thing is," Emily went on, "she called to tell us that they want to adopt Evelyn."

"What?" Jess shouted, jumping to his feet.

"Sit down, son," Michael said. "We need to talk about this rationally and—"

"But how can she just . . . all of sudden want to take Evelyn when—"

"Sit down," Michael repeated, putting a hand on his arm.

Jess did so, but his frustration was evident. In an attempt to follow Michael's advice, and talk about this rationally, Tamra asked, "Did you tell her that Jess and I want to—"

"Yes," Emily said, "I told her what you told me."

Tamra suddenly felt grateful for the prompting she'd gotten to tell Michael and Emily their intentions to adopt Evelyn, prior to leaving the country.

"She reacted much the same way you just did," Emily said. "She feels like Evelyn is supposed to be in her home."

"Great," Jess said with sarcasm. "So, now what? We have a custody battle and—"

"No, we will not!" Emily said. "We're family, and we will work this out in a mature, dignified manner. I understand Amee's feelings. She and Randy took guardianship of Evelyn when we left on our mission, but that last baby was unexpected and Randy started traveling more with his job, so Evelyn came here to stay with Sadie just until we could get home. But I know Amee's family loves Evelyn very much."

"So, what are you saying, Mother?" Jess asked. "Are you saying you're siding with Amee here?"

"I'm not *siding* with anything but what's right for Evelyn. God knows which home she belongs in, and He is where we need to turn for a solution."

Jess was more calm as he said, "I know in my heart that she's meant to be with us, Mother."

"Then you need to call your sister and tell her how you feel."

"But if she feels the same way, then . . ."

"Just call and talk to her; tell her how you feel. And we'll go from there."

Jess looked at his mother as if she'd just asked him to clean all the bathrooms in the house. Tamra suspected he'd rather clean the bathrooms, given the choice.

"Amee's not known for being easy to talk to," Jess said.

"Yes, well . . . she's still your sister, and that's where you have to start."

"How about a prayer?" Michael offered.

Jess sighed audibly. "That would be great, thanks," Jess said, looking into Tamra's eyes. She shared his concerns without a word being spoken between them, and she felt certain he knew it. She too felt that Evelyn was meant to be raised by them, and she didn't want this development putting a damper on their wedding, especially since Amee and her husband were supposed to be in the temple with them. She didn't want to start out their life together with strained feelings in the family.

In a way that was typical of their family prayers, they all knelt together and Michael offered a prayer that perfectly expressed Tamra's concerns. He asked that they would all be guided toward the Lord's will, and that the outcome would be what was best for Evelyn. He asked for hearts to be softened, and he prayed that all would go well for the wedding. He thanked Heavenly Father for Jess and Tamra's safe return, and expressed gratitude for having such a wonderful family, and for the love they shared. When his voice broke with emotion, Tamra had to wonder if this dispute between his children was weighing more heavily on Michael than he was letting on. Or was there something else?

Jess went straight to the phone to call Amee, saying as he dialed the number, "I'll never be able to sleep until I talk to her." Since he stayed in the same room to use the phone, it was evident that he wasn't opposed to being overheard. Michael and Emily stayed where they were, and Tamra did the same.

Following some strained small talk, Jess explained his feelings about raising Evelyn as his own. Tamra felt proud of the way he communicated what was in his heart without discrediting Amee's feelings. While he was obviously listening to whatever Amee had to say, Tamra sensed him becoming tense. Jess said little, but what he said was defensive and bordering on angry. Tamra heard Emily gasp when Jess said in a harsh voice, "He was *my* full-blooded brother." A moment later he slammed the phone down and groaned.

"That was completely inappropriate," Emily said, and Jess turned startled eyes toward her. "From the moment your father asked me to marry him, this family has never put *step* or *half* at the beginning of any relationship. It was your father's first marriage and my second, but he raised my daughters with as much love and concern as he raised our own children. The amount of blood you share with James has no bearing on this situation, whatsoever, and I think you owe your sister an apology."

Jess was relatively calm as he folded his arms over his chest and responded. "You're right, Mother, what I said was inappropriate and it has no bearing. I spoke in anger. But I think it wouldn't hurt for you to let my *sister* know that my rebellious youth and one attempted suicide have no bearing on this situation, either."

"She *said* that?" Emily gasped.

"She did," Jess said. "Next thing I know, she'll be telling me I don't deserve to raise my brother's child because I was driving the car he was killed in."

"She wouldn't," Emily insisted.

"I'm not so sure," Jess said and left the room. Tamra followed, praying that they could somehow get beyond this before the tension became any deeper.

Jess had little to say before he left Tamra at the door of her bedroom, but he eagerly responded to her suggestion that they begin a fast right then in order to know for certain they were pursuing the right course.

"And we must accept the Lord's will in this," she added gently, "whatever it may be."

Jess inhaled roughly. "Yes, of course," he said and moved down the hall toward his own room. He hesitated and turned back, adding, "Do you think I'm deluding myself when I believe in my heart that she's meant to be with us?"

"If you are," Tamra said, "then I am too. If we fast and pray, keeping an open mind, we'll know what the Lord wants us to do."

Jess nodded, offered a weak smile and went on to his room.

Tamra fell asleep praying, and woke up doing the same. The bulk of her day was spent consumed with wedding preparations, while Jess accompanied his father seeing to business in the stables and at the boys' home. Raising horses and wayward boys had been the family's work for generations. The two businesses were largely overseen by Michael, and Jess worked with him at every possible opportunity, helping where he was needed with the intention of taking it all over one day. Tamra knew his heart reached more toward the boys' home, as hers did, and it was easy to imagine the two of them living out their lives together, raising a family and working together to help the boys who came into their lives.

Jess and Tamra ate a late supper, long after the others had finished and Evelyn had been put to bed. They shared a long prayer both before and after the meal, then they cleaned up the kitchen and sought out Michael and Emily, who were seated on the veranda, holding hands. Their somber moods made Tamra wonder if they'd been discussing something difficult. Or perhaps they were just concerned about the issue standing between Jess and Amee; that was certainly difficult enough.

"What can we do for you?" Michael asked, motioning for them to sit down.

They sat close together holding hands before Jess said, "We have just finished fasting, and we've both done a lot of praying. We both feel more strongly than ever that Evelyn is meant to be raised here, with us as her parents. But . . . I don't know how to convince Amee of what I feel without making her angry."

Emily sighed, then smiled. "If you must know, your father and I both feel the same way. We believe she is meant to be with you."

Jess slumped visibly with relief. Tamra knew that having his parents' support meant a great deal to him. He lifted his face to look at his parents, asking humbly, "Would you talk to her? I'm afraid my emotions will get the better of me, that I'll get too defensive, even angry again. Will you?"

Emily sighed again. "I'll do my best."

"Thank you," Jess said.

* * *

Emily watched Jess and Tamra walk away, and Michael went into the house a few minutes later. Alone with her thoughts, Emily wondered why such a situation had to come up *now*. Of course she wanted the wedding to be perfect. She wanted to see her family gathered in the temple with no strained feelings between them. Jess and Tamra had been through so much, and they deserved to be happy together; they deserved to have their wedding free of discord and difficulty. But there were circumstances pending that the children were unaware of. Michael had made it clear he didn't want anyone else to know what was weighing on them until after the wedding. She understood his reasoning, but she couldn't help wondering if their knowing would help them see how petty such arguments could be. Of course, Evelyn's well being was anything but petty. Still, she sensed that for all her daughter's good intentions, there was some level of selfishness in her attitude. She'd told Jess she would talk to Amee, and

God willing, she would know what to say that might soften her heart and put this problem to rest.

Emily found Michael in his office on the main floor of the house. He was staring at the wall with a faraway look that had become familiar lately. But she couldn't think too hard about his reasons, or she'd simply fall apart. And right now, she didn't have time to fall apart.

"Hey there," she said, startling him. He smiled when he saw her, and she felt a momentary awareness of the full breadth of happiness he had brought into her life. For a moment she was speechless, too overcome with a mixture of heady emotions. She finally forced them back and smiled in return. "I need to call Amee," she said. "I was hoping you'd hold my hand."

"Of course," he said, reaching his hand toward her.

Emily scooted a chair close to his and picked up the phone. Once she'd dialed the number, she slipped her hand into Michael's and felt him squeeze it gently.

"Hello, sweetie," Emily said when Amee answered. "How are you doing?"

"Okay, I guess," she said as if she were lying.

"I assume you're still upset about Evelyn."

"Can you blame me?" Amee retorted.

Emily said nothing. She'd spoken to Amee the previous day and her efforts to point out that Amee's comments to Jess had been inappropriate had ended their conversation on a less-than-congenial note. She was hoping to keep a better spirit to this phone call, and prayed in her heart that Amee would soften herself enough to listen.

"We need to resolve this before the wedding," Emily said. "It's important for us to be together as a family and not have ill feelings."

"Well, if Jess would—"

"I need you to listen to me, Amee," Emily said gently. "Jess and Tamra have been fasting and praying. And you need to do the same."

"I guess I can, but it's not going to make any difference."

"No, it certainly won't," Emily said, "if that's the attitude you take into it. You have to be willing to find out what the Lord's will is in this, and then be willing to accept it. He knows where Evelyn is meant to be raised."

Amee's voice still sounded acrid when she said, "Well, maybe I don't want to fast and pray because I don't want to be told no."

"Is that what you think the answer will be?"

"I don't know. I just . . . want this to happen, and I'm afraid that . . ."

"Listen, Amee, if it's not the Lord's will for Evelyn to be raised in your home, can you honestly approach every challenge of raising a child, knowing deep inside that the Lord wanted her elsewhere? If you don't have the conviction in your heart that it's right, you can't possibly expect to have the Lord guide you in caring for her."

Amee was silent a long moment then said humbly, "Okay. I'll fast and pray."

"Good," Emily said, relief filling her completely, "and Randy should as well. This involves him as much as you."

"He will, of course."

"As I said," Emily added, "Jess and Tamra have been doing the same."

"And what if we get different answers?"

"Then we'll know that somebody is letting their own desires get in the way of the Spirit, and we'll have to try again."

Amee said little else and hurried to get off the phone. What could Emily do but pray that all would turn out well, and press forward with wedding plans? The family had endured many challenges, and she had no doubt they would successfully endure many more—some worse than others. But at the moment, this particular issue weighed heavily on her. It meant more to her than anyone could ever know to see her family united in the temple, peacefully. She had learned long ago, however, that her children were free agents, and life didn't always turn out the way she hoped. In this case, she prayed for a miracle. Under the circumstances, she could really use one.

* * *

Once again Jess listened to the recording on Amee's phone, and once again he left the same message. His sister had not called since that last conversation she'd had with their mother, and with the repeated attempts that he and Emily had made to call Amee, it was becoming evident that Amee didn't want to talk to them. While Jess couldn't help hoping that her reasons were wounded pride in having gotten the same answer that he'd gotten, he would feel uneasy until they were able to talk and clear the air. He couldn't keep from wondering if her reasons for cutting them off were related to a determination to get custody of Evelyn, with or without the approval of anyone else in the family. Would she get an attorney? Let it come between them?

Tamra repeatedly assured him that if Evelyn was meant to be with them, it would all work out. *But at what price?* he wondered. He wanted to get married without this dark cloud hanging over them. But he certainly couldn't do any more about it than he'd already done, so he did his best to put it to the back of his mind and focus on his forthcoming marriage to Tamra. The very idea of being her husband made everything that had ever gone wrong in his life seem right. She was amazing and he loved her. He only prayed that the wedding would come together without discord in the family.

Later that day, Jess found Tamra at one end of the lawn taking down clean sheets that had been hung to dry. When he realized she hadn't seen him, he sneaked carefully behind her and grabbed her. She shrieked and turned to hit him, laughing as he wrapped her in the sheet she'd just taken down. With her arms useless inside the sheet he started tickling her and she collapsed in a heap, kicking and screaming and laughing all at once. Jess stood back to catch his breath and admire his work while she wormed out of the sheet, yelling at him between her bouts of laughter.

He caught a movement from the corner of his eye and looked up to see his mother standing at the nursery window. She smiled at him and he waved comically. Tamra took advantage of the distraction and threw a sheet over his head, wrestling him to the ground to tickle his bare feet while he was too tangled in a king-sized sheet to stop her.

"Wretched woman," he growled once he'd wormed his way out. She ran away from him, letting the sheet flow out behind her like the cape of a superhero. He ran after her, following her in circles on the lawn until he caught hold of the other end of the sheet. Hand over hand he pulled her closer while she held the other end of the sheet. She gazed at him with a meaning in her eyes that completely dispelled his humor by the time she was close enough for him to reach out and take her into his arms. He kissed her as if the world might begin and end in that moment, then on a hunch he glanced up to see that his mother was still standing at the window. She smiled serenely. He smiled back and kissed Tamra again, wondering if his mother knew how it felt to be this happy. He felt certain she did.

The following morning, Emily announced at breakfast, "Your father and I are going into town later this morning; we'll be gone until evening, I believe. Everything's under control, so you should manage fine without us."

"What's up?" Jess asked, sensing something unusual in his mother's attitude.

"It's a private matter, for the time being," Emily said while she focused on clearing the breakfast table.

Jess wanted to demand, *What's that supposed to mean?* In all his life he couldn't recall his parents not giving some explanation for an outing, even if it was simply, *We just need some time away.* A glance from his father made it evident that questions would be left unanswered, so he said nothing. But the minute his parents drove away, he said to Tamra, "What do you suppose that's all about?"

"I don't know," she said as if it were nothing. "Maybe they just need to get out for a while. They've both been terribly busy with the wedding, and your father's always got Church business."

"If that's the case, why didn't they just say so?" he asked, as if she should have the answer.

"I don't know, Jess. Obviously it's none of our business. Are you worried?"

"Yes, I think I am."

"Well, if it's something to worry about, I'm sure they'll tell us. But I think you're just nervous in general. They're probably just . . . helping a family in the ward with a crisis, and since it's confidential, they didn't want to be specific."

"Okay," Jess said, liking that idea. "But they could have said, 'We're going to help a family with a crisis.' That would be more like them. They wouldn't have to tell us who or what."

"You know what, Jess," Tamra said, lifting Evelyn out of her booster seat beside the table. "You're getting all worked up over something that's none of our business. So . . . think about the wedding instead; get nervous over that. After all, in a couple of days, you can't back out. It'll be too late—you'll be stuck with me forever."

"Stuck?" he laughed. "Oh no, I'll be the happiest man alive. It's you who will be stuck."

"Never." Tamra laughed as well. "You will be no happier than me, I can assure you."

Jess and Tamra spent the day going over checklists for the wedding and packing their bags while they took turns watching over Evelyn. The following day they would be leaving for Sydney to meet friends and family members at a hotel near the temple where they would all be staying. Jess's sister, Emma, who was the only member of the family who hadn't yet been through the temple, would be watching over their nieces and nephews at the hotel during the wedding. Afterward, other family members and friends who were unable to attend the temple ceremony would join them at the same hotel to share a meal and celebrate the marriage. Jess and Tamra would then spend their wedding night in Sydney and honeymoon their way back home to celebrate with a reception at the house. Everything was as prepared as it possibly could be. For Jess, there were only two concerns. The first was whether or not Amee would even show up at the wedding due to her disgruntlement over Evelyn. And the second was his parents' mysterious trip to town.

"You know," Jess said to Tamra as they sat down to eat supper on the veranda with Evelyn. "I was thinking . . . maybe my parents are having marital problems. Maybe they're getting counseling and they don't want anyone to know."

Tamra shot him an appalled glare and shook her head. "Speculating will only drive you crazy, my dear. They are the most happily married people I've ever known. When they're ready to tell us what's going on, they'll tell us—if it's even worth telling. Just relax and forget about it."

Jess sighed and tried to convince himself that she was right, but he couldn't let go of an uneasy feeling that something was wrong.

Michael and Emily returned looking tired but perfectly normal, as if nothing in the world was wrong. Once greetings were exchanged, Emily asked, "Did you hear from Amee?"

"No, and I tried twice more to call her."

"I hope nothing's wrong," Emily said.

"The only thing wrong," Michael said, "is that she has caller ID and she doesn't want to talk to us. Let's just hope that Amee and Randy won't let the situation keep them from coming to the wedding as planned." He put his arm around Emily's shoulder and kissed her brow. "Everything will be fine, my love. The wedding's going to be perfect."

"I like that optimism," Tamra said. "Your son could stand to be a whole lot more like you."

"I'm working on it," Jess said. "But then . . . he's had a lot more practice at being optimistic; he's got a lot of years on me."

Michael chuckled. "I hope you're not trying to call me old."

"Of course not," Jess said, exaggerating his astonishment. "Mature; that's what I meant to say—you're mature."

Michael laughed, but stopped abruptly when Jess asked, "So, how did it go in town?"

Following a long moment of strained silence, Michael said, "As good as could be expected."

While Jess was wondering what he might ask to further satisfy his curiosity, Michael left the room hastily, obviously upset. Following such an abrupt gesture, Jess found it easier to say to his mother, "Something's wrong, isn't it?"

Emily sighed, then stated firmly, "Your father has a lot on his mind right now. All the two of you need to worry about is getting married—and enjoying every minute of it. These are precious days for the two of you, so make the most of them."

She smiled and left the room. Jess turned to meet Tamra's eyes. He felt certain she understood his growing uneasiness, but instinctively he knew his mother was right. He and Tamra needed to focus on the wedding, and enjoy every minute of it. He only prayed that once they were married the problem would be settled—whatever it was.

Chapter Three

Tamra's stomach filled with irrepressible butterflies as the small plane rose into the air and circled over the Byrnehouse-Davies and Hamilton station below. With Michael flying the plane, Jess sat between Tamra and Evelyn, who was securely buckled into her seat. She giggled when Jess pointed out the seemingly tiny horses in the corrals below.

"I'm always amazed at how beautiful it looks from up here," Emily commented.

"It?" Michael asked.

"Our home," she clarified. "I'll never forget when you brought me here with the girls, not long before *we* were married."

Michael smiled at his wife. "It was a pretty exciting day for me, too. But that wasn't the first time you came here."

"No," Emily heaved a nostalgic sigh, "coming here in college was pretty exciting as well."

"If we'd only known then . . ." Michael began, then became distracted as he took the plane to a higher altitude and headed south.

"What?" Emily asked. "How much trouble we were in for?"

"That too." Michael chuckled then glanced over his shoulder at Jess, Tamra, and Evelyn. "But I was going to say, 'If we'd only known then how happy we would be together, what would we have thought?'"

Tamra reached for Jess's hand. It was easy to imagine feeling much the same way many years ahead. Michael and Emily had endured many struggles and a great deal of heartache, but their happiness and their love for each other were deeply evident. Tamra wasn't so naïve as to think that marrying Jess would be the beginning of a blissful happily ever after. She knew their life together would have struggles and challenges, because that was the very nature of life. But she also knew in her heart that what they could accomplish together would far outweigh what either of them could have ever done alone. If they could share their lives with love and respect, living the gospel, raising a family, and trying to make the world just a little bit better, she could ask for no more than that.

"I love you," she whispered, and his smile provoked a fresh surge of butterflies. Tomorrow they would be married, and the dream she had once hardly dared entertain would then come true. Her wedding gown was carefully stowed in the back of the plane, along with everything else they needed to be married and embark on their honeymoon.

Jess kept Evelyn entertained the first hour of the flight with little trouble, then she became restless and whiny and they had to use a little more ingenuity. Emily gave them a few ideas, saying, "Your father and I flew from Utah to Queensland when Amee was about that age, and Alexa was one."

"How did you manage?" Tamra asked.

"I have no idea," Emily chuckled.

Evelyn finally drifted to sleep, allowing a calm reprieve for the remainder of the flight.

Tamra's excitement increased when they arrived in Sydney. When Jess kept laughing for no apparent reason, she had little doubt that he felt the same way. After they had arrived at the hotel and settled into their rooms, Emily went over a checklist with them to make certain they had everything they needed. When all was in order, everyone took a few minutes to freshen up before they went downstairs to a meeting room they had reserved for the family to gather. The only family member who actually lived in Sydney was Tamra's Aunt Rhea, her mother's sister. She was the first to arrive.

Rhea wore her bleached blonde hair ratted and poofed around her head. She wore high heels that were a pink similar to her lipstick, and dangling earrings in an equally flamboyant yellow, which matched her sweater. She wore a floral skirt in the same colors, over a figure that was far too thin, in Tamra's opinion. She was built much like Tamra's mother, with a thinness that became unattractive with all the smoking and drinking they did. But Rhea handled her liquor much better than Tamra's mother ever had, and she had eventually quit smoking after her husband had died of a stroke.

Rhea squealed with delight when she saw Tamra. They shared laughter and a firm embrace before Rhea took a step back and smiled through her bright lipstick. "How are you, dear?" Rhea asked. "I mean . . . I get your letters and I know what's been going on, of course, but . . . you're getting married tomorrow."

"Yes, I am," Tamra said and laughed again. "I'm great. How are you?"

"Couldn't be better. Oh, and here's the lucky groom." She grinned at Jess as he approached, and they too shared an embrace. "And how are you, young man?"

"Happy," he grinned and took Tamra's hand.

"Well, that's the way it should be," Rhea said. Tamra then turned to introduce her aunt to Jess's parents. "Rhea, I'd like you to meet Michael and Emily Hamilton, my almost-in-laws—Jess's parents. And this is my Aunt Rhea."

"It is such a pleasure," Michael said, eagerly shaking Rhea's hand.

"The pleasure's all mine," Rhea said. "Tamra's told me so much about you in her letters; what wonderful people you are."

"She's told us how wonderful *you* are," Emily said, shaking Rhea's hand as well. "Come sit down; let's visit."

Before they were seated, Rhea's attention was drawn to Evelyn, who was putting a puzzle together on the floor. "Oh, this must be little Evelyn," Rhea said, squatting down beside the child. "Hello there, little one," Rhea said, and Evelyn looked up with curious eyes. "I'm Auntie Rhea," she said in a singsong tone, "and I've brought you a little present."

Rhea reached into her purse and pulled out a large plastic locket on a pink cord, with a tiny dolly inside. Evelyn let out a delighted giggle as Rhea put the cord around her neck and showed her how to get the dolly out.

"Bribery," Rhea said, standing up straight. "Works every time."

Jess chuckled and Rhea added, "That's why Tamra came to my house every day after school when she was a little girl. It was bribery."

"You made great cookies," Tamra admitted. "But I think your company also had something to do with it."

Rhea smiled and sat down to visit with Michael and Emily. A few minutes later, Jess's oldest sister, Allison, arrived with her husband, Ammon, and their five children; they had all just flown in from Utah. They exchanged greetings and introductions barely in time for another of Jess's sisters to make an entrance. Alexa, her husband, Dale, and their five children had just arrived from California. Introductions went around again, while Tamra felt a growing excitement to think that she was finally becoming a literal part of this family. She had truly grown to love Jess's sisters, and with the absence of any sisters in her own life, she appreciated the way they had taken her in.

"Where's Emma?" Michael asked Allison.

"Oh, she's still up in her room primping," Ammon answered for his wife. "She'll be here in a few minutes."

Ammon got into a conversation with Rhea, while Allison and Alexa assaulted Tamra and Jess with questions about the forthcoming wedding, and the little cousins began to get reacquainted. Tamra was thoroughly enjoying herself until Alexa asked, "When's Amee getting here? I haven't talked to her for a while. She is coming, isn't she?"

"Last I heard, she was," Jess said, casting Tamra a concerned glance. "But then . . . we haven't talked to her for a while, either."

The mood was lightened when Emma arrived and immediately launched her typical greeting with Jess by literally leaping into his arms. He caught her efficiently and twirled her around while they laughed. Tamra always enjoyed seeing them together. Emma was Jess's only full-blooded sibling still living, since the other girls were from Emily's first marriage.

Once Emma exchanged greetings with her brother, she turned and gave Tamra an embrace that truly made her feel like a part of the family. Tamra introduced Emma to her aunt, then made certain Evelyn was all right. Allison's oldest daughter was watching out for her and seemed to be enjoying herself. A light buffet of sandwich fixings, and fresh fruits and vegetables, was set out. While everyone filled their plates, Tamra heard Emma say, "Oh, there's Amee. Now we're all here."

Tamra felt Jess reach for her hand even before they turned to see his sister come in the door with her husband, Randy, and their four children. Allison, Alexa, and Emma all rushed to greet their sister. Jess and Tamra held back, finding that Michael and Emily had moved close to them.

"Well, at least they're here," Emily said softly.

"Yes," Jess replied just as softly, "at least they're here."

When the others drifted toward the food table, Tamra felt Amee's gaze move toward them. Randy put his arm around her shoulders in an obvious gesture of support. They stepped forward and Tamra held her breath.

"Hello," Jess said in a kind voice, "I'm glad you're here."

"We all are," Emily added.

"Well, we're glad to be here," Amee said. She focused her gaze directly on Jess and added in a firm, quiet voice, "I owe you an apology. I . . ." Tears rose into her eyes and Jess reached out and took her hand. "I'm afraid I got carried away, and . . . I'm sorry for the awful things I said to you. We've both fasted and prayed, and . . . as difficult as it is, we both know that Evelyn should be with you."

Tamra felt as if they all heaved a deep sigh in unison. She felt tears come into her own eyes as Jess embraced his sister before he said, "I owe you an apology, as well. James is just as much your brother as he is mine; I was angry, and I'm sorry." Amee nodded and bit her lip while attempting a smile. Jess hugged her again and added, "Thank you, Amee. I prayed so hard that you would be here . . . that we could all be together, and . . ." He became too emotional to speak.

"However," Amee said with a smile, "I intend to be Evelyn's favorite aunt, and she must come and stay with me regularly. We should just make a tradition of having her stay for a few weeks every summer, at the very least."

"That sounds perfect," Jess said and embraced his sister again. Amee then embraced Tamra and her parents.

Everything truly became perfect when Brady and Claudia arrived. Tamra hugged them both tightly, pleased to see a light in her father's eyes that had been absent following his mother's death. He was obviously doing much better.

Tamra thoroughly enjoyed introducing her father and stepmother to all of Jess's family. She discovered that Rhea had only met Brady once, soon after he'd married Tamra's mother. Rhea and her sister had never been close, so Rhea quickly got along well with Brady and Claudia. As the evening progressed, Tamra was thrilled to see all of them huddled together with Jess's parents, talking and laughing like lifelong friends.

Surrounded by so many people they loved, and who loved them, Tamra felt deeply grateful. She appreciated Emily's idea to have this little get-together the evening before the wedding, which gave Jess and Tamra some time to relax and visit with family, since the wedding day itself would likely be very busy.

The party began to break up when those with children left to put them to bed. Knowing she was far too nervous to go to sleep yet, Tamra was relieved when Jess took her hand and approached their parents and Rhea, who were still visiting.

"Mind if we crash the older generation here?"

"Excuse me?" Brady said in mock offense.

"All right," Jess said, sitting between his mother and Tamra. "Mind if we crash the middle-aged generation here?"

"That's better," Emily said.

"Yeah, me too," Emma said, appearing from the hallway.

"Don't you need your sleep?" Michael asked as she sat beside him.

"Probably," Emma chuckled, "but it's too early to go to bed."

"What's on the agenda for you tomorrow, Emma?" Claudia asked.

"Oh, I get to be head babysitter here at the hotel, since I'm the only one who hasn't been through the temple yet."

Brady, Claudia, and Rhea all looked slightly confused, but Rhea said, "Oh, let me help you. It would be such fun, and we'll be having lunch here after the wedding anyway, right?"

"That's right," Emma said. "Hey, I'll take all the help I can get. I mean . . . some of the kids are older and they'll help, but . . . we're talking about fifteen kids here."

"Well, we'll come early for the lunch and put in a shift as well," Brady said.

"What a great idea," Claudia laughed softly.

"You really don't have to do that," Emma said. "We can manage and—"

"Oh, we'd love to," Claudia said.

Emma then said to her mother, "Have you decided yet if you want me to take them all over to the temple for pictures?"

"I think it would be nice," Emily said, "but as you just mentioned, with fifteen kids, I don't know if—"

"Well, we can help there, can't we?" Brady asked.

"Yes, you should have all of the children there; that would be wonderful," Claudia added.

"Are you sure you wouldn't mind?" Emily asked.

"It sounds delightful," Claudia said. "Besides, we're practically family."

"Yes, we sure are," Jess said, looking into Tamra's eyes. "We're down to counting hours now."

"And in another couple of hours, it will be the best day of my life," Tamra said.

"Isn't that sweet?" Rhea said. "They just make the cutest couple."

"Agreed," Brady said. Tamra turned warm from the attention and put her head on Jess's shoulder. She simply couldn't imagine being any happier. But the following morning as Emily helped the ladies at the temple adjust her dress in the bride's room mirror, she felt her happiness deepen. She'd never felt more beautiful, more fortunate, more grateful for the enormity of all she'd been blessed with.

When she was finally ready, Emily took both her hands tightly. Their eyes filled with tears in the same moment. "You know," Emily said, "I think my spirit knew the moment I saw you that you were meant to be my daughter; I couldn't have consciously recognized it at the time, but looking back . . . I just felt *something.*"

"And here we are," Tamra said. She fought to gain her composure, not wanting to get married with red, swollen eyes. "I believe my spirit knew the moment I arrived in your home that I was meant to be there." The tears overtook her as she admitted, "I love Jess so much."

"I know you do," Emily said. "And he loves you. You're the best thing that ever happened to him, Tamra. Whatever life brings you, the two of you will be able to conquer it—together. I've felt the connection between the two of you . . . so much like what Michael and I felt for each other." Emily gave Tamra a careful embrace and muttered close to her ear. "I love you dearly, my daughter."

"And I love you," Tamra whispered back. "Thank you . . . for everything. No woman has ever married into a greater family."

Emily laughed softly and eased back. "I did," she said.

Tamra smiled. "Yes, but . . . I have the added benefit of all you have contributed through the years you've been here. Jess is who and what he is because of all you and Michael have given him."

Emily got emotional again, but their conversation was halted when the temple worker told them it was time to go.

Tamra felt as if she would burst with happiness when she saw Jess, dressed in temple robes, and slipped her hand into his. Yet, her gratitude and happiness deepened further when they entered the celestial room together. His parents approached and Emily put both her hands on Jess's face as she whispered, "I believe James and Krista are here, and Tyson as well."

Tamra felt a subtle thrill. She hadn't considered the idea that family members from both sides of the veil might gather for such an event, but she felt certain it was true. Tyson was Emma's twin brother who had died soon after birth, and she considered it logical that he would be with his brother and sister-in-law who had been killed more recently. Tamra's mind wandered to the times she had felt a closeness with many of Jess's ancestors through reading their journals—most specifically, his great-great-grandmother, Alexa Byrnehouse-Davies. She wondered if Alexa might be here as well, along with her husband, her children, and grandchildren. Tamra then felt an undeniable warmth that seemed to confirm that her idea was indeed possible. Perhaps they were here—all of them—to witness this glorious event of the beginning of yet another generation in this great family. Tamra recalled Emily once telling her that since Michael was the only son of an only son of an only son, and since Jess was *his* only son living, the Hamilton line would end if not for Jess having a family of his own. Just one more reason to celebrate this day, Tamra concluded, looking into the eyes of this man she was about to marry. It was easy for her to imagine having his children and working together to raise them on the same land where generations before had lived out their lives.

"Are you ready?" Jess asked, startling her from her thoughts. He motioned toward the man in white who was apparently waiting to take them to the sealing room. Tamra took a deep breath and nodded firmly. She'd never felt more ready than this to embark on her future.

Tamra's happiness became all-consuming as she knelt at the altar with Jess across from her, holding her hand in his. While the sealer spoke the words of the ceremony, Tamra felt the love of all of Jess's family who were present, and she felt certain they were indeed surrounded by at least as many family members they couldn't see.

As they exchanged a kiss over the altar, Tamra instantly felt the full extent of how far they had come since they'd first met. They had fallen in love quickly, and something formless, yet powerful, had drawn them together. But they had struggled through much to arrive at this day. Tamra was grateful for their struggles, and for the hard-won evidence she had that together they could face difficulties and overcome them. She knew that their love and commitment to each other, and to the gospel, superceded anything else that might arise in this life.

When the ceremony was complete, Michael approached Tamra and embraced her tightly before he looked into her eyes and said, "My dear Mrs. Hamilton, you will never know what happiness you have brought me this day." He smiled and added, "Welcome to the family."

Tamra felt too moved to speak, but she knew that Michael understood as he hugged her again then turned to embrace his son. For a moment Tamra felt as if she were dreaming. And she had to remind herself that her deepest dream had come true. She was eternally bound to this man she loved so dearly, and she had become a part of this family—a family more wonderful than she had ever comprehended. She thought momentarily of the deep bond she'd felt with Alexandra Byrnehouse-Davies, and she was sealed into the same family. Tamra was incredulous at the thought.

Walking from the temple with Jess's hand in hers, and his ring on her finger, Tamra felt the warm spirit of the ceremony hover around them. Emma was waiting on the temple grounds with all of the children, along with Brady, Claudia, and Rhea.

"I dare say you're glowing," Claudia said when she greeted Jess and Tamra.

They looked into each other's eyes and Jess admitted, "Yes, I believe we are."

Following a long round of pictures at the temple, they all returned to the hotel where a beautiful meal was served to honor the newlyweds. Nearly every family member stood and expressed their love for Jess and Tamra, each offering a bit of advice. Tamra laughed and cried, holding Jess's hand in hers, acutely aware of the ring he now wore. She was glad Jess had insisted she wear her wedding gown to the luncheon. Not only did she feel more beautiful than she'd ever felt in her life, but just having it on helped convince her that this was not a dream.

Long after the meal was over, family and friends mingled and visited. Tamra began to wonder if this party would last all day. As if Jess had read her mind, he put his arm around her and spoke in a loud voice that quieted everyone else in the room. "Thank you for everything. We love you all, but we're blowing this party. We've got a honeymoon to see to. So . . . we'll see you next week and party some more."

Tamra let out a startled laugh as he scooped her into his arms. They left the room amidst cheers and applause, and he didn't set her down until they were in the elevator. An elderly couple got in with them, offering warm smiles in response to their wedding apparel. The other couple got off two floors up, and when the door closed again and they were alone, Jess took her in his arms and kissed her like he never had before. Tamra felt breathless with the realization that she was actually now his wife. There had been many times in her adult life when she had feared that certain aspects of marriage would provoke residue from the abuse of her childhood. She had prayed repeatedly to be freed from any such inhibitions or ugly reminders of the past. And looking into Jess's eyes now, she felt nothing but peace and sweet anticipation. Her gratitude deepened as she briefly contemplated the wondrous aspects of the gospel that had made it possible for her to shift the burden of her painful youth to the shoulders of Him who had already paid the price. She could never put into words the perfect peace and happiness she felt.

They stepped out of the elevator into an empty hallway and walked the short distance to the room they would share. Jess hesitated after he'd opened the door and took both her hands into his.

"Is something wrong?" she asked.

"No." He smiled and there was no missing the distinct sparkle of happiness in his eyes. "Everything is perfect. But there's something I want to say before I carry you over the threshold. It occurred to me a few days ago, and the idea settled into me in the temple. I need to tell you, but . . . it's a little sensitive so . . . bear with me."

"I'm your wife now," she said gently, putting her hands to his shoulders. "You should be able to tell me anything."

"I know, but . . ." He glanced down and cleared his throat. Tamra's heart quickened as she wondered what was coming. When he looked up again, there were tears glistening in his eyes. He took her face into his hands and pressed his brow to hers. "You already know that . . . I had many passionate escapades through my troubled youth. Even though it never went all the way, I . . . made some horrible choices and . . ."

"I know all of that," Tamra said when he hesitated. "It's all in the past."

"Yes, but . . . I must tell you that . . . what I learned to feel then was only dark and carnal. And when I fell in love with Heather, what I felt for her was everything I'd never felt before."

Tamra knew that he had met Heather at BYU after he'd emerged from his lengthy rebellious stage. She had encouraged him to serve a mission and had waited for him to return. It hadn't worked out between them, but Heather was a good woman and Tamra knew that at one time she and Jess had cared for each other deeply.

Jess sighed and went on, "What I felt for her was right and good, but it was never . . . dare I say . . . passionate? I mean . . . we always behaved ourselves but . . ." The intensity in his voice deepened. "Oh Tamra! Never in my life have I felt what I feel when I kiss you." He drew back only far enough to see into her eyes. "It's as if everything physical and emotional and spiritual all comes together in perfectly orchestrated harmony. I never realized until you came along the full damage that my indiscretions of the past had done. Those experiences deceived me into believing that passion was evil and wrong. I never imagined that being attracted to a woman could be so . . . passionate and so . . . righteous . . . at the same time."

He heaved a lengthy sigh, as if he were deeply relieved at having his words in the open. "I just want you to know," he added, "how deeply grateful I am for the love you give me, for your forgiveness and acceptance, and for letting me spend the rest of my life with you." He smiled and touched her face. "I love you beyond words."

Tamra felt tears splash onto her cheeks as she readily admitted, "I love you too, Jess. I never dreamed I could be so happy."

His smile widened and he let out a hearty chuckle before he lifted her into his arms and carried her into the room. "Welcome home, Mrs. Hamilton," he said and kicked the door closed.

* * *

The following day Jess and Tamra checked out of the hotel and went to the parking garage to find Tamra's car with "Just Married" written across the back window. Jess laughed as he unlocked the trunk. "Well, at least it's not full of newspaper and balloons." But he did check under the bumper before he added, "And no cans tied to the back."

"Since they're not here to see us off, they wouldn't get much pleasure out of such antics, now would they?"

"No," he said, helping her into the passenger seat, "but knowing Emma, she'd do something mischievous anyway."

"She's so much like you," Tamra said and Jess had to agree.

Tamra thoroughly enjoyed every minute of their sight-seeing as they slowly worked their way back toward home. She was glad now that she'd had to leave her car at her aunt's home in Sydney several weeks earlier before she'd gone to the States, and then had ended up flying home with Jess in the family's plane. Rhea had offered to drive the car to Queensland for the reception, but Jess had insisted that she fly home with his parents. She was thrilled with the prospect of spending some time with them, and the opportunity to help prepare for the reception. And of course, Michael and Emily had been equally thrilled with the chance to get to know Rhea better. Tamra was glad to have the car and be able to drive these roads with her husband at her side, taking time to absorb the beauty of Australia as they gradually came to accept that they were, indeed, married. Tamra knew that other family members were making the same drive, and some of them would be sight-seeing as well. But she was glad to not run into any of them. She wanted Jess all to herself.

A week after their marriage, they finally arrived at Byrnehouse-Davies and Hamilton Station, with the reception scheduled for that evening. As Jess drove the car onto the neatly groomed dirt roads,

Tamra glanced over her shoulder at the cloud of dust in their wake. How clearly she recalled the first time she'd come here, and how the dust in the rearview mirror had given her an obscure kind of peace, a physical reminder that she was putting the past behind her. She had instinctively believed then that she was taking a step that would eventually lead her to her destiny, but she never would have dreamed that less than a year later she would be married and calling this place her home. She reached for Jess's hand as the dirt road merged into blacktop and the iron archway that had served as the entrance to the station for generations appeared. And then the boys' home emerged, with the gables jutting out from the upper story.

"Wait," Tamra said, putting her hand on Jess's arm. "Stop here a minute."

"What?" he asked, putting the car into park.

Tamra leaned out the window to look up at the gables. "The first time I came here, I felt something . . . indescribably wonderful when I saw the gables. I remember thinking that I knew I'd made the right choice in coming here." She eased back and looked into his eyes. "But I never would have dreamed . . ." He smiled and she added, "Now I know that the gables had deep significance to your great-great-grandparents. It's as if they are somehow a tangible symbol of the great legacy that has come down through the generations in this family." She inhaled deeply and kissed Jess, touching his face as she did. "I just wanted you to know how grateful I am to be a part of that legacy."

Jess touched her face in return. "It is I who am grateful, my love." He smiled again. "Welcome home, Mrs. Hamilton."

"You said that at the hotel right after we were married."

"Yes, but . . . that was just our temporary home. This is *home.*"

"So it is," she said, and he drove on through the cluster of trees and around the bend to park beside the home where they would live out their lives together.

"We'll get our stuff later," he said, urging her out of the car. She was surprised when he took her around to the front door. She couldn't recall ever entering the house from the front beyond the first day she'd come here. But he went up the porch steps, opened the door and carried her over the threshold while she laughed with perfect happiness.

"There now," he said, setting her on her feet, "we're truly home."

Tamra threw her arms around his neck and kissed him. She was just beginning to enjoy it when they were discovered by his little nieces and nephews who had been playing in the lounge room just off the front entry hall. Little Evelyn was among them, squealing with excitement. Jess laughed and scooped her into his arms.

"There's my little Evie," he said, hugging her tightly. Tamra hugged her as well before she ran off to be with her little cousins. The adults emerged from the kitchen to see what all the noise was about, and the couple was soon assaulted by a round of hugs and laughter.

Michael and Emily walked with them out to the car to get their luggage and the carefully bagged wedding gown and tuxedo that would be needed that evening. They all went up the stairs together and approached the door to Jess's room—the room they would now share. On the door was tacked a little sign that read "Just Married."

"Oh no," Jess said, glancing at each of his parents who looked innocently amused.

"What?" Tamra asked just before Jess carefully opened the door then laughed. The room was filled with balloons, which were tied to every piece of furniture and clinging to the ceiling with brightly colored ribbons hanging from them. The carpet was littered with confetti, and on the bed was a large wrapped gift.

Tamra laughed and Emily explained, "Emma didn't figure it would be any fun to decorate your car when none of us would see you get in it, but she had to do *something.*"

"Why am I not surprised?" Jess said, stepping into the room.

"The gift is from your sisters," Michael said, "but I think you'd better open it when we're all together. In fact, I think you'd better just open it when you open the rest of them."

"And when will that be?" Tamra asked.

"This evening, of course," Michael said, "after the reception."

"It'll be better than Christmas," Jess said.

"Even though we don't really *need* anything," Tamra added.

"No, I don't think we do," Jess grinned and kissed Tamra.

"Get settled in and rest if you need to," Emily said. "There's food in the kitchen if you're hungry."

"Thank you," Jess said. "We'll be down in a while."

Michael tossed Jess a little smirk before they left the room and closed the door.

"Wow," Tamra said, looking around the room, "we're really home, aren't we?" She moved toward the window and sighed to see the familiar view.

"We really are," Jess said, embracing her from behind.

"I can't tell you how much it means to me to know that I'll never have to leave here." She turned in his arms and looked into his eyes. "I love you, Jess Hamilton."

He smiled and kissed her nose. "And I love you . . . Tamra Hamilton."

"I suppose we should get settled in," she said, glancing around the room. "And I think we'd better vacuum the floor." She scooped up a handful of the colorful confetti. "Or we'll have this stuff everywhere until our tenth anniversary."

"We might anyway," Jess said and went to get the vacuum.

An hour later they went down to the kitchen to get something to eat and found all of Jess's sisters there, talking and laughing while they worked at arranging cookies and slices of fruit bread on trays. They exchanged greetings as if it had been a year since they'd been together instead of only a week, then Jess and Tamra quickly became caught up in their conversation. Amidst the laughter Tamra looked around the room, attempting to comprehend that these four wonderful women had become her sisters. And Jess Hamilton was her husband. She felt truly blessed. A short while later her father and stepmother came into the kitchen, along with Michael and Emily. Tamra learned that her parents had arrived the day before and the four of them had been having a wonderful time; they were obviously getting along marvelously.

"Where's Rhea?" Tamra asked, recalling that her aunt had come home with Michael and Emily following the wedding.

"Oh, she's helping Sadie with the babies up in the nursery," Emily said. "They've been having a wonderful time."

They all flew into a panic when Emma looked up at the clock and gasped. They had less than an hour before guests would start arriving. But they were all ready on time, and the evening proved to be a huge success. Tamra enjoyed meeting friends and business associates of the Hamiltons that she'd never met before. And she was pleased to be congratulated by many ward members, the hired hands from the stables, the staff of the boys' home, and even the boys themselves. They all looked fine in their best clothes, and she was impressed with the way they behaved themselves. As each of them shook her hand in greeting, she felt deeply warmed to think of working with Jess in helping these boys. She'd gotten to know many of them quite well during her work there in the past.

Jess kept Evelyn close to him when she wasn't off following her little cousins around. The child often brought cookies or little sandwiches to Jess and Tamra, bringing hugs and laughter as well. After the receiving line broke up, Jess and Tamra cut the wedding cake and fed it to each other, then they both took off their shoes and shared a waltz. Others joined in and the dancing continued for more than an hour. By then, only family and close friends remained and the gift-opening frenzy began.

Tamra felt a little overwhelmed with the abundance of presents, especially when she realized that they would be living in a well-established household, where everything necessary was already in place. But it quickly became apparent that most gift-givers were aware of this. They were given bedroom and bathroom linens, books, decor items, CDs, and some kitchen items that could work with what was already there. The gift from Jess's sisters proved to be a beautiful picnic basket, complete with plastic dishes, lots of snack food, a bottle of non-alcoholic champagne, two goblets, a couple of books on strengthening marriage relationships, and gift certificates for a movie, a ballet, and two dinners out.

When all the gifts had been opened, Michael handed Tamra a large envelope.

"What is this?" she asked.

"You're supposed to open it to find out," Brady said.

"It was your father's idea," Emily said to Tamra.

"And a good one at that," Michael said.

"We all went in together," Claudia said.

Tamra exchanged a glance with Jess, reassured that he was as baffled—and perhaps as nervous—as she. Jess nodded to encourage her to open the envelope. It took her a moment to realize what she was looking at, and then she squealed with excitement.

"What?" Jess demanded, and she handed everything to Jess before she jumped to her feet and hugged her father, then Michael, then Claudia, then Emily. They were all beaming with pleasure as Jess announced to the curious onlookers, "It's a trip to Hawaii." He laughed then hugged all the parents before he turned to hug Tamra.

"And you're leaving tomorrow," Emily said.

"So," Claudia added, "it might be a good idea for the two of you to get some sleep and get your bags packed."

"I thought we'd already had a honeymoon," Tamra said and laughed again.

"Well," Michael said, "life can settle in pretty quickly once you get married. We all thought you could use a *real* vacation."

"Oh wait," Emily said. "There's one more gift; I almost forgot." She hurried into the other room and returned with a large, flat box wrapped in silver paper and a shimmery silver bow.

"Oh my," Tamra said as Emily set the gift on her lap and Jess put his arm around her. "Who is this from?"

Emily just smiled. Allison said with an enlightened voice, "Oh I know what it is."

"It must be the legacy gift," Alexa added with a little chuckle and Tamra's heart quickened.

"Well, open it," Michael urged.

Tamra carefully removed the bow and the paper. The box itself was silver, as well, and inside she folded back silver tissue paper to reveal some carefully folded white linens with intricately crocheted lace edging. Tamra and Jess both looked to his parents in question. Emily explained, "In her later years, Alexa became rather adept at crocheting lace, and she taught her skill to the other women in the family. There were many pieces that have been carefully preserved and distributed as wedding gifts among the family."

"We all have similar pieces," Amee said.

Tamra felt a deep warmth fill her at the implication, but she still wasn't completely certain who had made the contents of the box she was holding. And she was almost afraid to ask. She was relieved when Emily stepped forward and carefully removed each piece as she explained. "Michael's mother made this dresser cloth. His grandmother, Emma, made this tablecloth, and his great aunt, Lacey, made the other tablecloth. Alexa made the pillow slips."

"Alexa?" Tamra gasped.

"I take it you don't mean my sister," Jess chuckled.

"No," Emily smiled, "I mean your great-great-grandmother, Alexa Byrnehouse-Davies."

Tears rushed into Tamra's eyes so quickly that she had no chance to try and hold them back. Reverently touching the intricate, handmade lace, she pondered the deep affinity she had felt for this woman. She had felt like Alexa was guiding her from the other side of the veil to come to this place. And reading Alexa's journals had been one of the most remarkable experiences of Tamra's life. To be given something made by this woman meant more to Tamra than she could ever express. She met Jess's eyes, then looked up to see the serenity in his parents' faces, and she felt certain they understood when she simply said, "Thank you. No gift could mean more."

Emily helped refold the pieces and put them back into the silver lining of the box while Tamra regained her composure.

Jess and Tamra both expressed their appreciation to everyone present, especially to their parents, before they went up to bed. Before Jess turned out the lights, he kissed Tamra and whispered close to her ear, "I'm the happiest man alive, you know."

"No happier than I am," she said and kissed him back.

Chapter Four

Tamra woke the following morning and turned over to find Jess leaning against the headboard, reading a story to Evelyn. "Hi, Mommy," she said then turned her attention back to the book.

"Good morning, my love," Jess said. "Evelyn and I woke up early. I already told her we were going away for a while, but we'd bring her back a very special present. Isn't that right, sweetie bug?" he added more to Evelyn.

"I get a pwesent," she said firmly to Tamra.

Tamra chuckled and kissed Evelyn's little head before she kissed Jess. She couldn't imagine life getting any better than this.

When the story was finished they hurried to get their things together and get ready to leave. They went down to the kitchen with Evelyn in Jess's arms and found the family just finishing breakfast. While Michael made animal pancakes for Jess, Tamra, and Evelyn, much of the family hovered in the kitchen.

"Good thing we've got a big kitchen," Jess said.

"It is indeed," Emily said. "But before you start eating, you have one more gift to open from the family. We honestly forgot about it yesterday."

"This one's special," Emma declared.

"It must be pretty amazing," Tamra said. "I thought *everything* we got last night from the family was special."

"Well," Allison said, "it's not as special as those linens, but it does have a great deal of love in it."

Michael handed a large, soft, lightweight gift to Jess, who grinned and said, "I think I know what this is." He pulled the paper away and

Tamra gasped to see the quilt she had helped Emily and the girls make nearly a year ago, soon after she'd first arrived. Tamra knew it was a long-time tradition in the family to make quilts when all the women were together, and they were given as wedding and baby gifts from the family. She had found the experience deeply touching and nostalgic, but she never would have dreamed that the quilt she'd helped make would end up belonging to her and Jess. The back was made from a navy-colored, queen-sized sheet, and the top was a print fabric in blues and whites, with mountains and snowflakes, tied with white yarn. It would go beautifully with the color-scheme in their room, and Tamra had to wonder if Jess's mother might have had his marriage in mind when she'd chosen the fabric.

"Oh, it's incredible!" Tamra said more than once. "Thank you . . . so much. I have such good memories of making this quilt."

"We were all hoping then that Jess would have the good sense to marry you," Allison said.

"And it's about time he did," Amee added.

"But if you don't hurry and eat," Alexa said, "you're going to miss that flight to Hawaii."

Following a quick breakfast, Jess and Tamra shared farewell embraces with every family member, knowing they'd not see many of them for a very long time, given that they lived on different continents. It was difficult to say good-bye, but the anticipation of this incredible vacation made it easier. It was hardest for both of them to say good-bye to Evelyn, even though they would see her again soon. They truly felt as if she were their own.

Emma drove them out to the hangar and shared another long embrace with both of them. "I guess I'll see you again during my summer break. Well," she chuckled, "summer there, winter here."

"We'll look forward to it," Tamra said. "And thank you for everything."

"It's been great," Emma said.

"So, when are *you* getting married?" Jess asked her with a smirk.

"When I find a man worth dating, I'll be on the right track," she said. "Now hurry up or you'll miss that flight."

Within minutes Jess had the plane in the air and, once again, Tamra thought that life couldn't get any better than this. A week in paradise only added to the bliss she found in being Jess Hamilton's wife. Even being together almost constantly spurred no tension between them. She couldn't help thinking that all the struggles they'd endured together had helped them learn to communicate so effectively, and to appreciate how far they'd come and the love they shared.

* * *

The Hawaii honeymoon had been wonderful, but Tamra felt a deep thrill when Jess circled the plane low over the house to let his parents know they'd returned so they could pick them up at the hangar. Ten minutes later Jess helped Tamra out of the plane, and Evelyn came running to meet them. Jess laughed and scooped her into his arms.

"Did you miss Daddy?" he asked.

"I get a pwesent," she said and he laughed again.

"She's got a good memory," Emily said. "She's been talking about it all week."

"Yes," Jess said, "we got you a present, but we'll have to get the bags unpacked first."

Back at the house, Evelyn went upstairs with Jess and Tamra to help unpack. When Jess found the plastic sack with her present, he said, "I found it, but why don't we take it downstairs so Grandma and Grandpa can see?"

Evelyn giggled and ran out the door and toward the stairs, with Jess right behind her. Tamra grabbed another sack from inside her suitcase and followed. They found Michael and Emily in the library, sitting close together on the couch, looking through photo albums.

"I get a pwesent," Evelyn said, running toward her grandparents.

"We thought you should see her open this," Jess said. "You're going to love it."

"Jess picked it out," Tamra added.

"Okay," Jess sat down and held the sack out for Evelyn, "here you go."

The child giggled and took it from him. She sat on the floor and screwed her little face into deep concentration as she opened the sack and pulled out a doll dressed in a native Hawaiian costume, including a grass skirt. Evelyn squealed with delight and announced, "It's a pwitty dowy."

"It *is* a pretty dolly," Emily said.

"And look," Jess said, urging Evelyn back to the sack, almost more excited than she was, "there's something else."

A few minutes later Evelyn was dressed in her own Hawaiian print dress, with a grass skirt over it, and a lei of silk flowers. She giggled and danced with her new dolly, entertaining the adults for more than half an hour before she sat to undress her dolly.

"These are for you," Tamra said, handing a sack to Emily.

"Oh now, that wasn't necessary," Michael said.

"Well, it's certainly something you can live without," Jess said. "But . . . we wanted to."

Michael and Emily were both delighted with the shirt and dress in aloha prints, and Emily was quick to notice the quality of the fabric and craftsmanship. Jess explained that these weren't the typical flea-market variety for the tourists, but made by a reputable clothier.

"But which is mine?" Michael asked, holding the dress up to himself.

"Very funny," Emily said, grabbing it from him. Then to Jess and Tamra, "They're beautiful, thank you."

"Great for lounging on the veranda in the evenings, I thought," Tamra said.

"Oh yes," Michael said, putting the shirt on over the one he was wearing.

"So, what are you looking at here?" Jess asked, and they all gathered around the photo album with pictures of Jess's early childhood. A short while later Emily and Tamra went to the kitchen to see if Sadie needed any help with supper, while Jess and Michael stayed to watch Evelyn and look through the photo albums a bit more. Sadie had everything under control beyond setting the table. Tamra set out the plates and glasses while Emily gathered the napkins and utensils.

"So, it seems you had a good vacation," Emily said.

"It was incredible," Tamra said. *"Everything* is incredible!" she added with a little laugh. Then she became more serious. "I must thank you, Emily, even though words seem so trite. I am in awe of all you've given me." She put a hand on Emily's arm and looked into her eyes. "How can I ever tell you what it means to me to be a part of your family? The wedding and all the celebrations and the honey-moon were just so . . . incredible. But most of all . . ." Tamra's voice broke with emotion. "Most of all I want to thank you for raising such a fine man. I love him so much."

Tears rose in Emily's eyes before she embraced Tamra tightly, speaking softly. "It is I who am grateful, Tamra. I mean it when I say you are the best thing that ever happened to him." She drew back and put her hands on Tamra's shoulders. "Life will bring challenges, Tamra; there is no doubt about that. But I know in my heart that having you in his life will make whatever Jess has to face more bear-able—and the other way around, of course."

Tamra saw an intensity in Emily's eyes that almost frightened her. She could almost believe that Emily knew something she wasn't sharing. Was there some imminent *challenge* on the horizon that would test the waters of this new marriage? She wanted to ask, but Emily smiled away her tears and said, "It's so good to have you back, and to know that we're all a family now—as it should be."

A moment later Jess and Michael came into the kitchen, laughing heartily over Evelyn's antics. Jess situated her at the table and tied her bib before he turned and offered Tamra a quick kiss. "Hello, Mrs. Hamilton," he said.

"Hello," Emily and Tamra said at the same time, then they all laughed and sat down to eat.

When the meal was done, Emily said to Michael, "Why don't you help Sadie in the kitchen while I bathe Evelyn and get her to bed? Then we can all visit for a while before—"

"Actually," Jess stood and picked up Evelyn, *"I'm* going to bathe Evelyn and put her to bed—with Tamra's help, of course; I'm not so good at this fathering stuff, yet. But I need to learn. And now that the honeymoon is over, Evelyn is *our* responsibility." Smiling toward Sadie and his parents, he added, "You can help." He reached out a hand toward Tamra, "Come along, little mother, the princess needs a bath."

"I need a baf, Mommy," Evelyn said to Tamra.

"You certainly do," Tamra said, then added to the others, "Thank you for supper—and everything. It's good to be home."

"It's good to have you home," Michael said.

Tamra added, "We'll come back and help with the dishes after—"

"Don't worry about it," Emily said. "We've got it covered. We'll see you a little later."

"Actually," Jess said again, "I'm pretty beat. I think the jet lag is getting to me. And we have church in the morning, so . . . we'll see you tomorrow."

"Good night then," Michael said, and they left the room.

Evelyn insisted on walking up the stairs all by herself, but she let Tamra carry her new dolly. Jess chuckled occasionally at her almost constant chattering, and the way her little grass skirt wiggled as her tiny legs encountered each step. When the bath was finished, Evelyn could only be talked into putting on her pajamas by putting her new dress right beside her bed with the promise that she could put it on first thing in the morning to wear to church. Tucked in with her dolly, Evelyn listened, entranced, while Jess read her three stories and Tamra held her hand.

They finally left after giving Evelyn hugs and kisses, and the nursery monitor was put in Jess and Tamra's bedroom so they could hear any sound she might make. Once Jess and Tamra were settled into bed, Jess put his head on her shoulder and let out a deep sigh. "It's good to be home," he said. "I mean . . . it was such a wonderful honeymoon, but . . . it's just good to be home."

"I couldn't have said it better myself," she said, tightening her arms around him. A few minutes later she sensed that he was deep in thought and asked, "What's on your mind?"

Jess sighed again, "I just can't help thinking . . . a year ago my life was a mess. I nearly took my own life, for heaven's sake. And now . . . I can't even comprehend that kind of depression." He tightened his embrace. "I'm just so perfectly happy. Dad told me they'd already started the adoption proceedings. It's just as if this is how our life together is meant to be. I just feel . . . kind of in awe when I look at all we've been blessed with. And I can't help thinking about my ancestors; you've read all their journals, and you've told me so much about them that I never knew. But I think of all I have now that is so much a result of what they left behind, and I'm just . . . so grateful." He lifted his head and asked, "Do you think it's wrong to be so happy?"

Tamra laughed. "Of course not. I mean . . . it would be naïve of us to think that we could always be without problems or challenges." She squeezed his hand. "But we're together, and we are indeed very blessed. We've both had many struggles, and struggles will be a part of life." Tamra hesitated, thinking of Emily's words in the kitchen earlier. She felt a chill without fully understanding why, but she couldn't bring herself to mention it to Jess. Instead she went on to say, "But working together to overcome our challenges will keep us happy, just as your parents are. They've endured many struggles, but I doubt there are two people happier together."

"We're at least that happy," Jess said.

"That's true," Tamra agreed. "And I think it's important for us to continue to be grateful, no matter what happens. I remember Alexa once saying—"

"My sister?"

"No," she chuckled, "your great-great-grandmother, silly."

"Just have to clarify." He chuckled as well. "Go on."

"Well, I remember her saying in one of her journals how they had been blessed with abundance, and she was proud of the way Jess—her husband, not you—"

"Of course," he laughed.

"Anyway . . . how Jess had chosen to use all he'd been blessed with to build the boys' home and do so much good for others in this world. I think it's wonderful for us to have the opportunity to carry on that legacy, to be able to help the boys in our care, and anyone else we might feel prompted to help." She sat up and asked, "You haven't changed your mind, have you?"

"About what?"

"About taking over the boys' home eventually. I mean . . . Mr. Hobbs is continuing to have health problems, from what I hear, and—"

"No, I haven't changed my mind. I need to finish my degree, if only so I can learn all I can about how to help them. Hobbs is so good with the boys. It's truly what I want to do—what I *feel* I should do; I only hope I'm equal to the task."

"Oh, you'll be marvelous," she said intently.

"With you at my side, perhaps," he said. "You haven't changed *your* mind, have you?"

"About what?"

"About working with me in the boys' home. Of course, Evelyn needs to be cared for, and other children will come along, but . . . I've seen enough to know that *you* are gifted in dealing with those boys."

"No, I haven't changed my mind," she said. "I loved my time working there. We'll just have to work ourselves back in as we're needed."

"My thoughts exactly," Jess said, and she lay back down beside him.

* * *

The following morning proved to be a hectic challenge. Sadie didn't feel well and stayed in bed. Michael left early, as usual, for bishopric meetings, and Emily rode with him, taking along some reading she wanted to catch up on. Jess and Tamra took turns getting ready for church, checking on Sadie, and dealing with Evelyn, who was full of three-year-old stubbornness. They barely made it to church on time, and were glad that Emily had saved them seats. The moment he was seated, Jess met his father's eye from where he sat on the stand, flanked by his counselors. They exchanged a smile before Jess's attention turned to Evelyn trying to open her little bowl filled with dry cereal. Following the opening prayer, Jess was vaguely aware of the stake president standing at the pulpit to take care of a matter of business. He tuned in more attentively when he realized they were making a change in the bishopric. He recalled clearly the day his father had been put in as bishop, less than a year earlier. It had taken Jess completely by surprise, but he had known his father would be a good bishop and had a great deal to offer the people of this ward. Jess wondered if one of his counselors had come upon some challenges that made the calling too demanding; or perhaps one of them was moving away.

Jess felt his heart quicken then plummet to the pit of his stomach when he realized his father was being released. One of the counselors was made bishop, and a new counselor was called to take his place. Before he could express to Tamra his realization that something had to be wrong, he felt her squeeze his arm so tightly that it hurt. While the new bishopric was being sustained, Jess's mind sorted through the hints he'd noticed prior to the wedding that had pointed to something out of the ordinary. What had his mother told him? *Your father has a lot on his mind right now. All the two of you need to worry about is getting married—and enjoying every minute of it.* And he had. He'd enjoyed his wedding and honeymoon so thoroughly that he'd completely forgotten his concerns. And now *this!* He knew that bishops were expected to serve somewhere in the neighborhood of five years, depending on circumstances. He also knew that bishops often served in the face of many personal challenges. Why would his father be released now? What could possibly call for such drastic measures?

Jess was startled to see his father sliding onto the bench to sit beside Emily, while the new counselor took his place on the stand. Jess leaned forward to get his father's attention, much as he'd done the day Michael had been first sustained. Michael leaned forward, shrugged his shoulders and offered a wan smile, then he leaned back and put his arm around Emily. Jess noticed Emily squeezing Michael's hand tightly and his heart quickened further. *Something was dreadfully wrong!*

Michael and Emily were each asked to briefly share their testimonies, but neither of them said anything that gave a clue to what the problem might be. Through the remainder of the meeting, Jess found it impossible to concentrate. His stomach tightened into a knot that wouldn't relent. He was actually grateful for Evelyn throwing a fit so he could take her out to the foyer and move around a bit to release some nervous tension. But when he returned and sat down, just meeting Tamra's eyes reminded him that he was not imagining what he felt. There was simply too much adding up here, but for all his speculations, he just couldn't imagine what the problem might be. Or perhaps he didn't want to consider such possibilities.

Jess was hoping to talk to his parents once the meeting was over, but Emily rushed off to teach her Primary class, and his father hurried to the bishop's office with the new bishop. Jess took Evelyn to her Sunbeam class, then found Tamra standing outside the door to their Sunday School class.

"Are you okay?" she asked.

"Not really," he said. "Something's horribly wrong, and it was wrong before we got married. Everyone told me to relax and forget about it. Well, I certainly did. But I can't relax *now.*" Following a minute of silence he asked, "Am I crazy, or do you—"

"No, Jess, you're not crazy. It's evident something is wrong; I've sensed it, too. But whatever it is, they obviously didn't want it to put a damper on the wedding."

Jess groaned in frustration, grateful they were alone in the hall. "What did I say just last night? *Is it wrong to be so happy?*"

"Whatever is wrong, Jess," Tamra said, "we'll get through it together. Standing out here and letting your imagination run away with you isn't going to do anybody any good. Come on, let's go to class and see if we can get some distraction."

Jess went along reluctantly, but he wasn't comforted by the discussion on Job. If a faithful man could lose so much, then how bad could life get before it got better? Priesthood meeting was a little better, with the discussion focusing on the blessings of the temple and eternal marriage. Whatever might be wrong, at least they had eternity.

When the meeting was over, Jess collected Evelyn and met Tamra outside the Relief Society room. Before he could exchange a word with her, he was asked by two different ward members if everything was all right in the family. Jess could only force a smile and say, "Sure," before he hurried away with Tamra's hand in his. They found Emily having a quiet talk with one of her Primary students. She broke away only long enough to say, "You go on home. I'll come later with your father when he's finished with his meetings." Jess sighed as one more opportunity to get some information evaded him.

They drove home in near silence as Evelyn slept. Jess couldn't bring himself to speculate aloud on what the problem might be. The possibilities were just too frightening. Then he came up with one that he actually liked. "They're going on another mission," Jess said brightly.

"What?" Tamra asked, startled from her own thoughts.

"He was released because they're going on another mission."

"Maybe," she said, but it was evident she didn't believe it. She turned again to look out the window as he drove.

The minute they got home, Evelyn woke up in a better mood than she'd been in earlier. Jess and Tamra took her along as they both went to check on Sadie. "How you doing?" Jess asked.

"Oh, I've just got a little cold, I'm sure," Sadie said. "Evelyn had it while you were gone. I'm certain if I rest a bit I'll feel better."

"Is there anything we can get you?" Tamra asked. "Are you hungry, or—"

"The two of you will have to fix yourselves a sandwich, I suppose," she said. "I was going to get some dinner in for later when your parents got home, but—"

"Now, don't be worrying about that," Tamra said. "We'll just put in one of those casseroles you left in the freezer. Would you like a sandwich now, Sadie? Some orange juice?"

"Oh, that sounds nice," she said, "but you don't have to—"

"Oh, nonsense," Tamra said. "It's quite a hike down those stairs to the kitchen when you don't feel well. I'll bring something up for you in a bit. Do you need any medicines or anything to—"

"Oh, I've got all that here in my bathroom; thank you, dear."

"I'll be back in a while, then," Tamra said.

After changing out of their church clothes, Jess played with Evelyn in the nursery while Tamra made some sandwiches. When Jess heard Tamra back in Sadie's room, he met her there and couldn't resist asking, "Sadie, did you know they released Dad today?"

She looked somehow guilty before she said, "I'd heard it was coming."

"Do you know why?" Jess asked, sticking his hands deep in the pockets of his jeans.

She hesitated before saying firmly, "If your parents have something to tell you, they can tell you themselves."

Jess left the room without another word, fearing he'd get angry and badger Sadie into telling him what she knew. He was grateful for Tamra's bright mood, although it seemed somewhat forced, as she told Evelyn they were having a picnic on the lawn. Evelyn helped pack up the new picnic basket with the sandwiches Tamra had made, and some chips, cookies, and soda from the kitchen. They found a nice spot under a tree and spread out a blanket.

Listening to Evelyn chatter, and watching her play proved to be a good distraction. But after a few hours, Jess found himself glancing at his watch every three minutes, wondering when his parents would return. Tamra had everything ready for dinner, with a casserole kept warm in the oven, and Evelyn was almost being too good. When Michael and Emily finally arrived, Sadie was up, claiming to feel much better. Emily declared that she was starving and they sat right down to eat, as if nothing in the world were out of the ordinary.

Through the meal, Jess kept wanting to ask what was up, but at the same time he couldn't bring himself to do it. Something deep inside told him that once he heard what his parents had to tell him, everything would change. Again he tried to imagine what the problem might be, but such speculations only made his head ache. He kept hoping that one of them would naturally say something like, *So I guess you're wondering about the release,* but they said nothing beyond trivial conversation.

When dessert had been served, Sadie insisted on taking Evelyn for a walk. Jess was happy to let her do it, wondering if his parents didn't want to get into any serious conversation with the child present. Following minutes of unbearable silence while they all picked at their ice cream, Jess finally convinced himself that he couldn't bear the suspense any longer. He cleared his throat ridiculously loud before he forced himself to say, "You have something to tell us, don't you." It was not a question.

He saw his parents exchange a long, almost sad glance, before they both looked back at him and Tamra. "Yes," Emily said. He saw her reach for his father's hand across the table. Jess reached for Tamra's the same way. Emily took a deep breath and said gently, "Your father has cancer."

It took a minute for Jess to allow his brain to absorb the announcement. He felt Tamra squeeze his fingers tightly and knew she had absorbed it at the same moment. Cancer was one of the many dozens of possibilities that had flitted through his mind, but he'd dismissed it as an atrocity that he didn't even want to think about. Again he watched his parents exchange a long glance. The love and strength that permeated the air between their eyes left him as much in awe as in fear. When they said nothing more, he forced his voice enough to ask, "How bad is it? How do you know . . . for sure?"

Emily turned back to face them, speaking in a calm voice that seemed all wrong for the words she delivered. To Jess it seemed as though she was calmly telling him that they were passengers on the *Titanic* and it was sinking. "Well," she began, "some little problems started showing up just after Thanksgiving. They did a number of different tests, the last of which was a couple of days before the wedding—and it confirmed that the growths are malignant."

"Growths?" Jess echoed, hating the way that one word dashed his hope that something could be surgically removed and done away with.

Michael let go of Emily's hand to lean his forearms on the table while she put a hand on his back. He looked directly at Jess and said, "There are spots in one of my lungs, and in my liver. And there is more than one growth in my intestines." Jess felt Tamra's hand tighten further around his at the same moment everything inside of him tightened into one painful knot. He'd never been directly confronted with cancer before, but he was educated enough to know what he was hearing, even before his father clarified, "Once it has passed from one organ to another, the chances of getting rid of it are . . ." He sighed and glanced down. "Well, at best I can hope for it to go into remission."

"What are you saying?" Jess demanded, wishing it hadn't sounded so harsh.

"I'm saying that it may not be next week or next month, and if I'm really lucky it won't even be next year. But I *will* die of cancer."

Jess sprang to his feet, as if the shock and anger consuming him had nowhere else to go. "How can you just . . . give up that easy? How can you just sit there and say that—"

"Sit down, Jess," Michael said firmly. "I'm not finished yet."

Jess sank back into his chair, leaning his forearms on the table, exactly as his father was doing. Their gaze met across the table, and Tamra put a comforting hand on his shoulder.

"I didn't say we were giving up," Michael said. "There is a difference between giving up and being realistic. This is the real thing. It's cancer. It's one of the plagues of the last days, and it's hit home. But I am going to fight it with everything I've got—physically and emotionally. I'm not leaving my family until I absolutely have to. But being in denial and trying to pretend that it's not as bad as it is will only waste precious time. Ever since we lost Tyson, when he was just a baby, I've had a deep testimony that our lives are in God's hands—especially when we're trying to do what's right. When it's time for me to go, it's not going to do any of us any good to try and argue with Him. We all learned that well enough when we lost James and Krista—and when we *didn't* lose you. So, I am going to do everything in my power to fight this. And at the same time, we are all going to do our best to live life to its fullest, and make the most of the time we have left together in this life."

Jess leaned back and shook his head, attempting to digest everything he'd just heard, while an unexpected burst of emotion rushed into his throat. Tamra put her arm around him, but a quick glance at her showed tears on her face that mirrored his own heartache.

"Talk to me, Jess," Michael said.

Jess attempted to gain control of his emotion, but his voice broke nevertheless when he said, "I just . . . can't believe it. You were supposed to die an old man."

"I've lived a good life," Michael said. "I'm not really that young."

"You're not really that old," Jess countered. "I bet you could still whip me at a game of golf, and you could probably still outride me. You're supposed to get old and ornery . . . and I'd have to tell my kids to be patient with Grandpa because he's just old." He sniffled then almost shouted, "You're supposed to get old!" He heard himself sob and realized he was crying.

Michael reached both hands across the table and took hold of Jess's. He looked into his eyes and said, "I'm sorry, son. That's just not possible."

Jess sobbed again then fought to gain control. This was not the time or place to fall apart. But he had to ask, "How can you be so calm? So resigned?"

"Jess," Emily said gently, "we've known about this for weeks. We've had time to adjust somewhat. Don't think that this is easy for either of us. We've both felt the shock, the disbelief. We've both been angry, and we've both shed our fair share of tears. Now we're going to fight this thing to the best of our ability, and make the most of every day we have together."

Following a long moment of silence, Tamra asked, "Does the rest of the family know?"

"Yes," Emily said, "we told them all before they went home, after you'd left for Hawaii. We didn't want you worrying about something like this."

Jess groaned and squeezed his eyes shut. Tamra forced her voice to remain calm as she asked, "So . . . what now? Will you be starting chemotherapy soon or—"

"Already have," Michael said and stood up, pushing his jacket back enough for them to see a little fanny pack attached on a belt around his waist. The belt was hidden beneath the bottom of his waistcoat. He sat back down and unbuttoned the top button of his shirt to pull it open and show them, while he explained the porta-cath that had been surgically put into an artery in order to administer the medication without his having to remain in the hospital.

Jess jumped to his feet again and rushed toward the door.

"Jess?" Tamra said, attempting to follow him.

He held up a hand, saying firmly, "I just . . . need to be alone for a while."

Tamra sat back down slowly and turned to look at these wonderful people that she had come to love so dearly. She thought of when she'd first met them in a hospital in the Philippines. They had given her so much since that time; she felt far closer to them than she'd ever felt to any of her own family. And the heartache in their eyes was evident. At the moment she suspected their concerns were far more focused on Jess. An inner trembling that promised not to relent soon took hold of her.

Emily broke the silence when she said, "You must be patient with him, Tamra. He's already lost so much." Tamra nodded, knowing she meant the accident that had killed his brother, his sister-in-law, and his best friend. But then, hadn't those losses affected Michael and Emily as well? *They* had already lost so much, and now their time together on this earth would be drastically shortened. She felt an explosive emotion teasing at the perimeters of her shock, but she forced it down for the moment. She could cry later. Instead she reached her hands across the table; Michael and Emily each reached out to take one. She swallowed carefully and asked, "Is there anything I can do . . . to help?"

"All we need from you, my dear," Emily said, "is what we already know you will do. Just love Jess, be there for him. We'll get through this . . . together."

Tamra nodded and felt that sorrow again, threatening more boldly this time. She stood and managed to say, "I think . . . I need a little time alone, as well."

"Of course," Michael said, and she rushed from the room.

Chapter Five

Tamra had no idea where Jess might have gone to be alone. Wanting to avoid him, she went into the main stable. She knew that only the minimal care of the animals would be seen to on Sundays, and the hands wouldn't be there at this time of day. She sat down in the clean straw of an empty stall before the tears finally forced their way past every barrier. She cried long and hard, her heart aching for every member of this family that she had grown to love. She ached for Michael and Emily, for the love they shared. Thinking of her own love for Jess, she couldn't even begin to imagine how difficult it might be to face such a thing. And most especially, her heart ached for Jess. What Emily had said was true; he *had* lost so much. Of course, he had readily admitted just last night that they had much to be grateful for—and they did. When her tears ran out and her thoughts finally stood still, she determined to help him remember that very thing—day in and day out. They had to remember all they had to be grateful for. Still, it was difficult to imagine how they would ever get through this. With that thought, she cried some more.

An hour later Tamra finally emerged from the stable, certain she must look horrible. Ambling slowly toward the house, she noticed Michael standing at the highest part of the lawn, looking out over the stretch of land that merged into the mountains in the distance. She felt hesitant to disturb him, but she felt more compelled to share with him some thoughts that had crept into her mind.

"So, how are you doing?" she asked, standing beside him.

Michael glanced toward her then turned back to the view. "I'm okay. How about you?"

"I'm good . . . all things considered."

Following a minute of silence, Michael said, "And you came all the way out here to ask how I'm doing?"

"Is that so strange?" she asked.

"No, but . . ."

"There is something I'd like to say," she added, "but I wasn't sure if this would be a good time or not."

"Now's as good a time as any," Michael said. "We don't want to leave important things unsaid."

As Tamra absorbed the deeper meaning of his words, she felt that inner trembling again. "No, we don't," she said, glancing at the grass beneath her feet. "And this is something I've thought many times, but I've never said it out loud because . . . well, I wondered if it would really mean anything to anyone but me, or . . . I wondered if it would be out of line. But I am a member of the family now, so . . ."

"I'm listening," he said, turning to look at her and stuffing his hands deep into the pockets of his jeans, just as Jess would do. They were so much alike.

"Well," she chuckled tensely, wringing her hands, wondering why this seemed so difficult. Perhaps knowing the remainder of his life would be shortened dramatically put a greater urgency on admitting how much she'd grown to care for him. She cleared her throat and forced herself to begin. "You know that my childhood was not good. You know I only got to know my father recently, and I'm grateful for that, but . . . he was completely absent through most of my life. There were many men who came in and out of my mother's life who only made life worse for me. One of the things that helped get me through those horrible years was . . ." She laughed softly. "It sounds really silly to think of saying it out loud. I don't think I've admitted this to anyone, not even Jess. The thing is . . . some kids have imaginary friends, but I had an imaginary father."

Tamra glanced at him quickly to gauge his reaction. She saw nothing beyond a sparkle of interest in his eyes, which made it easier for her to forge ahead. "The funny thing is that . . . I didn't imagine him being with me, but rather . . . I imagined him living in some faraway land, and that one day he would show up and rescue me from my horrible existence. I remember lying awake at night imagining the things that he would write to me in lengthy letters, and . . . this might sound strange, but . . . the words that came through in those 'letters' are what pressed me to stick up for myself and make some changes in my life, even as young as I was."

Tamra looked up and found Michael looking directly at her, deep compassion showing in his eyes. She returned his gaze as she finally made her point. "I just want you to know that you are everything I imagined and more. I could not have dreamed up so wonderful a father, because I never could have comprehended so much goodness and courage in one man. I'm grateful to know my real father now; he's a good man and I love him. But . . . it's just not the same. Perhaps it's the fact that you and I share the gospel that makes a difference; maybe it was our meeting in the mission field, or the way I've come to know and love all the great ancestors you came from. I don't know. I only know that . . . I'm so grateful to be able to call you my father."

His eyes expressed humility before they glanced down. She turned away and tried to swallow the lump rising in her throat, but her voice still broke when she said, "When I made the decision to go on a mission, I was told in a priesthood blessing that by making the sacrifice to serve the Lord, many privileges and blessings would come into my life. And being taken into this family is evidence of that. I can think of no greater privilege or blessing than to be a Hamilton. So . . . I just wanted to say thank you—for raising Jess to be the man he is, for taking me into your heart and your home so completely, and for being the father I always believed existed somewhere."

Having said what she'd wanted to say, Tamra felt her tears press closer to the surface. Silence fell heavily around them until Michael finally said, "I'm not certain I deserve such praise, but I can assure you that making you a part of the family is a privilege and a blessing for every one of us. I believe I've said as much before, but I felt something special about you the first time we spoke. I truly believe you were meant to be a part of this family. And I've told you this before too, but your love and interest in my ancestors means a great deal to me. I think you understand *my* love for them even more than any of my own children."

Tamra nodded, suddenly too emotional to speak. She pressed a hand to her mouth and attempted to turn away. But Michael touched her shoulder and asked gently, "What is it, Tamra? What's wrong?"

She shook her head and managed to say, "I'm sorry. I didn't want to do this, but . . ."

"What?" he asked, putting his arm around her. "Tell me."

Tamra found her face against his shoulder as the tears refused to be held back any longer. Through a muffled sob she admitted, "I finally have a real father and . . . I don't want you to leave."

"Well, I'm not dead yet," Michael said with a chuckle.

"I know." She drew back and wiped at her tears. "I'm sorry, I just . . ."

"It's all right, Tamra," he said. "I'd rather have you telling me how you feel than trying to hold it inside. You just go ahead and cry."

As if his permission was all she needed, the tears let loose again and she allowed herself to feel the comfort of his fatherly embrace while she wept.

* * *

Jess locked himself in his room and cried long and hard. He couldn't believe it. He just couldn't believe it. Cancer was something that affected *other* people's families. Not this one! But it was. As his father had said, it was the real thing, and it had hit home.

As his tears subsided into shock, Jess felt sensations overtake him that were hauntingly familiar. The despair he'd encountered as a result of the accident was difficult to forget. But if nothing else, his experiences of the past had taught him one thing. He couldn't get through this alone. After endless months of suffering, he'd finally learned that the only path to get beyond it was accessed through prayer. And if he'd ever needed God's help, he needed it now. He didn't wait even another minute before he got down on his knees. Through a fresh bout of tears, he begged God to give him strength and understanding. He finally came to his feet with no obvious answers, but an undeniable peace. He knew, somehow, that everything would be all right. And he felt a sudden need to be with Tamra.

After searching the house to find it empty, he found his mother on the veranda with Evelyn and Sadie. He met his mother's eyes while she seemed to silently ask if he was all right, and he could feel her realization that for the moment, he was.

"Have you seen Tamra?" he asked quietly. Emily just pointed across the yard. Jess turned to see Tamra and his father standing at the highest part of the lawn. He went down the steps and started toward them, stopping a short distance away when he realized Tamra was crying on his father's shoulder. He was considering going back to leave them undisturbed when he caught his father's eye, and the sorrow he saw there tempted him to start bawling all over again. Attempting to lighten the mood, he took a deep breath and stepped toward them, pretending to be offended. "Hey there, old man, that's my wife you're hugging."

Tamra turned toward him, startled. Michael embraced her again and took her hand, saying with warmth, "She may be your wife, but she's *my* daughter."

At this Tamra started to cry again and Jess took her other hand. "What is it?" he asked, touching her chin. She just shook her head and put it to his shoulder. He held her tightly, saying in the lightest voice he could manage, "Stop that now, or you'll get me started again."

"That's not so bad, is it?" Michael said. "We could all use a good cry once in a while, and I've certainly been doing more than my fair share of it lately."

Jess met his father's eyes and saw the pain there. But he also saw a glimmer of the same peace he'd felt when he'd gotten up off his knees. He just had to believe that they were going to get through this—somehow. Three days later, though, Jess was still struggling with his feelings and finding it difficult to focus. He worked with his father back and forth between the stables and the boys' home. The work they did was familiar, and on the surface everything seemed as it always had been. The only noticeable difference was his father's lack of energy due to the chemotherapy. But ordinary moments became poignant as Jess found himself taking mental snapshots, as if he might never see his father doing such simple, everyday things ever again. Just seeing him saddle a horse, or talk quietly with a troubled boy suddenly became a trigger for Jess's tears. He'd either have to quickly excuse himself and hide, or force the emotion back until it made his head pound. He couldn't watch his father kiss his mother in greeting, or play with little Evelyn without feeling deep sorrow. Finding his parents once again looking through old photo albums, he felt a new level of understanding. They were reminiscing because their time together was drawing to a close. He tried to tell himself that a miracle could happen, that they still had years left together, but in the deepest part of him he truly believed that this was the beginning of the end, and denial would only rob him of what little precious time they had left together in this life.

Still, Jess found his ongoing grief difficult to cope with. Tamra was unceasingly supportive, and he found he could pour out his heart to her in the darkest part of the night; he could cry and curse and scream if he needed to, and she would still listen, still love him. And most of the time she wept with him. He prayed continually that he could get a grip on his emotions and not waste his time in tears behind closed doors, but when he wasn't crying he often felt angry, even though there was nothing or no one to be angry with. In the rare moments void of anger or tears, he felt overcome with a numb disbelief.

On Wednesday night, Jess had an especially difficult time falling asleep. He tried not to disturb Tamra, but he was grateful to have her close to him, even as she slept. Thinking of how thoroughly she had changed his life, he tried to comprehend how he might cope with his father's illness if he were still a troubled bachelor. The very idea sent a cold shiver through him. If nothing else, he was deeply grateful for her presence in his life. That in itself seemed tangible evidence that God existed and He was mindful of them.

Jess finally slept, but he woke in the dark with the memory of a disturbing dream. His father had lain dying in his arms, struggling to breathe, while his mother had sobbed and begged him not to go. He groaned and rolled over, relieved that it had only been a dream, but wondering if it might be some kind of premonition of things to come.

"What's wrong?" Tamra asked in the darkness.

"I didn't mean to wake you."

She snuggled close to his back. "I'm glad to be awake if you need me."

"I had a dream," he said.

"I suspected that from the way you were groaning in your sleep. Want to talk about it?"

"Not really," he said, "but I probably should. It's not complicated. I just dreamt my father was dying in my arms, and my mother was begging him not to go. I felt helpless and scared . . . but then, I feel that way all the time these days. Maybe I'm losing my mind."

"No, I don't think so," she said. "I think your emotions are perfectly understandable."

"But will it get any better?" he asked. "Or am I going to keep feeling this way until he goes . . . and beyond that? I've felt moments of peace, but they become more elusive. Is something wrong with me?"

"I don't think you're crazy, Jess, if that's what you're asking."

"And how would you know if I were crazy or not?" he asked lightly, turning toward her.

"Maybe I wouldn't," she said, kissing his brow, "but I know someone who would."

"Who?" he asked, lifting his head.

"Why don't you call Sean and talk to him? Maybe he can help you make sense of what you're feeling."

Jess mulled over the idea. How could he have forgotten so quickly how much Sean O'Hara had helped him finally heal emotionally from the accident that had caused him so much despair? Sean was practically like a brother to Jess. He'd been disowned by his family when he'd joined the Church, and Michael and Emily had taken him in while they had lived in Utah for a number of years during Jess's childhood. They had supported Sean on his mission and they had been like family ever since. When Jess had finally reached rock bottom not so many months ago, he had called Sean, who now worked as a psychologist. Sean told him exactly what he'd needed to hear—a perfect combination of psychological theory and gospel truth. And now, perhaps Sean could help him get through *this.*

"You know," Jess said, "I think that's a brilliant idea."

"Of course," she said facetiously. "You have a brilliant wife."

"Yes, I do," he said and kissed her warmly. "And I think I'll do just as you suggested, but I'll wait until it's a more convenient time of day for him."

"He'd probably prefer it that way," Tamra said, and Jess kissed her again.

At breakfast Jess said to his father, "Good morning. It's nice to see you alive."

Michael looked startled. "Okay, well . . . it's nice to *be* alive. Is there some reason for this comment?"

"I dreamt that you died. I just wanted you to know that it's nice to see you alive."

"I could agree with that," Emily said.

"So, what's on the agenda today?" Jess asked while he cut Evelyn's French toast into bite-sized pieces.

"Whatever it is," Emily said, "you'll be doing it without your father."

"I'm fine," Michael protested.

Emily scowled at him then turned to Jess and said, "He's been working too hard and he could barely get out of bed this morning. He needs to rest."

"What's wrong?" Jess demanded, suddenly certain that the cancer had grown out of control, and it had already taken over completely.

"It's just the chemotherapy," Emily said gently, as if she had read his mind. "The doctor told us it would make him tired; he's actually done very well, but today he's going to rest."

Jess felt a new awareness as he absorbed his father's expression. He'd always been strong and healthy, and having to give that up would not be easy for him. Hoping to ease his mood, Jess said brightly, "I'll see how everything's going and give you an update."

Michael nodded and left the table, his weakness evident. Emily followed him, leaving everyone in the room in concerned silence until Evelyn began talking about how her dollies were sick and she needed to take care of them.

Jess spent the better part of the morning with Murphy, the stable master, going over the books. Then he checked in with Mr. Hobbs at the boys' home before he returned to the house for lunch. But he found the kitchen empty and the house quiet. The main floor proved to be void of any human life so he went upstairs and finally found his father in bed, actually looking a little pale. Evelyn was sitting on the bed beside him, using her play doctor kit to check his blood pressure and give him a shot. Emily sat in a chair near the window, reading a book.

"Well, hello," she said when Jess entered the room.

"Where's Tamra?" he asked.

"She went into town to pick up a prescription for your father. Sadie went with her to catch the bus. She's going to stay with her son's family for a while."

"Why, what's wrong?" Jess growled, moving toward the bed.

"Sadie's daughter-in-law isn't feeling well and—"

"I meant with my father," Jess interrupted tersely.

"He's just having some nausea," Emily explained. "It's perfectly normal with the chemo. You're going to have to calm down, Jess."

"Sorry," Jess said, sitting on the edge of the bed.

"I'm just fine," Michael insisted. "And all this fussing and worrying isn't going to make me any better."

Jess sighed and forced back that seemingly frequent sense of panic.

"Gwampa got a shot," Evelyn said, holding up her little plastic shot needle.

"Okay." Jess gave a stilted chuckle. "Then I guess *Gwampa* is going to be just fine, isn't he?"

While Jess talked through the current business with his father, Emily went to the kitchen to fix some sandwiches. She returned with a tray so they could share lunch and be near Michael, but he refused to eat anything, insisting that he wasn't sure he could keep it down. When Emily returned to the kitchen with Evelyn in tow, Michael turned to Jess, saying severely, "Have you got a few minutes? Do you think we could talk?"

"Sure," Jess said, feeling his heart quicken as he took the chair his mother had just left in order to face his father more directly.

"How's the degree coming, son?" Michael asked.

Jess was surprised by the question, and it took him a long moment to gather his thoughts. Since he'd left BYU in the middle of a term last year, he'd been doing some classes via the Internet. "Uh . . . okay, I guess. You know I finished up the classes I'd been taking before the holidays, and it was your suggestion that I wait until the next semester to take any more; give myself some time to settle into married life. Isn't that what you said?"

"Something like that."

A thought occurred to Jess, and he had to ask, "When you made that suggestion, did you know you had cancer?"

"I suspected; I wasn't sure."

"Okay." Jess leaned back in the chair and stretched out his legs.

"Okay what?"

"Well," Jess struggled to put his thoughts in order, at the same time struggling with the ever-present grief. "I guess I have to say that . . . suddenly getting that degree doesn't seem so important, even though I really don't have much more to finish up." Following a minute of silence he added, "I assume you have an opinion on the subject, or was there another reason you brought it up?"

"I suppose you could say I have an opinion, although I think I'd prefer to call it . . . advice. Advice is something you can listen to, think about, and then you have to decide what's right for you."

"Okay, I'm listening," Jess said, unable to recall the last time his father had given him advice with a preamble.

"Education is a wonderful thing, Jess. My college degrees are something I worked hard for, and I'm proud of them. But in the whole vast scheme of life, I'm not sure they did me a great deal of good in the things that really matter. Education can be found in many aspects of life. It doesn't have to come with a piece of paper that you can hang on the wall to let people know you've met a certain list of requirements. I suppose a degree varies in value depending on the profession a person wants to pursue. Obviously, some occupations require degrees and we wouldn't want to go to a doctor who didn't have one. But for you . . ."

"For me?" Jess pressed when Michael hesitated too long.

Michael looked directly at him. "Those boys don't care whether or not you have a piece of paper that declares your ability to help them."

"But everything I can learn about psychology will help me help them better, won't it?"

"Perhaps, but . . . my grandfather was reputed as the best administrator this home has ever had. He had no college education. In fact, the only schooling he had was what he got here in the boys' home between the ages of eleven and eighteen. Prior to that time he'd never been in school. Personally, I think the education he got before he came here was the most benefit to those boys."

"But you just said he didn't get any education before he came here."

"No, I said he didn't go to school," Michael said. "He got his education on the streets, struggling to survive. He was street savvy, Jess. He knew how those boys thought, what made them tick. And he knew how the love he'd been given in the home had eventually transformed his life. I guess what I'm trying to say is that . . . I never would have chosen for you to spend those years of your youth in rebellion, but I have to confess . . . more than once it's occurred to me that the education *you* got on the streets will give you a level of insight into those boys that I never had."

Jess gave a dubious chuckle. "Is that something I should be proud of?" he asked with obvious sarcasm.

"I'm not saying we should make bad choices in order to gain certain experiences. But those choices are in the past; you've changed your life. Still, those choices are a part of who and what you've become, and the best thing you can do with those experiences is use them to help the boys in your care."

While Jess was trying to absorb all his father had said, Michael asked, "You haven't changed your mind, have you?"

"About what?"

"About taking over the boys' home once Hobbs can't manage it any longer."

Jess sighed. "Funny, Tamra asked me that question not long ago."

"And what did you tell her?"

"No, I haven't changed my mind. It is what I want to do—what I *feel* I should do; I only hope I'm equal to the task."

"If it's what you know in your heart you should be doing with your life, then you *will* be equal to the task. The most important thing you need is a genuine desire to help those boys. And I know you have that."

"Yes, I suppose I do," Jess said, wondering if the timing of this conversation was only coincidental. Taking a good, long look at his father, it was readily evident that he was being physically affected by this disease. Emily kept assuring him that it was only the chemo taking its toll. And maybe that was true. But what if the chemo didn't work? What if the cancer never went into remission? Jess knew enough to know that cancer was terribly unpredictable. Was it, at this very moment, eating his father's life away? Were his days numbered? Was this conversation meant to be some kind of preparation for Jess to officially take over the family businesses?

He was just trying to talk himself out of such a notion when Michael went on to say, "Now, I realize that those horses in our care don't have the tender spirits of the boys, but keeping the horse business successful is what keeps the boys' home running. The wealth that's been passed down through the generations would dwindle quickly if investments aren't managed properly. You've worked with me enough to know the basics of the business, and you have some education in that area as well. I'm confident you can handle it, but there's something you might not be aware of."

"What is that?" Jess asked dryly, trying to maintain his composure.

"With your inheritance comes many layers of responsibility that—"

"Whoa!" Jess erupted to his feet. "My *inheritance?* What are you talking about? *What* inheritance? You make it sound like you're going to die next week, or something. I don't want any *inheritance!"* He said it as if it were a dirty word.

Unruffled by Jess's outburst, Michael said calmly, "Sit down, Jess. What I have to say is important. I probably won't die next week, but I don't know *when* I'm going to die. My will has been in place for many years, and was adjusted following your brother's death. But you need to know what it says, and there are important things you should know that are *not* in the will. So, sit down and listen to what I have to say."

Jess exchanged a long gaze with his father while he reminded himself that he couldn't waste away their time together by giving into his childish fears and emotions. Still, it took every measure of self-control to keep those emotions in check as he returned to his chair, saying quietly, "I'm sorry. This is just . . . tough."

"Yes, it is, Jess. I thought I'd have another twenty years at least to do this kind of thing. I imagined that we would work together for so long that you would just naturally take it all over without a hitch. Of course, you have to understand that even though you told us years ago you wanted to take it all over, and I believed you meant it, you've had some pretty rough spells, and I wasn't certain it would ever come about. I have to say that I'm grateful you're finally here and settled with your sweet wife."

"Well, I'm glad of that myself," Jess admitted.

When Michael didn't go on, Jess cleared his throat and asked, "So, what exactly does this will say that I need to know? Maybe you should tell me and get it over with."

Michael sighed and closed his eyes for a long moment. Jess wondered if his frustration was due to Jess's attitude, or the very fact that he felt they needed to have this conversation. Perhaps both.

Michael sat up and leaned against the headboard of the bed. Jess sighed and hung his head into his hands. "I'm listening, Dad."

"It's all yours, Jess. All of it."

Jess shot his head up. "All of *what?*"

"Byrnehouse-Davies and Hamilton," he enunciated carefully. "It's all yours when I'm gone."

"What . . . I . . . the . . ."

"The land, the house, the boys' home, the stables, the racetrack, the—"

"I get the idea, Dad, but . . . you can't give all of that to *me.*"

"Are you questioning my judgment?" Michael asked.

"No . . . but . . . well, maybe," Jess protested. "What about . . . the girls? Your sister?"

"What about them? My sister inherited large sums of money at the deaths of both our parents. And it will be the same for your sisters. I'm grateful to know that they are all righteous, responsible people who will use it to better this world. That's the way it's been in this family, right from the beginning. The moment that money came into Jess Davies' hands, he used it to make the world a better place. He didn't think like a rich man; he didn't live like a rich man. And what he taught his children and grandchildren has been upheld through the generations. Instinctively he lived by the adage, 'Where much is given, much is required.' And we must live by it, as well. Your very reluctance to take what you're being given makes me all the more confident in giving it to you. I think you understand what comes with the inheritance."

"I'm not sure I understand *anything!"* Jess sprang to his feet again. "And don't tell me to sit down." He paced back and forth beside the bed. *"What* exactly am I supposed to understand?"

"What you're being given has more value than you could possibly comprehend, Jess—both monetary and otherwise."

"Precisely," Jess said. "So, why are you giving it to me? What about Mother?"

"Your mother has plenty of assets in her own name. Her every need will be met as long as she's living. But I don't want your mother to be responsible for all of this." He made a sweeping motion with his arm. "My father died when I was just a kid. My mother spent many years in charge of this estate. She had managers and administrators she could trust, but she still had to remain abreast of all that was going on, and I know it was a burden to her until I was old enough to take it over. My sister and her husband helped a great deal until not so many years ago. But your sisters are all settled elsewhere, except one. And Emma spends too much time in the States for us to expect her to marry an Australian who will want to settle here and share this home with you. I don't want your mother to be burdened with this. She can be a support to you. She's smart and she's tough. But you have to understand who and what you are. You have to take care of her as well as everything else that's being left to you. Yes, what you are inheriting is of tremendous value. But you will earn it, Jess, I can assure you."

Jess continued to pace, occasionally pausing to look at his father. The reality of this conversation was pushing his nerves to a breaking point. When Michael was quiet for a minute, Jess felt compelled to say, "Maybe that's the problem, Dad. What if I *don't* earn it? What if I can't live up to your expectations?"

Michael sighed deeply. "Stand still, Jess, and look at me."

Jess did as he was told, stuffing his hands deep into the pockets of his jeans. "Listen to me carefully. This is the one thing you have to remember when it gets tough."

Michael hesitated and Jess asked, "Okay. What's the one thing?"

"Well, it's not some magic formula. But I've just realized that I can't simply tell you that one thing without telling you where I learned it."

"Okay," Jess said.

"Sit down," Michael insisted and he did. "My grandfather outlived my father. After my father died, he sat me down and told me that one day all of this would be mine. He told me the story of how the land and the wealth had been acquired by his father-in-law, and the story of how he had come here off the streets to be raised in the boys' home and eventually become a part of the family. When I asked him how I could take care of such a big responsibility—and I was just a kid, mind you—he looked me in the eye and said, 'Your best is good enough, Michael.' And that's what I want to tell you, Jess. Your best is good enough. Some days your best won't amount to much. But most of the time it will be more than enough. Because you know something that the generations before us didn't know. I think they believed it instinctively, but they didn't fully understand it."

"And what's that?"

"They didn't have the gospel, Jess. We have a glorious understanding of the purpose of all we're doing, and we know that the Atonement is there to make up the difference—even through the ins and outs of everyday life. So, your best really is good enough. And given a little practice, everything you have to do here will become as natural as breathing and you will feel completely at home."

Jess sighed and looked into his father's eyes. He couldn't imagine *ever* feeling completely at home without him here. But it was becoming readily apparent that he had no choice.

Chapter Six

Through another lengthy silence, Jess tried to take in all that his father had said. Wondering if he would *ever* understand it, he instinctively turned his mind to prayer. While his prayer felt disjointed and lacking in fervor, he found his mind focusing on one point of what his father had just said. He finally found the voice to ask, "What *is* the story?" Michael looked disoriented and he clarified, "The story of how the land and the wealth were acquired. I'm sure I've heard bits and pieces, and I actually read Jess Davies' journals once, but there was a lot of drama going on in my life at the time, and I'm not sure I remember certain points. But . . . if it's going to be mine, it would be good for me to know where it came from, don't you think?"

Michael smiled, and while it warmed Jess, he couldn't help thinking how much he would miss that smile when his father was gone. "I didn't know you'd read his journals," Michael said. "That's great. You should read them again, and read the others as well. I can't tell you how grateful I am to have come from a journal-keeping family. I think I've learned more about life from those books than any other single source, except the gospel."

"I'll have to do that one of these days. But right now . . . I want you to tell me the story, the way your grandfather told you."

Michael sighed and became thoughtful before he began telling Jess of how Benjamin Davies had come to this country as a young man and had homesteaded this land. He fell in love with a woman whose guardian made it clear that she would not be married to a man with no fortune. Ben acquired enough money through mining gold to build a home and stables and get a few good horses. But the woman he loved had been manipulated into marrying Tyson Byrnehouse, whose father was the second son of an English lord, bringing with him to this country a vast fortune. A long-time feud had begun between the Byrnehouses and the Davies when both men loved the same woman. Following Benjamin's death, his son, Jess Davies, became the victim of that feud as Chad Byrnehouse spurred incidents that threatened all he owned, even his life. Alexandra Byrnehouse came into Jess's life in need of a job when Chad had turned her out following their father's death, and Jess put her to work training his horses for a race with everything he owned banked on her success. Alexa won the race and Jess's heart, but more trouble followed and they barely managed to hold onto the land that Jess had inherited. Through a series of events that were difficult and complicated, Jess and Alexa finally ended up inheriting the Byrnehouse fortune, and thus the Byrnehouse-Davies name was formed.

Jess Davies had immediately invested a good amount of money into founding the Byrnehouse-Davies Home for Boys, and he began traditions of aiding the aborigines and regularly donating large sums of money to other charitable foundations. Jess and Alexa's daughter, Emma, had married Michael Hamilton, who had come to the boys' home following an unspeakably horrible childhood. Michael had eventually taken over as administrator of the boys' home, committing his life to repaying all he'd been given through his association with the Byrnehouse-Davies family. The Byrnehouse-Davies name had ended during World War II when the only son of Jess and Alexa's only son had been killed in action. Michael and Emma's only son, Jesse, had then inherited the estate.

"And so," Michael concluded, "Michael and Emma are my grandparents; Jesse my father."

Jess felt surprisingly calm from the story he'd just been told. Listening to his father talk about their forebears, he could almost forget that they were now facing a new challenge that would inevitably tear them apart.

"You have a great name, Jess," Michael said. "I hope you'll never forget what it means simply to *be* Jess Michael Hamilton."

"The fourth," Jess added with a little chuckle.

"That's right."

Not wanting to break the spell, Jess asked, "How long did it take *you* to feel completely at home with the work here . . . for it to be as natural as breathing?"

"Well, truthfully, I don't know. There were some rough moments, but I always managed to get through them. For me, it seemed that once I had your mother and the girls here with me, everything just seemed to . . . fall into place."

Jess became lost in his thoughts through several minutes of silence, as Michael allowed him some time to absorb all that he'd said. When his mind came back to the present, he turned to meet his father's eyes. The reality of what they were facing settled in all over again. He had to admit, "I just don't know how I can do it all alone."

"You won't be alone, Jess; never alone."

"I know, but . . ."

"I know what you mean, son. And it's hard. If it's any consolation, I know what it's like to lose a father, and so does Allison."

"Allison?" he asked before he recalled. "Oh, yeah. I forget that Mom was married before."

"Yes, so do I," Michael said with something deeply sad in his voice, as well as his eyes. Jess wanted to ask what he was thinking, but Michael hurried to add, "I know this isn't going to be easy for you, but you have a great family, a great wife. And you are a great man."

"I don't *feel* like a great man," Jess said.

"If you did, you wouldn't be great," Michael said with conviction. "But you are, believe me."

"I guess I'll have to. But as long as you're around, you're going to have to teach me everything you know; I'm going to need all the help I can get."

"We'll just keep working together as we have been," Michael said. "The only difference being that . . . well, I just want us to be more open with questions and answers. I don't want to leave anything undone."

Jess nodded, suddenly unable to speak. The respite he'd found in the conversation ended abruptly as the severity of his father's illness engulfed him once again. He had to consciously will back his tears, feeling his head pound to compensate. Finding the silence uncomfortable, he turned toward the door, saying in a barely steady voice, "Mom sure has been gone a long time."

"I told her we needed to talk."

Jess nodded again, feeling a need for solitude, if only to relieve the pounding in his head. "Maybe I should . . . go and rescue her from Evelyn until Tamra gets back."

"Thanks for hearing me out," Michael said and held out a hand as Jess came to his feet. Jess took it and couldn't hold back the tears as his father squeezed tightly, at the same time saying, "I love you, son. And I'm proud of you."

"I love you too, Dad," Jess said and hurried from the room.

Alone in his bedroom, Jess let the full torrent of his emotions pour out. Recalling fragments of the conversation he'd just shared with his father, he felt overwhelmed and totally unprepared. He was grateful to have Tamra gone; he felt sure she had to be sick to death of his emotional state.

When he finally gained control, he noticed the time and realized if he didn't call Sean soon, the time difference would make it too late. He quickly found the number and dialed from his bedroom extension. A child answered and Jess asked, "Is your dad there?" A moment later Sean came to the phone. Jess tried not to sound as depressed as he felt when he said, "Hello there."

"Hey, kid," Sean said brightly. "How was the wedding? Sure wish we could have been there."

"Well, it was great," Jess said. "We missed you, but . . . Down Under's a long ways to go for a wedding."

"We've got a gift for you," Sean said. "But things have been pretty crazy so we haven't got it shipped off yet."

"Don't worry about it," Jess said. "We already have far more than we need."

"Well, you probably don't *need* this, but I think you'll enjoy it." Jess said nothing and Sean added, "So how's married life?"

"It's great," Jess said. "She's incredible. I'm still trying to figure out what I did to deserve her."

"I wouldn't wonder about that," Sean said. "You're an amazing guy; always have been."

Jess gave a scoffing laugh.

"So, what's up?" Sean asked. "You don't sound real chipper."

Jess cleared his throat and got to the point. "I guess you heard about Dad."

"No, what?" Sean asked, his voice expressing mild panic.

Jess groaned. "I thought they would have told you before now; I didn't want to be the one to tell you."

"Tell me *what?*" Sean demanded.

"You mean . . . you haven't talked to my parents since the wedding?"

"No."

"You haven't talked to Allison . . . or Emma?"

"No!"

"Well, you all live in the same city, for crying out loud," Jess insisted, as if he could convince Sean otherwise. "Why haven't you talked to them?"

"I don't know; they haven't called." The concern in his voice deepened. "What *about* your dad?" Jess said nothing while he attempted to gather his words. "Come on, Jess," he added. "He's been more of a father to me than my own ever was. Tell me what's going on."

Knowing he had no choice but to tell him, Jess took a deep breath and choked out the words. "He's got cancer; it's bad."

Jess heard him gasp, then all was quiet for a full minute. "I can't believe it," Sean finally said.

"That's a pretty common feeling around here," Jess said.

"And I can't believe Emma and Allison didn't call me."

"They probably thought Mom or Dad would tell you; if they're anything like me, they probably don't want to even think about it, let alone talk about it."

"I can't believe your parents didn't call me before now."

"Well, if it's any consolation, they knew before the wedding, but they didn't tell us until a few days ago. I guess they didn't want to ruin the honeymoon; they don't want us to worry."

"I can't believe it," Sean said again, his voice breathy. Following another minute of silence, Jess heard a sniffle, then another.

"You okay?" Jess asked.

"Not really, no," Sean said, his despair evident. If nothing else, Jess felt a little better to realize that if the psychologist was upset, then perhaps he wasn't totally crazy after all.

Jess gave him another minute before he asked, "Can we talk?"

"I thought you didn't want to talk about it."

"I don't, but if I can't get some grounding here, I'm going to lose my mind. And I'm afraid there's not enough of it left that I can afford to lose any more."

"So, let's talk," Sean said, his voice betraying his shock.

"Is now a bad time?"

"No, it's fine. I just . . . Geez, I just can't believe it. Where is the cancer? Can they do surgery or—"

"From what little they told me, there are growths in one of his lungs, his liver, and his intestines."

"Oh, good heavens," Sean muttered breathlessly. "I can't believe it."

"Like I said, that makes you a member of the vast majority. I don't think anyone who knows about it *can* believe it."

"So . . . how is he? How's your mom?"

"They both seem pretty resigned to the whole thing. I mean, Dad made it clear that he's not giving up, and he's going to make the best out of life and all that stuff, but he says he's got to face this realistically."

"At least he's not in denial. What about your mom?"

"Well . . . it's hard to read her on this. She told me they've known for a while and they've cried in private and dealt with it somewhat. I wonder if she's being brave for his sake."

"And what about you?" Sean asked.

"I'm an absolute mess," Jess said with a quavering voice that seemed to verify the statement.

"Like how?"

"I can't focus. I'm constantly trying not to cry, except for when I can sneak into the bathroom or something, and then I *do* cry. I feel *devastated!*"

"And it's been . . . what did you say? A few days since you were told that your father has terminal cancer?" Jess didn't answer; he was more preoccupied with the knot tightening in his stomach to hear it put that way. "I'd say you have every right to feel devastated, and to cry if you have to. Finding it difficult to focus would be an understatement. I think I'd be more concerned if you *didn't* feel like crying.

Holding all that emotion inside isn't good for you when it goes on too long."

"So what are you saying?" Jess asked. "Am I losing my mind or not?"

"No, Jess," he gave a stilted chuckle, "you're not losing your mind. You're *grieving*. You know, grief happens whenever we lose *anything*. We can grieve over losing a job, going through a divorce, lost time, moving away from an old home. Grief happens. The interesting thing about knowing that someone you love is going to die is that . . . well, most people tend to do the majority of their grieving before the death actually happens. It's completely different from losing someone suddenly—like when we lost your brother in that accident. There was no time to prepare, and the grief came when he wasn't around."

"I think that makes sense," Jess said. "Although, I think I would have preferred to have you tell me I was crazy. Or maybe I was hoping you could tell me something that could make me feel better."

"I can't tell you he's not going to die. Will anything short of that make you feel better?"

"No," Jess said, his voice strained. "But . . ."

"But what?" Sean pressed when he didn't go on.

"We're taught that the gospel can bring us peace. I know from my own experience that the gospel, more specifically the Atonement, is what healed me after the accident. So . . . I guess what I'm trying to say is that I almost feel . . . guilty, or like I *should* feel guilty because . . . I'm so upset."

"Let me explain something, Jess."

"I wish you would."

"I can tell you that I know beyond any doubt the gospel *does* offer a peace that cannot be found anywhere else. It gives us a deep understanding of life and death and the trials we endure here. Our Savior paid the price for our sorrow. And I promise you that if you earnestly seek that peace you will find it. However . . . grief is simply a part of this mortal existence. You don't have to grieve over a belief that you will never be with your father again, because you are blessed to know otherwise. But you do have to accept that you will be separated for much longer than you had probably been counting on. As the scriptures tell us, there is a time to mourn. And we would not commit to 'mourn with those that mourn' if mourning were not a part of life. If mourning goes on and on, becomes excessive or obsessive, then you'd have to get a grip. But there's a difference between a deep suffering that could be avoided if the burden were given to the Lord, and the natural sorrow we feel in losing a loved one. Am I making any sense?"

"Yes, actually, you are. I knew you would. That's why I called."

"Well, I'm glad *somebody* called." He sighed loudly. "I still can't believe it."

"Yeah, well, once you get through convincing me I'm not crazy, you can cry on my shoulder."

"Long distance?"

"Exactly. For as long as you want."

"Spoken like a true brother," Sean said, emotion tinging his voice again.

"So," Jess said, "can we talk about this grief stuff for a minute?"

"Sure," Sean said. "With the way I feel at the moment, I'm thinking I could probably use a refresher course. If I say all this out loud, maybe I'll remember enough to know that *I'm* not crazy."

"The thing is . . . sometimes I feel almost . . . Dare I say it? *Angry*. But there's no one or nothing to be angry with."

"That's true. Cancer is just one of those things. But when you found out your brother and his wife and your best friend were killed in that accident, were you angry with the guy driving that truck?"

"Not nearly as much as I was angry with myself," Jess admitted.

"Okay, well . . . the point being that anger is a natural part of grieving. Granted, I personally believe that anger is less likely to present itself when you have the peace of the gospel. If you understand and accept that a righteous man is taken from this earth when it is his time to go, and through the gift of the Holy Ghost you gain a personal witness of that, then . . . it's hard to be angry. Still, it takes time to come to terms with this kind of thing, and anger is normal. Shock, sadness, a sense of bargaining, and—"

"What's that?" Jess asked. "Bargaining?"

"Well . . . it's like . . ." He stammered a moment. "Let me give you a drastic example. Let's say you were inactive in the Church and smoking and doing drugs."

"As I once was," Jess admitted.

"Yes, but . . . I really wasn't thinking about that. It's just hypothetical."

"Okay, go on."

"So, you're living this lifestyle, you find out your father's going to die, and you start telling God, 'I'll turn my life around and go back to church if you'll let my father live.' Does that make sense?"

"Yes, it does," Jess said.

"But you have to remember that there's no required quota for grief. You may experience a great deal of one facet, and none of another. You may vacillate. Just remember that it's normal."

"So . . . is there anything I can do to make sure it doesn't get . . . out of hand?"

"Well . . . I think you should talk about it. Can you talk to Tamra?"

"Yes, of course."

"No, I mean . . . about the really honest, bare-faced guts of your feelings? Can you talk to her like that?"

"Yes, actually, I can."

"That's great," Sean said. "There are a lot of marriages that aren't that way. Don't take that for granted. And the only other thing I can say is to stay close to the Spirit. You'll find that peace you're seeking with time and effort, but . . . well . . . this is a rough thing. And you may have moments of grief come up and hit you for years after he's gone. Good heavens, I can't believe I'm saying this. I can't believe we're talking about your father."

"I guess that means you're experiencing some form of shock," Jess said in a mock professional tone.

Sean chuckled, then his voice turned grave. "Yes, I believe I am." A moment later he asked, "So . . . is there any time frame? Any specific prognosis?"

"Not that I know of. He's getting chemo, which is making him tired and nauseated. He said the best we can hope for is that it will go into some kind of remission. But we just . . . don't know. Earlier this afternoon he sat me down and started talking about my taking over the boys' home and the station, and how I would certainly *earn* my inheritance because it was a huge responsibility."

"Oh, help," Sean sighed.

They talked for a few more minutes before Tamra and Evelyn came looking for him. Jess wrapped up the conversation, then got off the phone. He repeated to Tamra everything he and Sean had discussed, while Evelyn colored in some coloring books that had been left on the bedroom floor. Jess cried, and so did Tamra, but given all that Sean had said, he had to admit that he felt a little better. At least he wasn't crazy—not completely, anyway.

The phone rang and Jess picked it up, surprised to hear that it was Sean calling him back.

"Hey, kid," he said. "I've just had a long talk with my wife and—"

"Yeah, me too."

"The thing is . . . I'm rearranging some vacation time, and . . . Well, do you think it would be all right if Tara and I came to visit, next week maybe?"

"I think it would be great," Jess said.

"I'd kind of like to surprise them, but . . . do you think there's too much going on, or—"

"I think it would be great," Jess repeated. "I'll do a little snooping and make sure there aren't any big conflicts, but I think it might perk things up around here. And maybe you can help us *all* come to terms with this stuff."

"Well, I'd love to do what I can, but mainly . . . I just want to spend some time with him. If there's no way of knowing how long it will be, well . . . I need to spend some time with him." Grief was evident in Sean's voice and Jess felt his own tears surfacing again. He agreed to call Sean back in a couple of days, and Sean was going to make tentative flight arrangements.

Michael came down to supper that evening, looking a little less pale. The medication Tamra had picked up apparently helped relieve his nausea, and he felt more like eating. Michael and Emily were both in good spirits, and the meal was enjoyable—almost normal. Jess managed to worm into the conversation an inquiry about his parents' plans for the coming week, and he felt confident that Sean's travel plans would work out.

When supper was over, Jess took Evelyn upstairs to bathe her while Tamra helped clean up the kitchen. Michael came to Evelyn's bedroom and shared story time with them before he went to bed early. Before going to bed, Jess and Tamra talked more about what was happening to their family. Long after Tamra had fallen asleep close beside him, Jess stared at the ceiling, contemplating all his father had said, as well as his conversation with Sean. He prayed for guidance and understanding, trying to add up the logic of the situation. He finally slept with some decisions in his mind, which he discussed with Tamra first thing the next morning while she was dressing Evelyn and putting her hair into little pigtails.

At the breakfast table, Jess spoke up right after the blessing had been said. "I've been thinking, Dad, about our conversation yesterday and . . . Well, I've discussed it with Tamra and I've come to some decisions."

"Such as?" Emily asked, seeming intrigued. Michael set his fork down and leaned his chin on his hands.

"Well, it's not complicated. I've just decided to put my education on hold for the time being." Looking directly at his father, he added, "I want to spend as much time with you as I possibly can. I want to learn everything I can from the man who knows more than anyone else the ins and outs of the family businesses." He paused and took a deep breath. "This is hard to say . . . it's no secret that we don't know how much time we have together, but then, for that matter, do we ever know how much time we have together?" Jess looked down in order to keep his emotions under control. "If we had known that accident was going to happen, wouldn't we have put more effort and energy into saying and doing certain things?" He chuckled tensely and set his elbows on the table. "I guess what I'm saying is that . . . maybe we should always live as if we don't know how long we'll have together, because we never do and . . ." He reached for Tamra's hand. "When it comes right down to it, our relationships are the most important thing."

Jess heard sniffling and glanced up to see all the eyes that were watching him were moist with tears. He chuckled again and said, "What? I'm not the only one around here who is a blubbering idiot?"

"Hardly," Emily said and dabbed her eyes with her napkin.

"Well, I *have* been a blubbering idiot, and . . . the thing is, I can't promise I won't cry at any given moment, probably over something stupid, but . . . I'm going to do my best to cope with this and just . . . well, make the most of what we have left."

Following a moment of silence except for the sound of more sniffling, Evelyn said with perfect innocence, "Why did you all be sad?"

Jess chuckled and leaned over to kiss the top of her head. "Because we're just a bunch of old, silly people," he said. She seemed to accept the answer and continued eating her scrambled eggs.

A moment later, Michael stood and leaned over the table to take Jess's face into his hands. He pressed a kiss to Jess's forehead, as if he were kissing a child, then he looked into Jess's eyes and said firmly, "I could not ask for a finer son, Jess. You will never know what a blessing you are to me, now more than ever." He smiled as he sat down and added, "I think your plan sounds marvelous."

While they all proceeded to eat in silence, Jess contemplated what his father had just said. *I could not ask for a finer son.* It only took a minute to recall all of the stupid things he'd done in his life to bring his parents grief. A number of incidents through his rebellious youth came to mind. And while he knew he had no accountability for the accident that had caused so much anguish for this family, it had taken him years to come to terms with it, and he felt certain his parents had worried a great deal through those years. His attempted suicide stood out as the most painful trial he'd brought on his parents. But still, after all of that, his father could look into his eyes and say with no reservation that he could not ask for a finer son. While he had no doubt that his father meant it, he found it difficult to believe that he could live up to the expectations that came with being the only remaining Hamilton, once his father was gone.

As his thoughts took hold fully, Jess set down his fork and put his face in his hands, but there was no concealing the fact that he was crying. When Emily passed him an extra napkin, Jess chuckled in an effort to force back a sob. "See what I mean?"

"It's okay, Jess," Emily said. "I'd far rather have you crying than have you holding it all inside."

"I agree emphatically," Tamra said, putting a hand on his shoulder.

Jess was relieved when his parents began chatting comfortably. A feeling of normalcy soon descended, and he was able to finish his breakfast. When they were all done eating, Michael rose and announced, "Jess and I will do up these dishes before we go see how business is coming along. Why don't you ladies go . . . for a walk or something?"

"Okay," Emily said, taking Evelyn to the sink to wash her hands and face.

After the women left with Evelyn, Michael cleared the table, and Jess started loading the dishwasher. When a particular thought wouldn't leave his head, he just forced himself to say, "Dad . . . I have a question."

"Okay."

"I know you've been aware of the cancer for a while now, and first of all I'd like to say that . . . I understand and I truly . . . appreciate the attitude you have—that both of you have—that you're going to fight this thing to the best of your ability, and make the most of every day we have together. But I guess what I want to ask is . . . well, Mom said that the two of you have cried, and been angry; that you've gone through shock and disbelief, and . . . given that, it's nice to know that how I feel is normal, but . . . what I want to ask is . . ."

When he hesitated too long, Michael said, "Stop stammering and just ask the question."

"Okay," Jess chuckled tensely and leaned against the counter. "I guess what I want to know is . . ." He looked up and met his father's eyes. "Have you come to terms with this? Have you found peace with it?"

Michael blew out a long, slow breath and looked briefly at the ceiling. "I can't say I'm ready to die, Jess. My instincts are screaming inside of me that I need to live and live long. My will to live is strong, but . . ." He paused and blew out another breath. "I learned a long time ago that the only way to find peace with the struggles in this life is to allow my will to be superceded by the will of our Father in Heaven. I know that denial would only rob me of precious time to prepare myself and my family."

Jess sighed and looked at the floor, folding his arms over his chest. "Okay, but . . ." He wondered how to explain that his question hadn't been answered.

"But?" Michael pressed, but Jess could only look at him, not certain what to say. The very fact that they were having such a conversation still felt surreal.

"I'm not sure what you're fishing for, Jess," Michael said, "but I can tell you this. I'm doing my best every day to have faith and press forward. And I—"

"Do you think if you have enough faith you could beat this, that you could get a miracle?"

Michael looked directly at him. "I don't think faith is some magic potion or some method of positive thinking, and if you come up with enough of it, you can make something happen. I think faith is learning to accept God's will and be at peace with it."

"And have you found peace with it?" Jess asked.

"I have," Michael said resolutely. "And maybe this is saying too much. If it is, forgive me, but . . . something deep inside of me . . ." He pressed a fist to his chest. "Something subtle, even formless, but impossible to ignore, leads me to believe that this disease *will* take me, that no miracle will intervene, and *if* it goes into remission, it won't relent for long."

Jess was amazed that he actually managed to control the emotions aroused by hearing his father say such things. He was relieved when Michael went on. "But I *do* have peace, Jess. That doesn't mean I *want* to die, or that I even feel *ready* to die. But I am *willing* to die when it is my time to go, and I know God wouldn't take me home if it *weren't* my time to go. Does that make sense?"

Jess nodded, fearing his ability to hold back his tears wouldn't hold up if he tried to speak. Again Michael continued. "There's something I want to say, Jess." His voice cracked and Jess looked up at him. After admitting that he was going to die, what would make him emotional? "I just want to tell you . . . how much I appreciate your attitude with all of this. I know it's tough, but . . . just seeing your effort to understand, and to . . . well, just your willingness to talk about it helps immensely. I'd far rather talk openly than pretend everything's okay. Your courage touches me and—"

"My courage?" Jess scoffed. "I feel anything but courageous."

"Yes, Jess, your courage. You're facing this head on, talking about it, trying to deal with it, and in my opinion, being pretty mature over the whole thing. This would be a lot tougher for me if you were in denial or . . . angry."

"I've had some angry moments, but . . . that won't get us anywhere, will it?"

"No, it won't. And I've had some angry moments as well, but . . ." Michael's voice broke again. "If nothing else, I want you to know that I'm glad you love your old dad enough to be upset." He chuckled. "It would be hard to think that losing me would be easy."

Jess chuckled as well, but with no trace of humor. "I can't even imagine how I will ever be able to . . ." He couldn't finish as grief flooded into his words, but Michael pulled him into a tight embrace, and they both cried. Jess found strength in knowing that at least they were in this together.

Chapter Seven

Jess finally got himself under control and returned to loading the dishwasher while his father washed a pan. Looking for a way to fill in a sudden silence, he said, "Dad?"

"Yes?"

"I've been thinking about our conversation yesterday, and there's a couple of things I'm not quite clear on. First of all . . . you said that with my inheritance came many layers of responsibility. I think you were trying to make a point, but I went off on a tangent and I don't think we ever got back to it."

Michael thought about it for a minute. "I think what I wanted to say is just that I've realized through the years, as I've grown to care for many of the people who have worked for us, that there's a certain responsibility to those people, beyond just providing them with a job. Some more than others. The point being that . . . well, I think the Spirit will guide you in such things. I just wanted to mention it."

Jess nodded, not wanting to think too deeply about those many layers of responsibility. He had to take all of this one day at a time, praying that they would have many, many days together yet.

Searching for another vein of conversation, he said, "Also, I have to ask exactly how Michael Hamilton—your grandfather—ended up marrying into the family if he'd been raised in the boys' home."

Michael grinned. "Oh, that's my favorite story. My grandfather was a rogue, Jess. He kidnapped Emma and Lacey for ransom and took them into the outback."

"You're joking," he chuckled.

"No, it's quite true."

"Well, come to think of it, I know I've heard the kidnapping story, but I guess I just . . . thought it was legend, or something."

"No, it's true. As I understand it, he fell in love with Emma in his youth. He stayed on to work in the stables after he graduated from the home. When Emma paid no attention to him, he left and ended up going to prison. When he got out, he came back and kidnapped her for ransom. But there was a mixup and he ended up getting Lacey, her foster sister, instead. So they had to come back for Emma. Somehow, through the escapade, Emma saw through Michael's façade and realized he loved her. He ended up, not so many weeks later, Emma's husband. And Jess Davies gave him the ransom money." He chuckled and added. "What I wouldn't give to know the *details* of that story. When they were still alive I was too young to really care about such stories, but now . . ."

"Well, when you see them again, you can ask them," Jess said, and then felt a little shocked to realize how soon that might be.

But Michael said straightly, "Yes, I'll have to do that. Maybe it will give me something to look forward to that will compensate for all I'm leaving behind." He chuckled tensely then said, "Perhaps we should get some work done."

"You mean besides the dishes?" Jess asked, trying to mimic his father's attempt to be cheerful.

Once the kitchen was in good order, they walked together to the boys' home, but Jess couldn't help noticing that Michael was moving a bit slowly and seemed to get out of breath easily. Once there, he relaxed in Mr. Hobbs's office while the three of them discussed some issues of concern. When they returned to the house for lunch, Jess slipped away to make a phone call before he joined the rest of the family in the kitchen. About halfway through the meal, Jess announced, "I'll be flying to Sydney the day after tomorrow. As you know, I'll likely be gone all day."

Michael and Emily both looked surprised. Tamra did well at pretending this was simply a mundane occurrence, even though she knew better. Jess managed to keep from smiling as he repeated the story Tamra had suggested they tell his parents in order to keep Sean's visit a surprise.

"The thing is, Tamra's aunt is having some challenges. It's not something she wanted us to discuss, but I do feel like I need to go and help her with a situation. I'll only need to be there a couple of hours, and I'll come right back."

"Okay," Emily said. "Tamra, if you want to go with him, we can certainly look out for Evelyn and—"

"Oh, that's all right. Jess can handle it, and I just don't think I'm up to the flight."

"You're not sticking around here because of me, are you?" Michael growled.

"Now, why would I do that?" Tamra asked, almost sounding insulted.

"If you think I'm not capable of taking care of myself enough for Emily to take care of Evie then—"

"I'm well aware that you've not become a crippled old man overnight," Tamra said. "And I'm not staying for any such reason. But since you brought it up, with Sadie gone, I think it's best that the two of you aren't left in charge of Evelyn. She's a handful."

"I'm a handfow," Evelyn said proudly and they all chuckled.

Michael nudged Jess and pointed at Tamra with his fork. "She's feisty when she wants to be." He smiled and added with affection, "Not unlike your mother."

"Indeed," Jess chuckled.

"Perhaps we need to be feisty to keep you Hamilton men in line," Emily said.

"And just for the record," Tamra added, more to Michael, "no one is attempting to coddle you or fuss over you, but it's my opinion that you should be a little less noble and stay down more. Everything around here survived while you served two missions, and Jess can learn much from you by talking in the bedroom. It's common knowledge that chemotherapy is tough on the body. So stop being brave and . . . read a book, or something."

Jess chuckled as he observed his father's widening eyes. A tense silence followed until Emily added firmly, "Amen."

Silence persisted until Tamra said, "I'm sorry. That didn't sound very respectful. Perhaps I should be a little more . . . restrained with my opinions."

"On the contrary, my dear," Emily said, "any one of the girls wouldn't have said any less, and you are certainly our daughter. Besides," she smiled at her husband, "I've told him that a dozen times, but he won't listen to me. Perhaps he'll get the idea if he hears it from both of us."

Michael sighed. Jess said, "I have to say I'm with them."

"Okay, fine," Michael said, "as soon as I eat I'm going upstairs to rest—but no coddling or fussing. I'm just a little . . . tired."

When they were finished eating, Emily took Michael upstairs, promising to find him something good to read. Tamra stayed to work in the kitchen with Evelyn close by, and Jess kissed them both before he went out to speak with Murphy and help him do some maintenance in the racing stables. He returned at supper time to find Tamra in the kitchen, tossing a salad. He put his arm around her from behind and kissed her neck, provoking a soft laugh before she turned to kiss him.

"How did your day go?" she asked.

"Fine. How about you?"

"Good. Evelyn's been a little more . . . demanding than usual, but she's still cute."

Jess went in the room off the kitchen where Evelyn often played. He sat on the floor beside her and she promptly sat on his lap with a stack of storybooks. Before he was through the second one, Tamra announced that supper was ready. Emily arrived a moment later, alone, saying, "Your father is worn out. I'll take a tray up to him as soon as we eat." She chuckled and added to Tamra, "I think you gave him permission to actually *admit* that he's worn out."

Tamra sighed. "I hope I wasn't out of line. I can get carried away with—"

"I told you before, my dear, I'm glad you said what you did—especially since you said it with love. I can assure you, if I felt there was a problem, I would discuss it with you."

"Yes, she would," Jess said, pretending to be frightened by the prospect of facing his mother. The women both laughed and they sat down to eat.

Without his father present, Jess couldn't resist asking his mother, "How are you holding up?"

Emily looked startled by the question. "I'm all right," she admitted. "It's . . . hard. But I'm all right."

"You don't have to be brave and noble either, Mother," Jess said. "I mean . . . you *are* brave and noble, quite naturally, but . . . what I'm saying is that you can talk to us. We're family."

"I know." She smiled and put her hand over Jess's on the table. "But really . . . for the moment, I'm all right."

"Just let us know if there's anything we can do," Tamra said. "Anything."

"Of course," Emily said. Jess exchanged a glance with Tamra and she felt certain that he shared her concerns. This had to be at least as difficult for Emily as it was for Michael, perhaps more so in some ways; or perhaps it was simply different. They could only pray that they would have the strength to bear the grief.

* * *

Early in the morning, two days later, Tamra drove Jess out to the hangar while Evelyn was still asleep and Emily listened for her.

"You be careful now," Tamra said, hugging him tightly before he climbed into the plane.

"I will," he said. "We should be back early evening. You know what to do."

"Of course," she said. "I'll see you then."

Tamra went back to the house where Evelyn was just waking up. After breakfast and a visit to Grandpa's room, she took Evelyn with her into town to do a few errands and to buy two weeks' worth of groceries for the family. They ate lunch in town, and Evelyn napped on the way home. They returned to spend the afternoon putting the groceries away and preparing supper. When the meal was ready, Tamra took a tray upstairs for Michael and Emily to eat together there. They were both obviously pleased with the idea, but while Tamra ate alone with Evelyn in the kitchen, she couldn't help thinking of how ill Michael had looked. She reminded herself, as she had dozens of times before, that the chemo was hard on a person, and just because he was bad off now didn't mean he was at death's door. Surely he had some good life left to live. She prayed that he did.

Tamra barely had Evelyn cleaned up from eating when she heard the plane circling low overhead. She made an excited noise that Evelyn imitated. "Come along, little bug. Let's go get Daddy."

"Daddy in da pwane," she said excitedly and Tamra carried her out to the Cruiser, buckling her into her seat. She let out an excited giggle when they pulled up beside the hangar just as the plane swept past them in a smooth landing. When it finally stopped and the engine died, Jess and Sean both got out, but Tamra was surprised to see only them. Evelyn ran into Jess's arms and Tamra greeted Sean with an embrace.

"It's good to see you again," she said.

"And you." He smiled, then tipped his head toward Jess. "He seems awfully happy, all things considered. Marriage agrees with him, I think."

Tamra smiled. "It certainly agrees with me. How were the flights?"

"Oh, long," he groaned. "I never remember how many hours it actually takes."

"Tara didn't come?" she asked, referring to his wife.

"No," Sean's disappointment was evident, "we had everything arranged, but our youngest is having some struggles, and then another of the kids showed up with a fever. She just didn't feel good about coming."

"Well, I'm glad *you* were able to come," Tamra said. "Michael and Emily will be thrilled to see you."

"I hope so," Sean said as he turned toward Jess, who was still holding Evelyn.

"Is this James and Krista's baby?" Sean asked, grinning at her while he touched her arm.

"Yes," Jess said proudly, "but until they can be with her again, she's ours."

Sean made a curious noise and Jess added, "The whole thing is being processed. Since my parents have been her legal guardians, it's not terribly complicated. It should be official before summer . . . I mean winter." He chuckled. "Which half of the world are we in? I lose track sometimes."

"We're Down Under and you mean winter," Tamra said, taking Evelyn from Jess. "Now help Sean with his luggage. Supper is waiting."

"Ooh, I'm starved," Sean admitted, and a few minutes later they were on their way to the house, Jess driving. They went straight to the kitchen, leaving Sean's luggage in the Cruiser until after they'd eaten. Jess insisted they were starving and they'd wait to spring Sean on his parents until after they'd eaten. Tamra heated their plates in the microwave while they started on some salad, talking and laughing just as she'd heard them do the last time they'd been together. She enjoyed hearing the normal banter between them, especially from Jess. She had to admit that, given the short time they'd known about Michael's cancer, they were all adjusting—to some degree.

Jess and Sean were nearly finished eating when Emily entered the kitchen, saying to Jess, "Oh, good. You're back and . . ." Her eyes fell on Sean and her mouth fell open for a long moment before she let out a squeal of laughter. "What are you doing here?"

"I came to see you and that ornery bloke you married," Sean said, coming to his feet. Emily rushed to embrace him while they both laughed, then Tamra noticed Emily's shoulders quivering and Sean's arms tightening around her. They were both crying. The moment Jess noticed the reason for their silence, he pressed a hand over his eyes and bit his quivering lip.

Tamra's emotions were quick to follow. At such moments she felt more angry than sad. Angry with cancer. Why did it have to even exist? Why had it become such a plague of the day they lived in? And why had it manifested itself in this family, *her* family? It ripped into her heart to see these people, whom she had grown to love so deeply, torn apart and grieving.

Emily finally drew back and wiped at her face, saying to Sean, "How did you know? I'm so glad you came."

"Are you?" Sean asked, putting his hands on her shoulders.

"Yes, oh yes."

"I was a bit worried that it might not be a good time, that I might be imposing while you're trying to adjust and—"

"You're family, Sean. We've been through too much together for you to feel that way." Again she asked, "How did you know?"

"No thanks to you or that husband of yours," Sean said with mock anger. "Jess called me to talk it through, assuming I already knew. Allison finally called to tell me yesterday before I left." A genuine edge of irritation crept into his voice. "If I'm family, I should have been told before now."

"Yes, you should have," Emily said. "I just assumed the girls would talk to you as soon as they got back to the States after the wedding. I should have made that request more clearly."

"Well, I know now and I'm here," Sean said gently, embracing Emily again. "So, tell me what I can do."

"We just need your company and a diversion, perhaps," Emily said.

"So, where is he?" Sean asked, sitting down to finish the last few bites of his meal.

"He's upstairs in bed," Emily said, then she went on to explain the prognosis and the effects of the chemo while Jess and Tamra cleared the table and finished loading the dishwasher.

When Emily had finished her explanation, Sean said, "Forgive me if I'm sounding like the family psychologist, but . . . how are you all doing with this? And how is *Michael* doing with this?"

"It wouldn't hurt to ask him," Emily said, "but truthfully, I think we're doing all right. It's hard, but we're certainly not in denial. We're talking about it, crying if we have to, and we're trying to be prepared and make the most of what we've got."

Sean smiled and reached for Emily's hand. "I wouldn't have expected anything less from you, *or* Michael."

"Would you like to see him now?" Emily asked, coming to her feet. "Boy, will he be surprised!"

"I hope so," Sean said.

"Hey," Jess said, "let's get your luggage and take it up while we're at it."

Jess and Sean carried the two suitcases up the stairs, with the women and Evelyn following. Sean commented, "One of these will be empty on the return trip. It's got your wedding present in it."

"Really?" Tamra said. "I can't wait."

"Well, we gotta see Dad first," Jess said.

"Bring it with you," Emily said. "Then Michael can see you open it."

"Great idea," Sean said. He left one suitcase in the room he always stayed in when he came, and he left the other just outside Michael's bedroom door.

"Hey, Dad," Jess said, entering the room first, with Evelyn in his arms. Emily and Tamra entered the room just behind him. "What's up?"

"Not much, why?" Michael set aside the book he'd been reading.

"Because I have a surprise for you," he said.

"Oh? I could use a surprise," Michael said. "Am I going to like it?"

"It's a good surprise, if that's what you're wondering," Jess said. "I picked it up in Sydney for you."

"Well, let's have it," Michael said, and Sean walked into the room.

"Hey, old man," he said with a genuine chuckle. "What are you doing lying around up here?"

"Merciful heaven!" Michael breathed, then he laughed and swung his legs over the side of the bed. "I don't believe it," he said and laughed again.

"Don't get up on my account," Sean said, but Michael rose to his feet and they shared a long, firm embrace.

"What on earth are you doing here?" Michael asked, taking hold of Sean's shoulders to look into his eyes.

"I heard a rumor that you were cavorting with the 'C' word."

"The 'C' word?" Michael laughed and sat back down on the edge of the bed.

"Well, it *is* an ugly word, isn't it?" Sean said, taking a chair nearby. Emily sat in the other chair available, Tamra on the end of the bed and Jess on the floor with Evelyn.

"Yes, it is," Michael said. "But in case you're testing us, *Doctor* O'Hara, we're not afraid to say it. It's not easy, but we do manage to spit it out."

"I'm not testing you," Sean said. "If you must know, *I'm* having a rough time saying it—at least in relation to you. I think I'm still in shock."

"Well, that comes and goes around here," Michael admitted, looking at the floor. He looked up and smiled. "But if the 'C' word got you to come here, it might almost be worth it. It's good to see you."

"And you," Sean said. "So," he added, rubbing his hands together, "I'm counting on beating you at chess, having at least one picnic, long talks on the veranda in the evenings. What else do we get to do?"

"You can help Jess fix some fence lines," Michael said, "if you think you're up to it."

"Oh, I'm up to it," Sean said, his voice expressing delight, as if Michael assigning him a chore were tantamount to winning a great sum of money.

"Well, good. Because I'm really trying not to feel guilty lying here most of the time, but there's a great deal of maintenance that got out of hand through two missions and some dramatics in between. Murphy's short on help at the moment, so . . . if you could put some hours in helping Jess, it would be a great blessing."

"I consider it a privilege," Sean said. "Thanks for asking."

"Thanks for coming," Emily said.

"Okay," Sean said, "I can't stand it any longer." He hurried to get the suitcase he'd left in the hall. He laid it on Michael and Emily's bed and unzipped it. "We were going to ship this, and then when I decided to come, I just brought it with me. Fortunately my neighbor had this suitcase—exactly the right size." He pulled back several layers of bubble wrap and added, "I hope it's still in one piece. I prayed it would be."

He finally lifted out a gift wrapped in silver paper with a huge navy ribbon tied around it. Its size and shape suggested that it was something to hang on the wall.

"Well, open it," Sean said, setting it on the bed beside Tamra. He closed the suitcase and set it aside.

"Help me, Jess," Tamra said.

"I already told you that we don't need anything," Jess said to Sean.

"Yes, and I already told you that you probably don't *need* this, but I think it will have meaning nevertheless."

"Of course," Tamra said, then she gasped as a framed print of the Savior came into view. "Oh, it's beautiful!" she said breathlessly.

"You don't already have something similar, do you?" Sean asked.

"Not that's ours," Jess said. "But this will go perfectly in our bedroom."

"Good," Sean said. "Tara picked it out."

"Well, she has excellent taste," Tamra said, still admiring the picture.

"Yes, she does," Sean said with a chuckle. "After all, she married me."

"Indeed," Emily said with a little smirk.

Jess and Tamra each embraced Sean and thanked him again for the gift, then they took Evelyn with them to find something to hang it with, leaving Sean to visit with Michael and Emily. After they hung and admired the picture, they bathed Evelyn and put her to bed. They found that Michael was already asleep, and Sean and Emily were in the lounge room visiting.

"Mind if we intrude?" Jess asked, setting the nursery monitor on the coffee table.

"Not at all," Emily said, and they soon realized that Emily was telling Sean in more detail how the cancer was discovered and their reaction to it. Hearing points he'd never heard before, Jess wondered if Sean was simply easier for his mother to talk to, or if perhaps his own overly emotional state had made her hesitant to open up. Whatever the reason, Jess was glad to hear her opening up now.

They visited until nearly midnight, sharing tears all around more than once. The following morning, Sean went out with Jess right after breakfast to help with the fences. Jess enjoyed this opportunity to share memories and candidly discuss the present struggles. He was truly grateful to have Sean as an unofficial member of the family, and equally appreciative for his visit. He knew that taking a week off work and paying for the flight couldn't be easy, but he was grateful.

Through the next few days, they finished up the fences between long visits, a couple of picnics, and a worsening of Michael's illness from the chemotherapy. On a particularly warm afternoon, Sean went with the women and Evelyn into town to help them do some shopping. He wanted to pick up some little gifts to take home to his family. While they were gone, Jess entered the kitchen to see his father sitting at the table, reading a book. A pot simmering on the stove made it evident that Michael was keeping watch over whatever was cooking. The only thing unusual about the scene forced Jess to comment. "Dad, you're wearing a hat."

Without looking up, Michael adjusted the low, flat-brimmed hat that he typically wore to ride or work out in the sun. "Yes, I am," he said and turned a page.

"But you're inside. You never wear a hat inside. New fashion statement?"

"Something like that," Michael said and finally looked up. "Most of my hair fell out last night. I shaved the rest off because it looked so ridiculous, but I'm not quite ready to be bald in public."

Jess felt a bit stupid for bringing it up and hurried to say, "I'm sorry. I shouldn't have—"

"Shouldn't have what? Commented because I'm wearing a hat in the kitchen?" Michael chuckled. "I really didn't expect anyone to not notice. It's not a problem, son."

He stood up to stir the contents of the pot on the stove and Jess hurried to change the subject. "You're cooking?"

"Yes, actually. I was in the mood for chili."

"Well, no one can make it like you," Jess said. "I'll be looking forward to it."

Michael wore the hat the remainder of the day in spite of some teasing from Sean, but he came down to breakfast the next morning without it. Jess was used to seeing his father wearing his hair cut short and worn close to his head, so the change wasn't terribly drastic, as it might have been at other times in his life when Jess knew he had worn it thicker, as Jess did. In the middle of breakfast Jess commented, "You know, I could go with your fashion statement, Dad. People wouldn't be able to tell us apart."

Michael gave a scoffing chuckle and Jess added, "But if I don't have hair over my ears, people will be able to tell what a rebel I once was."

"How is that?" Sean asked. Jess lifted his hair off of one ear and leaned toward Sean. "Oh, I see," he chuckled. "How many earrings did you have in that ear?"

"Six, eight, I don't remember," Jess said.

"Keep your hair, Jess," Michael said. "I think I'm getting used to it, anyway." He gave Sean a mocking scowl. "It wouldn't hurt for *you* to stop making bald jokes, however."

"Now, if Emily had lost her hair, I wouldn't be making jokes, but hey, it's you, Michael."

Michael smiled. "Yes, it's me. And I must admit that it's worth a couple of bad bald jokes to have you here."

"The feeling is mutual," Sean said, and the subject was changed.

On the final day of Sean's visit, Michael felt better and was up and around even more. That evening while Evelyn slept, they all sat out on the veranda, watching dusk descend and the stars come out. In the midst of their comfortable conversation, Sean asked Michael, "You lost your father when you were young, didn't you?"

"I did," Michael said.

"Do you remember him well?" Sean asked.

"Not as well as I'd like, although I do have some very clear memories, and most of them are good. He was a good man."

"How did he die?" Tamra asked. "I don't know that you ever told me."

"Wasn't it cancer?" Sean asked, and Jess shot his head up abruptly from where it had rested on the back of the chair. Tamra's heart quickened as she sensed his surprise, and . . . What? Fear, perhaps?

"He got cancer when I was about eight," Michael said. "But it wasn't the cancer that killed him. From what I understand, it was discovered early and he responded well to the treatments. But he had a weak heart; always did. In fact, that was the reason the air force wouldn't take him during World War II, which probably saved his life then. Anyway, after the cancer treatments he was just never the same. He became terribly ill and was down in bed most of the time. He finally died when I was eleven."

"I didn't know he had cancer," Jess said, his voice expressing some degree of panic.

"Ooh," Sean said, "that ugly 'C' word."

"Yes, it is," Jess said as if he weren't amused.

"I'm sure we told you," Emily said. "Perhaps it's one of those stories that passed over your head in your youth."

"Perhaps," Jess said, then with eyes pinned on his father, he asked, "Do you know what kind of cancer he had? Do you think it's hereditary?"

"What are you saying?" Tamra demanded before Michael could answer. "Do you think *you* are likely to get it as well?"

Jess didn't answer, but his eyes expressed his concern. Michael sighed and leaned his forearms on this thighs. Looking directly at Jess, he said, "Listen to me, son. I don't know if it's hereditary. I don't know what he had exactly, and there's no one living who *would* know. I can tell you this, however, I believe we all have an appointed time on this earth, and as long as we're doing our best to live righteously, we will only be taken when that time comes. My father lived the life he was meant to live, as I have, and as you will. You need to take care of yourself, do your best to stay healthy, and enjoy your life. Regular cancer screenings wouldn't hurt."

"For all of us," Emily added. "The 'C' word," she said almost facetiously, "is a fact of life. It *is* becoming increasingly more common, and we need to do our best to be responsible about such things and listen to the Spirit. That's all anyone can do."

Jess sighed and leaned back. He knew that what his parents were saying was true; he could feel the verity of it. In truth, he wasn't concerned about his own mortality any more than any other human being would be. But one point troubled him and he had to ask, "If you had caught it earlier, do you think that . . ."

His words faded into a silence that no one seemed prone to break until Emily finally spoke in a voice tinged with emotion. "If your father was meant to survive the cancer, the Spirit would have alerted us to a problem more quickly."

Through another long silence, Jess grasped her deeper meaning. While a part of him had come to believe that cancer would take his father, he had clung to the deep hope for a miracle that would erase it from his father's body and give him many more years of life. Hearing such words cut away at his hopes, and he felt one of those angry moments close by as he clarified, "What you're saying then is that he's *not* meant to survive the cancer?"

Emily sighed loudly. "I'm saying that through much fasting and prayer, I instinctively believe that this is the beginning of the end, and we need to be prepared."

Jess turned to his father, perhaps hoping Michael might offer some opposing point of view, that he might suggest he'd had feelings to the contrary. But Michael just nodded slightly, as if to echo his wife's words. Jess sprang to his feet and hurried down the veranda steps, onto the lawn. He quickly walked to the back of the house where he couldn't be seen by the others. Pacing back and forth, feeling the cool grass beneath his bare feet, the anger melted quickly into raw fear. How could he live without his father? How could he live up to all that would be left to him in his father's absence? How could life ever be *right* without the great Michael Hamilton at his side, guiding him, loving him unconditionally, wrestling with him in the grass, making animal pancakes and telling Jess about the latest book he'd read? How could this be right when it felt so wrong?

Please God, Jess muttered silently, *tell me how this could be right when it feels so wrong! I don't understand!* He lost track of how many times he repeated his plea, pacing like a caged animal, while his emotions threatened to burst out of him like a volcanic eruption. He gasped and stopped pacing when a thought entered his mind with quiet force. Three simple words: *appointed unto death.*

Jess suddenly found it difficult to breathe. He pressed a hand to his chest and sat abruptly on the lawn. He felt as if the Spirit had just told him something powerful, but he wasn't quite grasping it, or perhaps he didn't want to. Trying to search his fogged mind, he realized that he didn't have the full answer, he only had a clue. He jumped to his feet and walked around the house to the front door, hoping to avoid his family, were they still on the veranda. He was grateful to be alone as he took the front stairs three at a time and rushed to his bedroom, reaching for the scriptures on the bedside table as he sat on the floor beside the bed. He went to the topical guide and quickly found the reference for the words he'd heard in his head. Doctrine and Covenants 42:48. He found the page, then the verse, while the book quavered in his trembling hands. There in black and white it read, "And again, it shall come to pass that he that hath faith in me to be healed, and is not appointed unto death, shall be healed."

"Oh help," Jess muttered aloud, feeling the truth pierce his heart. His father had been appointed unto death, and he knew it. Just as his parents knew it. And now that he knew, his mother's earlier words came back to him with force. *I instinctively believe that this is the beginning of the end, and we need to be prepared.*

Jess pressed his face into his hands and cried until he felt Tamra's hand on his shoulder. She sat beside him and he collapsed into her arms, sobbing like a child.

"What is it?" she asked quietly.

"It's true. We're going to lose him, and we have to be prepared."

"I know," she said. He raised his head and looked into her tear-filled eyes. It was true. She *did* know. And while he wanted to ask her how long she had known, and how it had come to her, he felt more inclined to just hold her and feel the comfort of her presence. He couldn't help but silently thank God for sending him this sweet angel to help carry him through the struggles of this life. In spite of all he was destined to lose, he had gained so much through Tamra's love. A definite peace settled around his heart. He felt the reality of the Comforter. He knew that somehow they would make it through.

Sean's leaving was difficult for all of them. Their farewells had an added poignancy with the uncertainty of Michael's illness. But Emily reminded them, "When you stop to think about it, we never know when any one of us might be taken from this earth. While I'm grateful for the time to prepare, there are moments when I think that knowing ahead of time can be harder."

"I think I agree with that," Sean said, setting his luggage down on the veranda. He sighed loudly and added, "Maybe this isn't appropriate, but . . . there are moments when I wish that I was a literal part of the family." His eyes focused on Michael. "It would be nice to know I was included in the next life."

Michael offered a slight smile and stuffed his hands into the pockets of his jeans. "If you have to be a *literal* part of the family to be together in the next life, you're not the only one in trouble." Sean looked mildly alarmed, while Jess felt completely baffled. Michael looked out over the lawn and added, "I know in my heart that God is a just God. In my opinion, eternity would not be celestial without those I love around me, whether they are literally sealed to me or not." He smiled again at Sean and added, "Don't worry, kid, it'll all work out."

Sean nodded with moisture in his eyes. Jess wanted to ask his father to expound on what he'd just said, but they needed to leave or Sean wouldn't make his flight to the States. When the farewells were completed, Tamra drove Sean and Jess to the hangar and saw them off in the plane. On the flight to Sydney, Sean told Jess, "I can't say for certain, but . . . I have a feeling I'll see him again . . . in *this* life, I mean."

Jess clung to the idea. To have his father live long enough for Sean to see him alive again would be a miracle. It could only happen if Michael's cancer went into some sort of remission, a blessing that Jess longed and prayed for. He was almost beginning to accept that this loss was really going to happen, but he hoped that God would be merciful enough to allow them a little more time together, time when Michael wasn't sick with chemotherapy side effects. It was his deepest hope.

Chapter Eight

The same day that Michael began his second round of chemotherapy, Sadie finally returned from an extended visit with her son's family. A few days later, an urgent knock at the bedroom door woke Jess out of a sound sleep. He grabbed a robe and rushed for the door while he called, "I'm coming." He pulled it open to see suppressed panic in his mother's eyes.

"What's happened?" he demanded, his heart plummeting. Tamra appeared at his side, looking as alarmed as he felt.

The worst possibilities flitted through his mind before Emily reported, "I'm taking your father to the hospital. It's not an emergency, but he's been throwing up for hours and I think he's dehydrated."

"Do you want me to go? To take him? Should I—"

"No, we'll be fine. I'll call when I get there. But would you call your sisters?"

"I'd be happy to, but . . . what should I tell them?"

"I just promised to keep them informed. We must go."

Jess helped his father out to the car, startled by his weakness. He watched them drive away then returned to his bedroom, knowing that any attempt to sleep was futile. The clock read just past four. It would be midmorning in Utah, so he decided to just get up and call his sisters.

"Where you going?" Tamra asked.

"I'm going to make those phone calls, at least the ones that won't wake anybody up."

"Hey, before you do," she said, "I've been thinking that . . . perhaps we should have a family fast. I know that many of us have fasted more than once over this, but I don't think we've ever done it all together. And since it's Thursday and . . . well, in the States it's Wednesday, but it still works. We could do it this Sunday, beginning Saturday evening."

"I think that's a splendid idea, my love," Jess said. He kissed her quickly and got dressed before he went down to the office where he sat behind the huge antique desk in the chair he'd seen his father occupy countless times. For several minutes he just sat there, an almost eerie sensation hovering around him. Sitting in his father's chair might have once been an entirely unnoticed occurrence. But under the circumstances, it seemed somehow symbolic, a premonition of sorts. He thought of the generations before him who had sat behind this desk to oversee the matters of this estate. He felt both weighed down by the burden, and deeply comforted by the belief that those men would always be behind him in spirit.

Jess set his elbows on the desk and leaned his face into his hands. He prayed for several minutes before he finally dialed Allison's number in Utah. He knew she was a busy woman, and prayed that she would be home. She had a great deal of strength and faith, and he always felt better after talking to her. She answered right off and they talked for nearly an hour. He felt comforted to hear her admit that she too had felt that Michael's death was imminent. "But not necessarily soon," she added. "I've prayed very hard about whether or not I should drop everything and make another trip out there, because I want to spend some time with him, some real quality time. And I've just felt peaceful, as if it's all right for me to finish up some projects I've got going, and the right time will come. So, I guess we'll see. We're tentatively planning two weeks this summer—winter for you. I've talked to the others about it a little. I was thinking it would be nice to have all of us together and just . . . go to the beach or something. Remember when we all went to that place in Cairns before you and James went on your missions? There are so many things to do there, enough variety to keep everybody happy. And we can all spend some time on the beach. But I think about how we'd all crowd into Mom and Dad's hotel room and play those stupid card games, and how we'd stay up talking half the night. Honestly, it's one of my best memories, and I think it's the last time we were all together. When

James got married you were on your mission, and then . . . we lost him." Following a moment of silence she added, "So what do you think? Could we pull it off?"

"I think it sounds great. I say we just do it. Set a date that will work around everyone's schedule as much as possible, then we'll just hope everyone can make it. Do you want me to talk to Mom and Dad about it?"

"Would you?" she almost pleaded. "I've hesitated to bring it up, wondering if it would sound presumptuous of me. I mean . . . they paid for everything last time, and I'm sure they'd have to again. Just taking the time off work and getting there can be a real challenge for some of us, but . . . it's important, don't you think?"

"I do. And I really think Mom and Dad can afford it." They both chuckled, and he added, "Besides, according to Dad, our inheritances should put us all ahead. We can pay for it with that if it would be easier."

"He was talking about our *inheritances?"* She sounded appalled.

"Yes."

"And he was serious?"

"Yes. I told you he's trying to be prepared, and he's trying to prepare me to take everything over."

Allison sighed loudly. "Forgive me, but I think if I were you, I'd feel terribly burdened by such a prospect."

"Well, yeah, but . . ."

"But?" she pressed.

"I just . . . feel like it's what I'm supposed to do. I've always felt it, I suppose. I'm not sure I feel worthy of it. I have serious doubts as to whether I can live up to what I'm being given."

"You're going to be a rich man, Jess."

"He tells me I'll earn it."

"I'm sure you will."

"And it all seems so trivial," Jess added. "I'm sure you'll agree that the money has always been a blessing, and Mom and Dad taught us to handle it well. But . . . this inheritance stuff just feels so . . . crass under the circumstances."

"Yeah, I know what you mean."

They went on to discuss Tamra's idea of the family fast. Allison heartily agreed and promised to talk with Emma about it, and update her on all that was happening. Since her work and school schedule was pretty tight, Jess catching her on the phone could be a challenge. But Allison lived under the same roof. Jess asked how Emma was doing with this whole cancer thing. He was pleased to hear that the two of them had talked it through a great deal, and shed many tears. It was hard but they were coping. It was nice to know he wasn't the only one experiencing such emotions, and at least as nice to know that they weren't in some level of denial.

Jess wrapped up their call, then he called his sister Alexa, who lived in California. Their conversation was similar, although lacking in some of the depth he was able to share with Allison. Her feelings about the cancer were along the same line. She was thrilled with Allison's family vacation idea, and felt certain they could pull it off. And she was pleased with the fast and committed to having her family members who were old enough participate. Again he was amazed, although he figured he shouldn't have been, to realize that the Spirit had guided her to the same conclusion concerning their father, and she was doing her best to be prepared.

By that time it was late enough for Jess to call his sister Amee in Adelaide. He was amazed to have found all of them home on the first try. But the conversation with Amee immediately felt different. Instead of concerned inquiries about their father's health, she rambled on with irrelevant chatter. Jess finally said, "Don't you want to know how Dad's doing?"

Following tense moments of silence, Amee said, "How *is* he doing?"

"He's in the hospital at the moment."

"Why, what's the matter?" Her voice revealed an excessive panic, especially in comparison to her initial indifference.

"He's got cancer, Amee."

"I know *that,*" she insisted, as if it were somehow his fault. "But he's getting chemotherapy, right? He should be fine, right?"

"Yes, he's getting chemo, but this round is making him even more ill than the last one. It's been pretty rough."

Jess expected more questions about how the chemo had been affecting Michael, and how their parents were handling the whole thing. He expected some conversation about their own struggles in dealing with it.

As siblings they were all in the same boat and were dealing with many of the same emotions. At least that was the feeling he'd gotten talking to his *other* sisters. But Amee didn't seem to want to talk about it at all. He made one more attempt to bring it up, but the topic was carefully steered elsewhere. When she finally ended the call, Jess hung up feeling frustrated and confused. After contemplating the issue for several minutes, he went in search of his wife. He found her in the upstairs hall, doing a typical aerobic dance routine that she did every other day for exercise. He couldn't resist sneaking up behind her and putting his arm around her waist.

Tamra gasped, then laughed as she turned in his arms and he eased her into a simple dance step. "Ooh," she said, looking into his eyes, "we haven't danced for a while."

"Too long," he said. "You should point out my neglect when I go more than a week without dancing with my wife."

"I'll try to keep track," she said, and he picked up the tempo. She easily followed his lead and he laughed as he guided her through a series of exaggerated twirls and a dip.

"You haven't lost your touch," she laughed as he straightened her back up and continued to dance.

"Of course not," he said with mock arrogance, followed by a humble chuckle.

"Do you remember the first time we danced . . . right here in this very room?"

"I do," he said. "And I believe you were wearing the same cute little skirt."

"We were practically strangers, you know."

"I was falling in love with you," he admitted in a voice so tender that Tamra felt a rush of goose bumps. "I'm still falling in love with you, Tamra Hamilton," he added, "more every day."

"The feeling is mutual, Jess Hamilton."

They danced until the music ended, then they collapsed side by side on the floor, holding hands, looking toward the ceiling. "Where's Evelyn?" he asked.

"Sadie took her for a walk to see the horsies after breakfast. You missed breakfast. I hovered at the door of the office to tell you it was ready, but you were obviously in deep conversation so I figured you'd show up if you got hungry."

"I didn't get hungry," he said, recalling the most recent of his phone conversations.

"What's wrong?" she asked, leaning on one elbow to look down at him.

"Talking to Allie and Alexa went great, and Allie said she'd keep Emma posted. But Amee . . ."

"What?"

"She's in denial, plain and simple."

He told her more details of their conversation and appreciated her insight when she concluded, "You can't force Amee to acknowledge what's going on. Eventually she'll have to face it. All you can do is keep her informed to the best of your ability, and let her come to terms in her own way. Trying to tell her she's in denial will only make her angry, won't it?"

"I'm sure you're right," he said then went on to tell her Allison's idea for a big family vacation in the summer. "Well, it will be winter for us, but beautiful weather in Cairns. If we plan on, say . . . July, Dad should be past his treatment schedule, and doing better . . . we hope."

"Well, I think it's a marvelous idea."

"And . . . I hesitate to say this, but . . ."

"But what?" Tamra pressed.

"What if he doesn't go into remission and we're simply unable to go because he's too ill or . . . dare I say it? What if he's gone by then?"

Tamra sighed. "I think we should just plan it and hope for the best. It will give us all something to look forward to, and if we have to change plans, we'll change plans."

"Do you think Mom and Dad will be put off by the idea?"

"Not at all. We should talk to them about it right away, I think—since your sisters gave you that assignment."

"Yes, it seems they did." Jess then recalled the obvious. "They're at the hospital. Maybe we should call and see what's going on. Mom probably didn't try to call because she knew I'd be talking to the girls."

"Good idea." Tamra jumped to her feet and held out a hand to help Jess up. He took her into his arms and kissed her before they went to the bedroom where Jess phoned the hospital while Tamra showered.

"What's the report?" she asked, emerging from the bathroom in a blue, terry cloth robe, towel drying her hair.

"He's fine. They've got him on an IV to get some fluids in him as well as some stuff to help the nausea more than what he'd been taking. They're keeping him for a couple of days. I was thinking we should go visit him and . . . well, we could just make a day of going into town. Mom said we could bring Evelyn in for a brief visit. There are a few things I need to do in town. We could visit, do errands, and have lunch out, then go visit again before we come home."

"Sounds perfect," Tamra said. "Why don't you grab some toast or something to hold you over while I get ready?"

Jess got himself and Evelyn ready to go and met Tamra out on the side lawn. The drive into town was pleasant while Evelyn sang her rendition of the songs she'd been learning in her Sunbeam class in Primary. They found Michael and Emily both in good spirits aside from Michael's disgruntlement over having to be in the hospital at all.

"He needs something to read," Emily said. "The television doesn't have much to offer."

"Well, we'll get you something while we're out," Tamra said. "What would you like?"

"Do you think you could find me a couple of good novels that are clean that I haven't read yet?" Michael asked.

Jess snorted a chuckle. "Yeah, and we'll just find a needle in a haystack while we're at it."

"We'll certainly do our best," Tamra said.

"A couple of magazines wouldn't hurt," Emily added. "You know what he likes."

Evelyn sat on the bed beside Michael while he showed her the funny tube going into his arm. She giggled when he made the bed go up and down, and she sang him her Primary songs.

"Oh, you are such a grand singer," Michael said as she squirmed down from the bed. "You make Grandpa feel better already."

"I sing Gwampa a song," she announced proudly to Jess.

"Yes, and it was such a beautiful song," Jess said, picking her up. "Should we go get some lunch and find Grandpa something to read? Then we'll come back and you can sing to him again."

Evelyn nodded eagerly and Tamra said, "We've got a number of errands, but we'll be back before we head home."

"I'll look forward to it," Michael said.

Lunch went well, the highlight being Evelyn's attempt to converse with the servers as if she were an adult. With their errands completed they returned to the hospital, having found one good novel that Michael hadn't read and seemed pleased with, and a handful of magazines, a crossword puzzle book, and some balloons to brighten his room. Evelyn sang to him again and Michael read her one of the storybooks that she'd brought along. They finally left when Michael's supper was brought in. His appreciation for their visit was evident, and Jess wondered how accustomed they would all become to such things before this was over.

"Hey," Jess said to his mother, "do you want to ride home with us? I'll bring you back in the morning. It won't hurt to leave a vehicle here and—"

"No," she said, "thank you anyway, but I'm staying here tonight. I brought some things on a hunch. They already said that I could."

"Okay, well . . . if you need anything, just call. We'll come back tomorrow."

"Thank you," Michael said.

Jess was pulling the Cruiser onto the highway when Tamra said, "We forgot something."

"What?" Jess asked, sounding panicked. He glanced over his shoulder and added lightly, "We have Evelyn."

"Yes, we certainly do," Tamra said, and Evelyn giggled as if she'd picked up on the humor. "But we forgot to talk with your parents about the vacation."

Jess sighed. "So we did. We'll just have to talk about that tomorrow."

"Is there anything you have to do that would keep you from going back in the morning?"

"I'll check with Murphy and Hobbs early and see what we need to do."

Jess and Tamra had only been home a short while when Sadie came out to the veranda to tell them that the bishopric was there. Jess carried Evelyn into the house with Tamra at his side. They entered the lounge room and the three men who made up the new bishopric came to their feet.

"What brings you all the way out here?" Jess asked after they'd exchanged handshakes and greetings. They were all seated and Jess added, "Dad's actually in the hospital and—"

"Yes, we've just been to see your parents there, actually," the bishop said. "But we wanted to visit with you, as well, and see what we might be able to do to help."

"Well, that's very kind of you," Jess said. "But you could have called. It's an awfully long drive out here just to—"

"We wanted to see you," the bishop said gently. "We know that finances are not a problem for your family, but the circumstances can't help but be a strain. And that's what we're here for."

Jess felt suddenly emotional and turned away, trying to hide his discomfort. He figured he'd done rather well at learning to cope with his father's illness and face it head on. He'd gotten over being emotional at every turn. But looking into the bishop's eyes, he was struck with the fact that not so many weeks ago his *father* had been the bishop, and Jess had believed that he'd live to be an old man who would be around to guide him and his children with the love and wisdom he'd gained through the years.

Before Jess could get control of his thoughts or his emotions, Tamra said, "Your visit is very much appreciated, Bishop. There *is* something you could do." Jess turned to her in surprise as she added, "We are having a family fast this weekend. We're praying that Michael can get through his treatments without so much illness, and that we might be blessed with some kind of remission that could give us some quality time together."

"Oh, of course," the bishop said.

One of the counselors added, "We can get the Relief Society sisters to call through the visiting teaching network and ask ward members to join your fast."

"That's exactly what I was thinking," Tamra said. "Michael and Emily are handling all of this relatively well, but I suspect it's more difficult than they're letting on. Surely so many prayers on their behalf would buoy up their spirits and give them hope."

"I'm sure that they would," the other counselor said. Jess wished he could remember their names. But he was more preoccupied with this amazing woman he had married. She was levelheaded enough to think of something that would have never occurred to him. Her wisdom and insight continually amazed him. How he loved her!

"Is there anything else we can do?" the bishop asked. "Anything at all?"

Jess cleared his throat and managed to say, "Your offer is very much appreciated, Bishop, but we have a lot of good help around here, and we're blessed to have our needs met."

"I would hope that you'd not be too proud to call and let someone in the ward know if any needs arise."

Jess nodded and said, "No, Bishop, I won't be too proud, I promise. I think we've been given a pretty big dose of humility."

"Yes, I'm sure you have," one of the counselors said.

A moment later the bishop added, "Could we give each of you a blessing? We did the same for your parents. The power of the priesthood can be a great boon during such times."

Jess nodded, again too emotional to speak. How grateful he was for these good men and their insight and compassion. The blessings given to him and Tamra were full of strength and peace, and the spirit of their visit lingered long after the men left. Jess felt deeply comforted by an aspect of his life he'd not considered before. They were greatly blessed to have the gospel in their lives and the knowledge it afforded them through such adversity, but he'd not considered the blessing of actually being a member of the Church with the support system it offered. He'd been aware of the Relief Society being in touch with his mother, and a few meals had been brought to their home. But he'd not fully considered what that support meant. The bishop's visit had been a tangible evidence of God's love for their family. Angels were truly among them.

The following morning Jess had already spent a couple of hours with the stable master before breakfast. As soon as he'd eaten with Tamra, Sadie, and Evelyn, he went to the boys' home to go over a few things with Hobbs and talk with a boy who would soon be eighteen. Jess was pleased to find that he had some very specific goals and seemed well adjusted. It was a report that he looked forward to passing along to his father.

By midmorning they were on their way to the hospital again. They found Michael seeming more down than they'd seen him since they'd been told about the cancer.

"What's up?" Jess asked, looking directly at his father.

"What do you mean, *what's up?* I'm wasting away in this bed. That's what's up."

"You don't look like you're at death's door just yet," Jess said, and one corner of Michael's mouth twitched upward. Tamra felt certain Michael far preferred to have them address the subject head on. It was evident he appreciated Jess's attitude. "So what's up?" Jess persisted. "You look pretty glum."

Michael blew out a long breath. "This is just getting old . . . and I haven't been here that long. I wonder how much worse it will get before . . ."

Jess saw his parents exchange an anxious glance. He did the same with Tamra, wondering what to say. He hoped his instincts weren't too far off base when he quickly added, "Before we all go on vacation, you mean?"

"Vacation?" Michael echoed, like a child would have said *candy.*

"It was Allison's idea," Jess said, taking a chair near the bed. "But I told her I'd talk to you about it, which means . . . if you hate the idea, she can take the blame, but if you love it, I'd be happy to take the credit."

Emily laughed softly and Tamra gave Jess a nod of encouragement. He jumped right in, repeating everything Allison had said about her idea. "And Cairns is the perfect place," Jess said. "There's plenty of variety to keep everyone happy, and just like Allie said, the best part would just be that we're all together. We can play games, have long talks, and just . . . be together. Of course, Allie said you'd probably have to pay for it; you did last time, of course. But I figure you could just take it out of our inheritance. It would be money well spent. That's my opinion, anyway. So, what do you think?"

"I think it's a marvelous idea," Emily said eagerly.

"Dad?" Jess asked when he hesitated.

Michael sighed and Jess was afraid he wouldn't like the idea. Or perhaps he sensed that he wouldn't live long enough, or be in good enough health to make it a feasible plan. After a long moment of silence, Michael said, "I think it's the best thing I've heard since you decided to get smart and marry Tamra."

Jess chuckled and tossed Tamra an affectionate glance. They talked for nearly an hour about details of what they might do, while a distinct light came back into Michael's eyes. They discussed the possibility of Michael's health not being good, but he insisted that he would go and be with his family if he had to go in a wheelchair. The possibility of his dying before then wasn't brought up. Before they left, they told Michael and Emily about the family fast, and how the bishop's visit had broadened it to a ward fast. The tears that rose in both their eyes confirmed how much this meant to them.

Michael returned home the following day, seeming better both physically and emotionally. He found Jess on the veranda in the early evening and sat beside him.

"It's good to have you home," Jess said.

"It's good to *be* home," Michael said with a deep sigh, as if he were literally taking his surroundings into himself. "I want you to promise me something, Jess."

"Anything," he said, "provided it's within my capacity, of course."

"Of course," Michael said. "And it is. I don't want to die in a hospital. Chances are it will happen slowly, and if being in the hospital is not serving any distinct purpose for prolonging my life with any kind of quality, I don't want to be there. My parents both died here at home. We hired someone to be with my mother when it became necessary. Do whatever you have to, but don't make me die in a hospital."

Jess forced back a thrust of emotion and said firmly, "I promise, Dad."

Michael heaved another deep sigh, expressing keen relief.

Following several minutes of silence, Jess felt compelled to ask something that he'd pondered a great deal. "Are you afraid to die, Dad?"

"No," he answered with no hesitation then shifted his eyes to the horizon. "There was a time when I would have been, but not now. No, fear is not the problem, son."

"What's the problem, then? Or shouldn't I ask such questions?"

"You can ask me anything you want. I'd rather talk about it and be prepared than pretend it's not happening. In fact, I think that has to be one of the great blessings of cancer and other such illnesses."

Jess let out a dubious chuckle. "Blessing? Using the word *cancer* and *blessing* in the same sentence sounds like an oxymoron to me."

Michael chuckled. "True, but . . . if you have to look for silver linings—and you do—I have to say that I'm grateful for this time to prepare. We didn't get that blessing when James and Krista left us. In fact, your mother and I had not even seen them for well over a year. And while we knew it was meant to be, I couldn't help wishing that I'd just . . . had the chance . . . to say certain things. So," he turned to look at Jess, "we need to take advantage of that chance now. Ask me anything you like, Jess. There are so many things I want to tell you—to teach you—but I don't know what of my feelings or life's experiences will really matter to you. So ask."

"Okay," Jess said, but it took him a few minutes to fully take in all that Michael had just said. He finally remembered his question and asked, "So, what is the problem, if it's not fear?"

"It's separation," Michael said and inhaled deeply. "I just . . . don't want to leave, not yet anyway. I've imagined your mother and me growing old here together, and even if one of us left before the other, I just always thought there wouldn't be many years in between. But now I have to accept that I will likely be leaving her alone here for a good long time. I want to take care of her. I want her to be happy. And I don't want to leave my children . . . my grandchildren. I believe in my heart that I will be aware of my loved ones and their progress from the other side, at least to some extent. But I also understand that there are experiences unique to this earth life. And while there are many promises in the eternities that I have to look forward to, I just . . ." His voice broke with emotion and he was silent for a minute before he finished with more composure. "The problem is separation, son."

"Yeah, I see what you mean," Jess said. "I guess that's the problem for me too." He sniffled and wiped a hand over his face. "I just don't want you to go, Dad." Michael put a hand on Jess's arm. "At least it's only temporary," Jess added. "I can't imagine how people cope with this if they have to wonder about such things. I'm so grateful to know that it's only temporary."

"That's right," Michael said with firm conviction. "The separation is only temporary. Don't you ever forget that."

A few minutes later, Michael said, "I want you to know that I'm really grateful for that vacation we're planning. I already called Allie and told her, but I wanted you to know that the timing of your bringing it up was . . . well, it was good. I'm really trying to not let this get me down. I don't want to spoil what time I have left by being grumpy or depressed, but there are moments when it's just . . ."

"Hard," Jess provided.

"That's right, and . . . I have to say that the very idea of having something so great to look forward to is just . . . well, it helps. I can't imagine anything I would rather do in this world than to have my family all together like that, except perhaps having them together in the temple. But of course, there are some who can't be there yet and . . . well, I would still like to get there before I go as well."

"Perhaps we can work that out, too."

"Perhaps," Michael said, "but for now, let's just work on making that vacation happen."

"So," Jess said, "we're just going to be positive and count on making it happen, right?"

"Right," Michael said. "And I don't know if it's worth anything, but . . . I couldn't sleep last night, and I prayed long and hard. I told the Lord that I didn't think I could live with getting my hopes up over being able to enjoy such an event with my family, only to have them dashed by being too ill to make it happen. I asked—no I *pleaded*—for Him to allow me this one opportunity before I have to go. All I can tell you is that I felt . . . calm, and very much at peace. I really believe it will happen, so . . . yes, we're just going to count on it."

Jess smiled. "In the meantime," Jess said, "I bet I could still beat you at chess."

Michael scoffed. "I don't recall your *ever* beating me at chess."

"There's always a first time," Jess said, and he went into the house to get the chess set from the library.

A daily chess game became a well-established habit. Between moves, Jess would talk with his father about life, love, and business. The blessings of fasting and prayer were readily felt as they all agreed there was more of a feeling of peace within the family, and Michael felt less ill. Between the chemo treatments, Michael would gradually gain more strength and was able to accompany Jess to the stables and the boys' home, and he would spend some time cooking. He taught Jess how to make animal pancakes and chocolate mousse at Tamra's insistence. During the chemo treatments, Michael tended to be down more, and occasionally would have to spend a day or two in the hospital, which he loathed. But the illness never got quite as bad as it had the night Emily had rushed him to the hospital. Michael spoke often of his plans with the family once the round of treatments was finished. Family, friends, and ward members prayed and fasted regularly that he might be blessed with a significant remission. Tests showed that the chemo was showing some improvement, as the growths appeared to be shrinking; faith and hope grew in contrast.

Jess appreciated the blessing he had of living in the same home with his parents and being able to spend so much time with his father. He couldn't deny the dark cloud hanging over their situation, knowing that the best they could hope for was some form of remission. But he did his best to remain positive and be grateful for every hour they had together. Tamra remained perfectly supportive of the many hours he spent with his father, and he was pleased to see that she too spent many hours with him, especially when he had to stay down because of a chronic lack of energy. Michael enjoyed having Evelyn close by, and the two of them shared many hours of reading stories and coloring, with Jess or Tamra keeping an eye on them to be certain Michael didn't get overwhelmed.

Emily set up an easel in the bedroom where she could explore her interest in oil painting and be close to Michael when he needed to rest. It was something she'd done on and off throughout her life; she'd even taken related college courses, but she had put it aside while she served two missions and coped with everything else that had occurred in recent years. Now, she admitted that it gave her something to occupy her time and her thoughts, and Michael seemed to enjoy keeping track of the progress of her projects.

Tamra thoroughly enjoyed her opportunity for long conversations with Michael concerning his family's history. She had come to the Byrnehouse-Davies and Hamilton Station feeling instinctively drawn to his ancestors, and she had avidly studied the journals of those who had gone before him. While Jess appreciated the stories of his ancestors, Tamra found that Michael had a deep love for them that she related to. She told him more than once of the deep kinship she felt with Alexandra Byrnehouse-Davies, his great-grandmother, and his thrill at Tamra's appreciation of Alexa was evident. He too had a profound love and respect for this woman, which deepened the bond between the two of them. He told her more than once of how he appreciated her love for their history, which was more than any of his own children had ever expressed. And while his own love ran deep, and he'd researched the family's background extensively, he'd lost sight of some of his feelings, and her interest had rekindled his love for the great family he'd come from. He also admitted that being reminded of those who had gone before helped him feel more at peace with the prospect of coming together with them on the other side of the veil.

"It will give me something to look forward to," he said while coloring a picture with Evelyn, "which might compensate just a little bit for having to leave all of you behind."

"I'm going to miss you, Michael," Tamra said, and he reached for her hand.

"I'm going to miss you too," he replied. "But I'm not dead yet. So, why don't you help me hobble down the stairs to the kitchen and we'll make some chocolate mousse."

"Do you think you're up to it?" Tamra asked.

"If I get tired I'll just . . . tell you what to do."

"It's a deal," Tamra said.

"We make chocut," Evelyn announced with excitement, leading the way down the stairs.

"A woman after my own heart," Tamra said, and together they laughed.

Chapter Nine

Michael was feeling relatively well, between treatments, when the family's solicitor made a personal visit to the home with the news that Evelyn's adoption was now final. Because he was practically a friend of the family, the solicitor stayed for lunch. That evening the family went out to dinner to celebrate. Nothing had changed beyond a technicality, but Jess admitted more than once how good it felt to know that Evelyn was officially theirs.

"It's too bad you don't smoke," Tamra said.

"Why is that?" Jess asked with a chuckle.

"You could hand out cigars, since you've just become a father."

They all laughed heartily and Michael said, "The stable hands would probably appreciate a good cigar. But I think you should pass out candy bars instead."

"I just might do that," Jess said.

A couple of days later, Tamra presented Jess with a box of candy bars, each with a cute little note attached that read, "It's a girl." He laughed and thoroughly enjoyed giving one to every employee around the stables and in the boys' home. Those who were close to the family expressed their delight in seeing how it had worked out for Evelyn to be raised by Jess and Tamra. Jess couldn't help but agree. In his heart, he would have preferred that James and Krista had lived to raise their daughter. But he knew it had been their time to go, and in their absence, being Evelyn's father deeply thrilled him. He loved her more than he could tell.

A couple of weeks later, Tamra sat brushing her hair out just after she'd gotten into her pajamas. Jess sat in bed reading from the Book of

Mormon until Tamra said, "You know that line in your patriarchal blessing that says you'll have children and carry on a great family legacy?"

"Yes." Jess looked up from the book and gave her his full attention. "What about it?"

"Well, I was thinking about the first time your mother mentioned that to me. It was when you were struggling so much, and you had declared you would probably never marry."

Jess made a scoffing noise. "Glad I got over *that* idiotic idea."

"Yes, so am I." Tamra laughed softly. "Anyway, I remember your parents saying that since your father is the only son of an only son of an only son, and your brothers are no longer with us, and Evelyn being a girl, the Hamilton line would end with you unless you have a son. I don't remember anything they said after that, but I know that I felt like seeing the line go on would really mean something to your parents, your father especially."

Jess sighed and turned to look toward the window. "I'm sure it would. It's too bad he may not live long enough to see it happen."

"Maybe he will," Tamra said.

Jess turned abruptly to look toward Tamra. "Are you trying to tell me something?"

"Yes," Tamra said with a little laugh.

Jess got out of bed and abruptly knelt beside her. He took the brush from her and set it aside, taking her hands into his. *"What* are you trying to tell me?" he asked, looking into her eyes.

Tamra offered a serene smile. "I'm telling you that if your father lives another eight or so months, he will see the Hamilton line continue through his son. And there's a fifty-fifty chance that it will be a boy."

Jess's heart quickened and joy rose into his throat. He tightened his hands around hers and his voice squeaked as he asked, "Are you sure?"

She smiled again. "Yes, I'm sure. I picked up a home pregnancy test today because my cycle is late. It's clearly positive. But I thought I'd go into town tomorrow and get a more accurate test at the clinic, just to be absolutely certain."

An emotional laugh erupted from Jess's throat and he hugged her tightly. He drew back and took her shoulders into his hands. "Have you felt ill? Are you okay? Shouldn't you be—"

"I'm fine, Jess." She laughed softly. "I think it's a little soon for any illness. It will probably kick in any day now, but . . . we'll just take it on. Some women don't get ill."

"And some do," he said. "When my mother had the twins she was terribly ill and—"

"Then I'm certain she'll be able to give me all the help and advice I need," she said and embraced him tightly. "Oh, Jess. I love you. Nothing could make me happier than to have your baby."

Jess returned her embrace, nuzzling his face into her luxuriant hair, if only to hide the feelings overtaking him. He simply couldn't find words to tell her how much her love meant to him, and he felt certain there could be no greater expression of that love than bringing this child into the world. Even the likelihood of losing his father took on a different perspective with this tangible evidence that life would go on, and one more generation of this family would come forward.

Jess found it difficult to sleep that night as the news settled into him. He was going to be a father. Of course, he was Evelyn's father, and he couldn't imagine loving any child more than he loved her. Still, this child would be his own flesh and blood, a literal product of the love he shared with Tamra. He prayed long and hard that his father would live to see this child born, and he found comfort in conjuring up a vision in his mind of seeing Michael holding that child in his arms. He knew that this child's gender had already been determined, and whether boy or girl, it would be loved just the same. But he couldn't help hoping it would be a boy, for the very fact that his father could live to see the Hamilton line continue through a child that would carry on the name. In his heart he knew that Michael would not live long enough to see *another* of his children born. He simply hoped that eight or so months wasn't too much to ask for.

Jess asked his mother if she and Sadie could look out for Evelyn while he and Tamra went into town. They eagerly agreed and a quick visit to the clinic affirmed that Tamra was indeed pregnant. The official due date was January sixteenth, and Tamra commented with sarcasm, "Oh, the holidays will be fun. You can just roll me up to the table for Christmas dinner."

Jess laughed and said, "It will be a pleasure, Mrs. Hamilton."

They celebrated over lunch in a fine restaurant that they never would have dared take a three-year-old into. Then Jess insisted that they go shopping. He bought Tamra some maternity clothes, even though she sincerely hoped she wouldn't be needing them for many weeks yet. And he just had to buy *something* for the baby. While the home was already equipped with the basic furniture needed for a baby, Jess bought a bedding set for the crib that was decorated with classic Winnie the Pooh. "Perfect for a boy or girl," he announced. But the newborn-sized outfit he insisted on buying was definitely for a boy. The stuffed rabbit he had to buy, however, was pink.

"So," Tamra said on the way home, "how do you think Evelyn will like having a baby brother?"

Jess chuckled. "It could be a sister."

"Maybe," Tamra said, "but I really think it's a boy."

"You do? Why?"

"I don't know. I just . . . believe it is. I guess we won't know for a while yet."

"Nine months, you mean; well, eight and a half."

"Actually, they can tell with an ultrasound much sooner than that. About halfway along, I believe."

"Really?" Jess said and chuckled. "Well, to answer your question, I think Evelyn will make a very good big sister."

"Yes," Tamra agreed, "I believe she will. We should get her a new dolly so that she can take care of her baby while we take care of ours."

"Excellent idea," Jess said. "What will we name it?"

"Jess Michael Hamilton, *the fifth,* of course."

"Of course," Jess said and laughed again. "And if it's a girl?"

"I have no idea. We'll have to work on that."

That evening after supper had been eaten and the kitchen cleaned up, Jess and Tamra went with Evelyn to find Michael, Emily, and Sadie all visiting in the lounge room. They sat down and Emily motioned toward the plastic sack Jess carried. "What have you got there?"

"Stuff," Jess said and pulled out a little wrapped package which he handed to his father.

"What is this?" Michael asked.

"It's a present," Jess said, as if he were deeply offended, then he chuckled.

"What's the occasion?" Michael asked, and Jess just shrugged his shoulders.

Michael cast Jess a dubious glance, then slowly opened the package. He lifted the lid on the box and folded back the tissue. "I don't think it will fit me," he said lightly, then the implication seemed to dawn on him as his eyes widened toward Jess, then Tamra, who couldn't hold back a little laugh.

"What is it?" Emily asked impatiently and Michael held up the tiny outfit.

Emily and Sadie both gasped and Jess said, "It's for your grandson. Well, if it's a girl, she can certainly wear it. I guess girls can get away with wearing boy clothes more than the other way around."

"Are you saying what I think you're saying?" Emily asked.

"If you think I'm saying that we're going to have a baby, then yes, I guess you're right."

Sadie gave a delighted laugh. Emily laughed and jumped to her feet to embrace Jess, then Tamra. "Oh, that's wonderful news," she said just before a stilted sob turned everyone's attention to Michael. He rose and left the room abruptly. Jess heard footsteps on the stairs and felt his heart sink, wondering what could be wrong, although it wasn't difficult to imagine. While he was waiting for his mother to leave and go after him, she only nodded toward Jess, saying quietly, "I think *you* need to talk to him this time."

This time? Jess echoed silently in his mind. How many times had his father been overtaken by such emotion that he'd been unaware of? For the most part, Jess had seen him calm and resolute. Discouraged at times, but never so emotional. He quickly concluded that he couldn't think too hard about that; he just had to hurry and catch up with him, if only to do as his mother had asked. He didn't know what he was going to say, but he had to at least try and talk to him.

Jess found his father's bedroom door slightly ajar, but no light on. He knocked lightly and heard his father growl, "What?"

He pushed the door open and saw Michael silhouetted against the window. An occasional sniffle revealed his despair.

"You okay?" Jess finally asked, leaning against the doorjamb.

"Sorry about that," Michael said. "The last thing I wanted was to put a dark cloud over your good news."

"You *are* happy about it, then?" Jess asked.

"Oh, yes!" Michael turned toward him. "More happy than you could possibly imagine. I suppose that's part of the reason I got so emotional." He shook his head and turned back toward the window. "It hasn't been so long since I had deep concerns for you, Jess. I can't tell you how many times I've prayed that you would just be able to get past your grief . . . settle down, have a good life, a family. And you have. My prayers have been answered."

"What's the other part?" Jess asked, taking a seat and putting his feet up.

Michael heaved a deep sigh and stuffed his hands into the pockets of his jeans. In a cracking voice he admitted, "I want to live to see this child born."

"And why shouldn't you?" Jess asked. "It's not so many months. I'm counting on it, myself."

"Okay, maybe that's not so unreasonable a hope, but . . . I want to see it grow. I want to hold it and play with it and see it go to school and see its brothers and sisters come into the world."

Jess swallowed hard and said the words his father had said to him the day he'd told them he had cancer. "I'm sorry, Dad, that's just not possible." He added the thought that appeared in his mind, "At least not from this side of the veil. But maybe you can do more for your grandchildren on the other side." Jess chuckled and leaned his head back. "Maybe with your influence my sons won't turn out as stubborn and bullheaded as I was."

Jess was relieved to hear his father chuckle as he admitted, "I'll see what I can do."

Following several minutes of comfortable silence, Michael added, "Don't tell your wife I said this, but . . . I can't help hoping it's a boy." He chuckled and added, "Not that I have anything against girls, but . . ."

He hesitated and Jess guessed, "But before you leave you'd like to see the Hamilton line continue through a son who would carry on the name."

Michael sighed. "Is that selfish of me?"

"No, Dad. I'd like to see that, too. But you know what? If it's going to be a girl, it's already a girl. But whether you see me have a son before you go, or after, I promise you that your name will go on, and I will teach my son what it means to be a Hamilton."

Jess heard his father take a long, deep breath and blow it out again. "Maybe we should go see how much I've upset your mother this time," he said.

This time, Jess echoed silently, once again, realizing he'd only seen the tip of the iceberg of what his parents were struggling with. But in a strange way he felt deeply comforted to know that his own grief was not so far from theirs. They all had something in common; they loved each other, and preparing for this untimely separation was tough. But they were in it together, and he was grateful.

"Let's do that," Jess said, coming to his feet. "Oh, and . . . we forgot to eat dessert."

"Was there dessert?" Michael asked, moving toward the door.

"Yes, I made chocolate mousse. I still don't get it as fluffy as you do, but I'm working on it."

"Fluffy or not, it's chocolate. And your mother tells me that chocolate always makes a person feel better."

"Maybe she's right," Jess said, and they both laughed.

* * *

The following afternoon, Jess found Tamra in the bedroom where she was folding laundry and putting it away.

"Hey, come here for a few minutes," he said, taking her hand.

"What's up?"

"Nothing. I just want to . . . show you something—sort of. Where's Evelyn?"

"She's with your mother. Why?"

"Just wanted a few minutes alone," he said, leading her to the upstairs hall. He pushed a button on the stereo then guided her to the center of the floor, holding her close to dance slowly as the music began. He smiled at her and added, "I just thought we should dance . . . to celebrate."

"Celebrate what?" she asked.

"That we're having a baby, of course." He chuckled and held her a little closer.

"Of course," she said and laughed softly, pressing her head to his shoulder.

"For some reason I thought of this song when I woke up this morning, and I had to listen to it. It just . . . expresses how I feel, so I wanted to share it with you. Listen," he said. She recognized the band as Creed, and the song "With Arms Wide Open" was one she knew well. She tuned her ears into the lyrics, feeling them touch her in a personal way. *Well I just heard the news today; it seems my life is going to change. I close my eyes, begin to pray, and tears of joy stream down my face . . . Well, I don't know if I'm ready to be the man I have to be. I take a breath; I take her by my side. We stand in awe; we've created life.*

Tamra drew back to look into Jess's eyes, not surprised to see them glistening with the hint of tears. "I love you," he murmured and pressed a hand to the side of her face. "I never imagined that I could be so happy. Even in the face of everything that's happening with my dad, I'm still just . . . happy."

Tamra sighed and kissed his lips. "I love you too, Jess." She smiled. "And no one could be happier than I am."

Jess sighed and tightened his embrace as they continued to dance. "As long as I have you, somehow I know I can get through anything."

"The feeling is mutual."

"Well, then," he said decisively, "everything's going to be all right."

"Yes, it is," she agreed and kissed him again.

* * *

Only two days later, Tamra woke up and immediately ran into the bathroom with dry heaves, then she went back to bed, moaning that she felt horrible. Jess got Evelyn up and dressed, but when they appeared in the kitchen with the report that Tamra was ill, Emily went straight upstairs with some crackers and herbal tea.

"Your mother has experience with these things," Michael said almost proudly. "She'll take good care of her."

"I'm sure she will," Jess said, unable to help feeling worried. "But . . . how bad does it get?"

"I suppose that depends on the woman," Michael said. "The results will be worth it; I promise."

It quickly became evident that Tamra's mornings were going to be horrible. She generally felt better before lunch, and afternoons weren't too bad, but by evening she was exhausted and feeling sick to her stomach again. Jess was grateful for his mother's help and support, both with Tamra and Evelyn. When some problems arose in the boys' home that took a great deal of Jess's time, and his father began another round of chemo, he was grateful for Sadie's help with Evelyn so that Emily could watch out for Michael. But he declared that this family had gone over the edge when Tamra and Michael began comparing notes on who had thrown up more on any given day.

"You people are *sick,"* Jess said with disgust, then everyone broke into laughter.

"That would be the problem," Michael added, and Jess finally got the pun.

When Tamra went to see a doctor for her first exam, he gave her some medication to help with the nausea and heartburn. It made such a difference that she wished she had gone to see him earlier. She began to get better control of her symptoms as Michael eased out of the worst effects of that round of chemo. Tamra insisted they have a picnic to celebrate feeling better, and Jess found the little excursion particularly gratifying, even if they'd only ventured out as far as the trees in the backyard. Just to hear his father laughing and enjoying life was like a miracle. He had a long way to go to get his strength back, but after a few more rounds of chemo, he would have the opportunity to do that. They had much to look forward to.

"You know," Michael said after they'd eaten and visited for quite some time, "I'd really like to get on a horse."

"I don't know if that's a good idea," Emily said. "You don't have much strength and—"

"You're fussing, Emily," he scolded lightly, coming to his feet. "Jess will take good care of me. Won't you, Jess?"

"Sure I will," Jess said and followed his father toward the stable. He turned back to give his mother a reassuring nod, but she didn't look convinced.

Jess insisted on saddling the horses, and Michael asked if he'd help him mount. Jess was a bit startled by his father's weakness and was tempted to protest, as his mother had done. But once Michael was in the saddle he seemed fine, and Jess felt certain a brief ride would do wonders for his spirit.

"You okay?" Jess asked.

"I'm fine."

Jess mounted and said, "Okay, let's go. But we're taking it easy and we're not going very far."

"Agreed," Michael said, and they trotted out into the afternoon sun.

Jess was pleased to see how his father enjoyed the ride, and he didn't argue when it was time to call it good and go back. He noted his father looking a bit pale just before they entered the stable. While Jess hurried to dismount, he said, "Hang on a minute and I'll help you down."

He barely had his foot out of the stirrup when he realized that Michael was getting down on his own. A second later Michael landed flat on his back with a deep groan. Jess rushed to his side and dropped to knees. "Are you okay? What happened?"

"I just . . . got a little light-headed all of a sudden," Michael insisted. "I'm fine."

"You don't look fine," Jess said. "Are you hurt anywhere? Are you—"

"It just . . . knocked the wind out of my lungs; I'll be fine."

Murphy soon appeared and demanded, "What happened?"

"I'm fine," Michael insisted, and tried to sit up, but obviously got dizzy again. Jess quickly moved behind him and Michael ended up leaning his head back onto Jess's chest.

Murphy ran out saying, "I'm going for help."

"If you make any emergency calls I will fire you!" Michael hollered.

"Well, there's nothing wrong with your vocal cords," Jess said with a chuckle.

"I'm fine," Michael repeated.

"You're not fine. Stop being so proud."

"Okay, but I don't need an ambulance out here to—"

"No, I can take you to the hospital myself as soon as Murphy gets back to help me get you to the Cruiser."

"I don't need to go to the hospital," Michael argued.

"Why don't you just be quiet and do what you're told?" Jess said with mock authority.

"I'm still your father," Michael said.

"Yes," Jess said more seriously, "you're still my father, and I'm going to make certain you're all right—whether you like it or not."

Michael said nothing.

* * *

Tamra and Emily cleaned up the picnic lunch while Evelyn went upstairs in Sadie's care, then they went together to the laundry room. They talked and laughed while Emily folded clothes out of the dryer and Tamra pretreated some stained items to go into a load of whites. They were startled when they heard the side door open and Murphy holler loudly, "Emily! Are you here?"

"What is it?" she demanded, stepping into the hall.

"Michael's collapsed in the stable and—"

"Good heavens!" She rushed out the door with Tamra and Murphy following. "Is he all right? Did you leave him alone? Is he—"

"Jess is with him. He's coherent enough to threaten to fire me if I made any emergency calls. I figured I'd leave that up to you."

"Thank you, Murphy," Emily said. "Why don't you pull out the Cruiser in case we need to take him into town?"

"Be glad to," Murphy said, apparently pleased with an assignment.

Emily rushed into the stable with Tamra at her side. They slowed drastically at the same time, as if they both sensed the tenderness of the moment and felt a desire to observe it before intruding. Tamra felt almost moved to tears to see Jess sitting on the ground, his father stretched out, his head leaning against Jess's chest. Michael held tightly to one of Jess's arms that was wrapped around him. She heard Emily take a ragged breath, as if to sustain herself before she quickened her pace again and demanded, "What happened?"

Both men turned their heads toward them. "I'm fine!" Michael bellowed. "I'm just too blasted light-headed to stand up, but . . . I'm fine."

"Now, that's a contradictory statement if I ever heard one," Emily said, dropping to her knees beside him.

Jess met his mother's eyes and saw his concern mirrored there. Was there something wrong beyond the effects of the chemo? Was this a normal side effect combined with simply overdoing? Or was there something more?

"What happened?" Tamra asked, also kneeling close by.

Jess quickly explained and Michael added once again, "I'm fine. Just help me into the house and—"

"No," Emily insisted, "we're helping you into the Cruiser and we're going to get you checked out, just to make sure you're fine."

"Blasted woman," Michael muttered as Jess carefully urged his father to his feet, with Emily standing close beside him to help keep him upright. It only took a few steps to realize how weak Michael really was. Emily was obviously relieved when Murphy appeared to take her place, helping Michael to the Cruiser that he'd parked right outside the stable doorway.

"Okay," Michael said, sliding onto the seat, "I think you've convinced me that I'm not fine."

"Very good," Jess drawled as if he were impressed. On a hunch he turned to his mother and asked, "Do you want me to take him?"

She looked up at him with huge tears in her eyes and nodded firmly. "I need some time alone," she barely managed to say. She squeezed Michael's hand and closed the door.

Jess got in and Michael growled, "Where's your mother?"

"She said she needs some time alone," he said and drove away before Michael could question it.

Following several minutes of silence, Michael asked, "Did I do something wrong?"

"No, Dad, you didn't do anything wrong. I enjoyed our ride together, but obviously it was just . . . a bit much. At least, I hope that's all."

"Well, I hope so too." He looked out the window. "You know, I could never say this to your mother but . . . I have moments when I almost wish I could just go in an accident or something, quick and easy; get it over with for all of us."

"Yes, well I can see why you can't say that to Mother. I'm not sure I appreciate it myself."

"And why not?"

"We all want you here just as long as possible."

"Why? So you can fuss and worry and have to drop everything to take me to the hospital? And what about your mother? What do you suppose she's doing right now? Time alone? She's bawling her eyes out."

"Probably. She's got to cry once in a while, and I don't believe she wants to upset you."

"I suppose."

"And I think you scared her."

"I think I scared me," he admitted quietly.

"So what was all that 'I'm fine' stuff back there? Just gotta be tough, I suppose?"

"I suppose," Michael said even more quietly.

At the hospital it was declared that Michael had suffered a case of heatstroke. He was put on an IV to get some fluids into him. When he admitted to the nurse that he'd had some vomiting earlier in the day, she suggested with only subtle disdain that he shouldn't have been out in the sun with such an obvious loss of fluids.

"Okay," Michael said to Jess when the nurse left the room, "next time I'm taking a sports drink along."

"Good idea," Jess said. "I'm going to call your wife."

"Call your wife while you're at it," Michael said. "And tell them both that I love them and I . . ."

"What?" Jess asked when he hesitated.

"And I'm sorry if I scared them. I'll try not to do it again."

Jess smiled. "I'll tell them."

Jess could almost see his mother slump with relief through the phone when he told her the diagnosis.

"I'm sorry I made you step in again for me like that," she said. "I just . . . knew I'd be a blubbering idiot, and that wouldn't help him feel any better."

"I know, Mom. It's okay. I understand."

"Does your father understand?" Emily asked.

"Yes, I think he does actually."

"Tell him we'll be up to see him in a while. Sadie's going to stay with Evelyn."

"I'll tell him. Be careful."

Tamra and Emily arrived a couple of hours later. Jess lowered his magazine when they walked into the room. Emily rushed to Michael's side and leaned over him, embracing him tightly. He returned the embrace as far as it was possible with the IV in his arm.

"I'm sorry," she muttered tearfully, looking into his eyes.

Michael touched the tears on her face. "There's nothing to be sorry for," he said.

"I wish I was stronger . . . for your sake. I should be strong enough to be there when you need me."

"You would have been if there had be no options," he said. "But it's okay." He glanced toward Jess. "I told you he'd come in handy one of these days."

They all chuckled, which broke the tension somewhat. But Jess felt compelled to take Tamra's hand and urge her into the hall with him. He leaned back against the wall and admitted with a breaking voice, "Okay, now I think it's my turn."

"What's wrong?" Tamra asked, glancing around to assure herself there was no one standing close by.

"I managed to keep it together until . . . Oh, help." He covered his eyes with his hand. "When I see them together like that . . . and I think of how I would feel if I were losing *you,* I can't even imagine what they must be going through. He told me on the way here that he could never tell Mom, but there were times when he wished he could just die in an accident or something and have it over with."

"I can't blame him really," Tamra said. "I mean . . . we all want him here as long as possible, and there are advantages in being prepared, but there are disadvantages as well. Didn't Sean say that this kind of death brings on most of the mourning before it happens? Well, your dad has to be here to see it all. And people who die quickly don't spend time mourning their own deaths. But *he* is."

"I never thought of it that way."

"And don't you think he has to wonder how bad it will get before it's over? Cancer can be so ugly, Jess. He's got to be scared, at some level, of what he'll have to go through."

Jess choked back a sob and said, "I never thought of that, either."

"Well, don't think about it too hard. The best we can do is try to understand what he's going through and be there for him to lean on."

"Well, I'm glad you're here for *me* to lean on."

"The feeling is mutual," she said, resting her head on his shoulder. He held her tightly and squeezed his eyes shut, silently thanking God for giving him such a sweet wife—and such incredible parents. *Please don't let them suffer too much before this is over,* he added, then forced back his sorrow and said, "Let's go see if we can dig up something chocolate. That'll perk them up."

"Good thing your dad can eat whatever he wants," Tamra said.

"Yes, that *is* a good thing," Jess admitted, figuring chocolate might make them *all* feel a little better. Less than an hour later they returned to Michael's room with a large carton of chocolate ice cream and disposable bowls and spoons.

"Hey there," Jess said to his father, "you don't look so good. Maybe some chocolate will perk you up."

Michael sat up in bed with an eager chuckle. Emily commented, "He may not look so good, but he's still a great kisser." Michael gave a startled laugh which spread through the room.

"Well, thank you for sharing that with us, Mother," Jess said.

"That's why I married him, you know," Emily added facetiously. "Because he was such a great kisser."

"Is that why?" Michael asked. "I thought it was because of my Australian brogue."

"That too," Emily said and laughed. "Oh, and there was the fact that I wanted my children to look like you."

"It worked," Tamra said, squeezing Jess's hand.

"Yes, it did." Emily smiled at her son as he held out a bowl of ice cream toward Michael.

"Except that I have more hair," Jess said, and Michael playfully slugged him in the shoulder.

"Do you want ice cream or not?" he asked, pulling the bowl out of Michael's reach.

"Give me that," Michael said. "I'm still your father, and when I get my strength back, I bet I can still wrestle you to the ground."

"Not if you're going to end up here," Emily scolded and Jess gave his father the bowl.

"What are you going to do with the rest of that before it melts?" Michael asked, motioning toward the carton. Jess shrugged his shoulders. Tamra left the room for a few minutes and returned with several staff members and another patient in a wheelchair. Jess served ice cream to everyone amidst a great deal of laughter.

While Jess enjoyed his own cold chocolate, he wanted to tell his father how deeply grateful he was that he hadn't been taken suddenly in an accident, but he figured he'd save it for another time. For now, he was content just to enjoy the moment.

* * *

Jess left his parents at the hospital and took Tamra home. The following morning he phoned his sisters to give them the latest update. This time he spoke to Emma instead of Allison, which was nice. Her busy schedule of work and school didn't allow such opportunities very often. The other calls were typical. Everyone was concerned but adjusting to the progress of their father's illness—except for Amee, who didn't want to talk about it and seemed convinced that once the chemo treatments were finished it would all go away—forever. Jess just reported the news and let it drop, but he couldn't help being concerned.

Chapter Ten

Weeks after Michael's visit to the hospital, Jess could hardly sit still through the hours while his parents went into town for a number of errands, including a visit to Michael's oncologist to discuss the results of some tests taken recently, and where they should go from here. Would they recommend more chemo? Stop the treatments because they weren't doing any good? Maybe add radiation treatments to the regime? Had the cancer spread? Or would the news actually be good?

When the Cruiser finally pulled into the yard, Michael was actually driving—something he'd not been doing much of lately. Jess and Tamra hurried out to meet them with Evelyn in tow.

"Well?" Jess demanded after typical greetings had been exchanged.

"Well what?" Michael asked, then he laughed. At least he was laughing, Jess thought. But was it happiness or denial?

"What did the doctor say?"

Michael and Emily exchanged a long glance, then they both laughed.

"What?" Jess practically screamed, and they laughed again.

"It's gone," Emily finally said. "Not a sign of it anywhere."

Jess felt tears overtake him before he had a chance to say anything. He caught a glimpse of Tamra crying as well as he shared a long, firm embrace with his father.

"So, no more chemo?" Jess asked, wiping at his tears.

"Not until it comes back," Michael said.

Jess had to ask, "Are they sure it will?"

"Yes, son. It can't have spread as far as it had without metastasizing elsewhere. We simply have to enjoy each day and try not to worry about that."

"And so we will," Jess said, and they all went into the house.

Michael quickly regained his strength, seeming more like himself every day. He slowly worked himself back into accompanying Jess through his work days, while plans for the great family vacation became more concrete. Since they'd told no one else in Jess's family about the baby, they decided to announce it when they were all together.

A beautiful plant was delivered for Michael with a card from Tamra's father and stepmother. The card simply said, "Congratulations on your victory. Our prayers are with you. Brady and Claudia."

"Isn't that sweet?" Emily said.

"And dare I ask how they knew?" Michael added.

"Oh, they know everything," Jess said. "They e-mail back and forth with Tamra every few days."

"They know about the baby, then?" Emily asked.

"Oh, yes, I couldn't resist. My dad has no blood grandchildren. This is quite an event for him. They're terribly excited. They're hoping to come out soon after he's born."

"He?" Michael questioned.

"I just think it's a boy," she insisted.

"I guess we'll just have to wait and see," Emily said.

"Whatever it is," Michael said, "the child will be adorable and loved."

"Of course," Jess added. "Either way, we'll know next week."

"We will?" Michael asked, looking practically dumbfounded.

"We have an appointment for an ultrasound," Tamra said. "You'll come with us, won't you?"

"If we're invited," Emily said.

"Of course," Jess insisted. "The more the merrier."

Michael laughed as if the joy simply couldn't be contained.

Tamra smiled at him and asked, "You won't be embarrassed to see my bare belly, will you?"

"I won't if you won't," Michael said.

"Does Rhea know about the baby?" Emily asked.

"Of course," Jess said. "She's more excited than I am. And that's pretty excited."

"I don't think anyone is more excited than *you* are," Tamra said.

Michael and Emily exchanged a warm smile and he reached for her hand. Jess did the same with Tamra, grateful beyond words for the life he'd been blessed to live.

A few minutes later, Michael asked Tamra, "And what of your mother? What has she said about the baby? I assume she knows."

Tamra sighed and her countenance darkened slightly. "I write to her every week or two; I have since Christmas. But I've only gotten two letters in return, both of them brief and not necessarily warm. Still, that's an improvement over the past and I'm grateful. I've not heard anything since I sent news about the baby. I'll let you know when I hear."

"Well, perhaps when she sees pictures she'll be a little more excited at the prospect of being a grandmother," Emily said.

"Perhaps," Tamra said, appreciating her positive attitude.

The day of the ultrasound appointment, Sadie volunteered to watch Evelyn while the others went into town. Jess couldn't help feeling nervous. He felt almost guilty for wanting so desperately to have this child be a boy. He knew that a baby girl would be every bit as loved and wanted. But the timing . . . He simply couldn't help hoping, and if it *was* a girl, he knew he'd adjust to the idea in a matter of minutes. He only hoped she would forgive him if she knew from the other side how he was feeling.

They ended up sitting in a waiting room for over half an hour, while Tamra and Emily both casually looked through magazines, and Michael and Jess both fidgeted nervously. And a little teasing from the women didn't lessen their nerves any. When they were finally called back by a young female technician with short dark hair, Michael seemed to relax, but Jess became even more jittery. When Tamra laid back on the table and bared her belly, Jess said, "Are you sure there's anything in there? You hardly look pregnant enough for us to be able to tell what kind it is."

"She's much taller than I am," Emily said. "The baby has room to spread out more. By the time I was this far along, I looked *really* pregnant."

"You did have a way of blossoming," Michael said. "But then, that last pregnancy was twins."

"You had twins?" the technician asked. "Oh, it's fun to find twins. Did you make the discovery through an ultrasound?"

"Yes, we did actually," Emily said.

"At first I thought we had a baby with twenty fingers," Michael joked.

"And how old are your twins now?" the technician asked.

Emily answered, "One of them died soon after birth; the other is in college. She's our youngest."

The technician smiled, then turned her attention to Tamra's belly as she squirted some kind of gel onto her skin which made Tamra gasp then giggle. "It's cold," she announced. As the instrument was rubbed over Tamra's lower belly, images came up on the monitor.

"Amazing," Michael said, peering closely. "That's a lot more clear than the last time I saw one of these done."

"That was a long time ago," Emily reminded him.

"You've not been in on this with any other grandchildren?" Tamra asked.

"No, actually. Except for Evelyn, they were all born elsewhere. And we were on a mission when she was born."

"So you were," Jess said, tightening his gaze on the monitor. He laughed when the technician pointed out a beating heart, then he nearly cried after she'd done a number of measurements and stated that there were no obvious problems with the baby, and the size appeared right for the projected due date.

"The doctor will look it over and call you in a couple of days if he finds anything of concern," she said, "but from what I can tell—and I've done thousands of these—you have a potentially healthy baby here. Do you want to know what it is?"

"Yes," Tamra said eagerly. "Can you tell?"

"I knew the minute I turned the machine on," she said. "Let me show you. He's turned just right to give us a perfect view."

"It's a boy?" Jess squeaked and exchanged a long glance with his father, whose joy was evident.

"Beyond a doubt," the technician said. "No shadows or guessing with this one. Congratulations, you've got a son."

She turned off the machine and helped Tamra wipe the excess gel off her belly. Michael took Tamra's hand to help her sit up, then he took hold of her shoulders and kissed her forehead. He looked into her eyes and said tenderly, "Thank you, my dear Tamra. Now I can die happy."

"I don't think I like the way you put that," she said. "Don't you want to hold him before you go?"

"Yes, I do," he said. "And I'm going to do my best to make that happen, but . . . just in case, I want you to know how happy this makes me."

Tamra smiled at her father-in-law, not knowing what to say. She noticed the technician looking a bit concerned as she fussed with putting everything in order. Tamra quickly said to Michael, "I knew it was a boy. Perhaps there's a reason that God would send a son now."

"Perhaps," Michael said and took a step back.

Emily embraced Tamra, then Jess. "Thank you for bringing us along. It truly is wonderful to have the two of you together, and to know that you'll have this child."

"Yes, it is," Jess said.

"We'll wait outside," Emily said and ushered Michael from the room.

"Sorry about the dramatics," Jess said to the technician. "We're good at that lately."

"Well, I've seen more dramatic responses in here if you must know, but . . . I can't help wondering why—"

"My father has cancer," Jess explained quietly. "He's in remission, but they don't expect it to last long. He's the only son of an only son of an only son. And my only brothers have died. Our having a son means a great deal to him."

The technician smiled at Jess with empathy showing in her eyes. "I think that's understandable. I wish you the best . . . all of you."

"Thank you," Jess said, and helped Tamra down from the table.

Michael took them all out to lunch, then he insisted they go shopping. Emily and Tamra stood back and laughed together a number of times as these men they loved made such a fuss over buying baby clothes and accessories. When Tamra declared that they had plenty of time to get what little else the baby would need, Jess insisted that they needed to buy Evelyn a new baby doll. He took great care in picking out just the right one, and some clothes and a little bathtub to go with it. For more than two hours after they'd returned home, Jess helped Evelyn bathe and dress her baby. After four baths he declared, "Boy, she's a clean baby. Did you know Mama's going to have a new baby? And he's going to be your little brother." Evelyn then started calling her baby "little brother" even though it was obviously a girl baby. Jess just laughed and insisted that it was Grandpa's turn to dress the baby. Michael put down his book and took obvious joy in helping Evelyn with her new project, while Jess found equal joy in sensing the fulfillment in his father's eyes. All things considered, they were truly blessed.

* * *

By the time they set out for the great family vacation, Michael was feeling almost as good as new. His hair had even grown back in to its normal length. Tamra had completely gotten past the nausea of her pregnancy, even though she still hardly looked pregnant except in certain clothes. They arrived in Cairns late morning, and the remainder of the family trickled in through the afternoon, the last of them arriving just after six. Reunions were filled with laughter and hugs, and even a few tears, and many declarations on how good Michael looked—and how good it was to see him. Jess noticed that his father's emotions were close to the surface, and he couldn't help wondering if Michael's thoughts were tuned to the likelihood that this might well be the last time the entire family was together. Jess noticed that Amee was the only one who didn't want to talk at all about the cancer, but after a few questions were answered, the issue seemed to be put away and Jess figured it was just as well. With the disease in remission, and being together as they were, perhaps taking Amee's attitude would be best for the time being. If he could pretend it would never come back, he could enjoy this time with no dark clouds hanging over them.

The second night there, all of the adults gathered together in Michael and Emily's room, while the children were off to bed, older ones staying in the rooms with younger ones to look after them. Jess was surprised to hear Michael say, "Now that we're all together, I would like to introduce you to the newest member of the family."

They all looked suspiciously at each other, as if to guess who might be pregnant. Jess was amazed at Tamra's ability to keep a straight face. After a long, grueling minute, Michael stood and took Tamra's hand, urging her to her feet. "Tamra, of course," he said, "is the newest member of the family, since she married Jess."

Everyone groaned, except Jess, who laughed. "Oh, you had us going there for a minute," Amee said.

"I'm not done yet," Michael added and they all became immediately silent. With an arm around Tamra's shoulders, he tentatively pressed a hand to Tamra's belly and said with a tenderness in his voice that bordered on reverent, "Let me introduce you to the newest member of the family: Jess Michael Hamilton, the fifth, who will be appearing in January."

Amidst the rumble of excitement and questions and congratulations, Jess knew that three of his sisters had perceived the deeper meaning to their father's announcement. The tears in their eyes let him know that they were well aware of what this meant to Michael. Amee only seemed pleased that Jess and Tamra were expecting.

For the next ten days, the family shared a wide variety of outings in the area, and also took advantage of a rented meeting room in the hotel where they all gathered for many games and activities. They took several pictures and had the video cameras running often to capture the memories. No one seemed to want to talk about this oasis of time ever coming to a close. A family portrait was taken, with every member wearing brightly colored polo shirts that Emily had purchased and brought with her. But for Jess, his favorite times were the late evening conversations among the adults. Memories were shared, enhanced by photo albums that Emily had brought along. And Allison kept a tape recorder running through a number of evenings while Michael and Emily spoke of their childhoods, their coming together in college, being separated for years, and coming together again. They talked back and forth of their marriage, their children, their struggles, and the good times they'd shared. They teased and laughed, and even cried a little, while Jess just tried to absorb every moment clearly into his memory, grateful for the pictures and recordings that would help preserve this precious time. Allison promised to send each of her siblings both an audio copy and a transcription of everything she recorded. It was easy for Jess to imagine just how priceless they would become once his father was gone.

When the vacation drew to a close, good-byes were difficult. The reality of the cancer's imminent return became evident in the tearful farewells that Michael shared with his daughters, although Jess couldn't help noticing that Amee seemed much less emotional than the others. She kept her farewells brief, then was nowhere around while the other girls lingered with their father until the last possible moment. There was talk of all of them getting back together for Christmas, "As long as Michael pays for the trip," Allison's husband said lightly just before he exchanged an emotional embrace with his father-in-law. Michael was deeply serious when he looked at Ammon and responded, "It would be worth any amount of money to have you all together again."

"Then we'll plan on it," Allison said.

The drive home was quiet beyond Evelyn's typical antics. It was as if they all instinctively knew that even if they were ever together again as a family, it would never be the same. Jess had to wonder if that meant the remission would indeed be brief, as the doctors had suggested it might be. He tried not to think about that, but rather focused his mind on all they had to be grateful for. They had been greatly blessed to come this far, and he had to keep that in mind.

They arrived home to find that Sadie had missed them terribly, although they suspected that she'd missed Evelyn most. After they had showered Sadie with all kinds of ridiculous souvenirs, she served them roast chicken and her special gravy.

Over dinner, Michael said, "I really want to go to the temple."

"Oh, that sounds wonderful," Emily said. "Do you want some time to rest up first or—"

"I was thinking we could leave in a few days, spend four or five days in Sydney, get in several sessions." He turned directly to Tamra. "I was hoping the two of you could come along, and perhaps we could have the chance to visit with your aunt while we're in the city."

"Oh, I'm certain she would be thrilled," Tamra said eagerly. "As I would be. It would be great to see her *and* go to the temple."

Sadie chimed in saying, "Next you'll be asking if I'll look out for little Evelyn while you're gone and the answer is yes, I would love to!"

"Well then," Michael said. "Let's do it. I think I'll call Amee and see if she could meet us for at least one session."

"Splendid idea," Emily said, and Jess couldn't help hoping that his sister would accept the offer. Some time together might help her come to terms with the reality of her father's cancer. But Michael reported the next morning that his call to Amee had not gone well at all. She insisted that she was just too busy to make it and they would just have to try another time.

"I asked her what she was doing and she just evaded the question," Michael said. "I suggested we might not get another chance and she became terribly eager to get off the phone."

Emily sighed. "I'm worried about her, Michael."

"Yes, so am I," Michael said. He went on to explain how he had regular long phone conversations with the other girls, and even their husbands, as well as lengthy e-mails back and forth. He felt that their relationships were good and they were doing their best to accept the cancer and its ramifications. "But with Amee," he said, "she's become steadily more withdrawn from me since the cancer came up."

Tamra suggested, "Perhaps she's trying to prepare herself by getting used to living without you."

"Perhaps," Michael said. "I hadn't thought about that, but it has some logic, I suppose."

"Or maybe she's just in denial," Jess said. "She never asks how Dad is doing, and if I bring it up, she changes the subject."

"I don't know." Emily sighed again. "I only know I'm worried about her. I fear that for whatever reason, she's simply not willing to look at something that eventually will have to be faced. I fear she is wasting this precious time we have to prepare. I've tried to talk to her, but it's the same. She just doesn't want to talk about it, and we can't force her to do something she doesn't want to do."

Jess said, "I wonder if she could possibly appreciate what a great opportunity it would be to go to the temple together, when it's so far away and we get there so rarely."

"I as much as asked her that," Michael said.

"Well *I* appreciate what a great opportunity it is," Tamra said brightly. "And I'm looking forward to it. I think I'll go call Rhea and see if we can take her to dinner one evening while we're there."

"Splendid idea," Michael said. "Find out what her favorite restaurant is."

"I already know," Tamra said and went to make the call.

The trip to Sydney turned out to be a huge success. Michael felt great and they were able to attend half a dozen sessions together over the three days they stayed in the city. They also did some sealings. Jess felt a deep poignancy as he contemplated how his parents might be feeling as they realized this could very well be their last time together in the temple. But this sweet symbolism of the blessings of eternity was a source of deep comfort in facing the tragedies of this life.

They enjoyed a delightful evening with Tamra's aunt Rhea. Observing his parents' interaction with this woman who lived a lifestyle so different from their own, Jess was struck with how loving and nonjudgmental his parents were. He'd grown up seeing them interact with many different kinds of people, but it had never occurred to him how very good they were at it. He realized then that they were an amazing example of being in the world but not of the world. Their convictions ran deep, and they would never fluctuate on their values and standards. But that didn't keep them from sharing genuine acceptance and friendship with all kinds of people. This realization, combined with their many hours together in the temple, left Jess deeply grateful for the kind of people he'd been born to. He thought of Tamra's difficult upbringing and all that she'd had to rise above, including some serious abuse, and his gratitude deepened for being given so much.

They returned home from Sydney to find Sadie and Evelyn both in good spirits and doing well. Jess and Tamra extended their little vacation a day and took Evelyn into town to buy some new shoes and have lunch out. They returned home and helped Sadie prepare a picnic for the entire family, and they ate supper on a blanket under the trees on the side lawn. After they'd eaten, Michael laid down on the blanket and quickly fell asleep. Evelyn begged to go for a walk, so Tamra took her hand and set out toward the back of the house. Jess helped his mother and Sadie take the remnants of their picnic back into the house, and then he caught up with Tamra and Evelyn near the wrought-iron fence at the edge of the huge yard where Evelyn was smelling flowers. The fence surrounded a little graveyard, where every member of the family who had lived here had been buried since Ben Davies had first homesteaded this land in the 1850s. Evelyn ambled through the open gate and skipped between the gravestones while Jess and Tamra strolled behind her.

Tamra had come to this place a number of times, always fascinated with the names and the dates on the headstones that coincided with the many journals and family history records she had pored over since she'd first come to live here. She pondered the contrast between the very old stones of Jess's ancestors, and the newer pieces of his brother and sister-in-law—Evelyn's parents. And she was struck by the thought of losing another family member to death. She couldn't help wondering how long it might be before Michael joined his loved ones here. But of course, this was only the final resting place for the bodies that were cast aside. The real reunion with family would occur when their spirits met on the other side of the veil. Still, she had a thought she felt compelled to share.

"You know, Jess," she said, bending over to brush some dirt off of his great-great-grandmother's headstone, "this place is going to be incredible when the resurrection occurs."

Jess chuckled and looked around. "It certainly is. What a family reunion *that* will be."

They walked slowly on while Evelyn skipped back and forth, full of four-year-old energy. Coming to the fence opposite the gate, Tamra commented, "You know, whoever put this fence up must have had great foresight."

"How is that?"

"Well, I know that your great-great-grandmother said in her journals that the graveyard was surrounded by an iron fence; she spoke of it when her first baby died and was buried here. So it's been here a long time. And yet it still surrounds the graves and there's room for more."

"Yes, I suppose you're right," Jess said, glancing around himself. "It must have seemed awfully big when there were only a few graves here."

"So, whoever put the fence up must have had some measure of vision regarding their posterity. Of course, those who settled elsewhere have been buried elsewhere, but still . . . this will be a busy place when that resurrection happens."

Jess chuckled again. "One way or another, I plan to be here when that happens."

Tamra squeezed his hand. "And I plan to be with you."

He smiled and kissed her quickly before they wandered back through the gate. As they walked back across the sloping lawn, they found Michael, Emily, and Sadie all seated on the veranda, watching the sun go down.

"Do you suppose," Emily asked as they were seated and Evelyn climbed onto her grandfather's lap, "that everywhere in the world has such beautiful sunsets?"

"I would imagine," Michael said. "We saw beautiful sunsets in the Philippines . . . and Africa as well."

"That's true," Emily said. "And serving missions there made me appreciate many beauties, but . . . maybe I'm just partial to Australian sunsets because it's home."

"I think I could agree with that," Michael said, and a contented silence fell over the group. Even Evelyn remained fairly quiet, seeming to appreciate the serenity of the moment.

Once dusk had settled, Jess took Evelyn upstairs to give her a quick bath and get her ready for bed. Tamra helped put the kitchen in order and put in a load of laundry before she went upstairs to find Jess reading a story to Evelyn in her room. A few minutes later Michael and Emily came in and they all knelt together for family prayer.

With Evelyn tucked into bed, Michael and Emily went to their room, declaring the need for an early night. "All that traveling's caught up with me," Michael said through a yawn.

Jess and Tamra went to the sitting room off their bedroom, where Jess read aloud from the *Ensign* while Tamra did some hand sewing on a quilt block that would eventually be worked into a little quilt for the baby. When Jess finished the article he was reading, he became quietly thoughtful for several minutes before Tamra asked, "What's on your mind?"

He sighed and turned more toward her. "I was just thinking how much my gratitude for the gospel keeps deepening. I've felt it work very dramatically in my life in the past, but lately I just feel sort of a . . . gradual deepening of . . . Well, it's difficult to describe, but . . . I guess I just feel an underlying feeling of peace and calm, and a deep gratitude for the knowledge we have that makes the prospect of losing my father to cancer actually bearable. And the same applies to any other difficulty that might come up." He sighed again. "I'm just grateful."

"Well, so am I," she said, reaching for his hand. "I'm especially grateful for eternal marriage. Going to the temple again made me really appreciate what an incredible blessing that is. To know that we'll be together forever is just . . . so completely comforting when you think of all we're up against in this life. It's like . . . death is the ultimate opposition, but the resurrection has triumphed over that. And the eternal sealing of families makes it all truly worthwhile."

"I couldn't have said it better myself," Jess said. "I can't even imagine how I would cope if my parents weren't sealed for eternity."

Jess yawned noisily and proclaimed, "I think I need to get some sleep. I've got some major work to be catching up on tomorrow."

Tamra continued her needlework for a short while after Jess had gone to sleep, wondering why an uncomfortable feeling was hovering in her mind. She tried to place where in the conversation it had begun, and why it would have left her ill at ease.

She got ready for bed and slipped quietly between the covers without disturbing Jess, but she fell asleep without knowing why she felt uneasy, and she woke up with the feeling still there. Long after breakfast was over and Jess had gone to the boys' home with his father, she finally pinpointed that something hadn't felt right when Jess had expressed his gratitude for his parents being sealed together. When she had finished some laundry and set the kitchen in order, she took Evelyn to the library and sat her on one of the big leather sofas with some storybooks. With Evelyn occupied, Tamra opened the drawer that contained the Book of Remembrance where she had once found the records of all the temple work that had been done for the family. She understood the reason for her uneasiness when she found a marriage certificate for Michael and Emily, but the marriage had been performed by a bishop, not many months after Michael's baptism date. He wouldn't have been able to go to the temple at that point, so it made sense that they had been married civilly, but there was no subsequent sealing certificate. She wondered if the certificate had been misplaced, but looking at other records, she found no record of a sealing date, although she did find a record of Michael's endowment date. Tamra felt confused and baffled, and subsequently more uneasy. She wondered how to question Michael and Emily enough to appease her curiosity, without sounding nosy or obnoxious. She reminded herself that they were family, and surely there was some simple explanation. Surely they would be able to help her understand her confusion so that she could put the idea away. Perhaps Jess would know the answer and she wouldn't even have to bring it up with his parents. She met him for lunch in the cafeteria at the boys' home, but the meal was typically filled with talk and teasing between them and the boys, and there was no opportunity for serious conversation before Jess had to hurry back to Mr. Hobbs's office and get on with some paperwork.

Jess was late arriving for supper, but once the meal was over, Tamra offered to wash up the dishes if Michael and Emily would look after Evelyn. "And Jess can help me," Tamra said with a smile toward him.

Jess winked as he said with mock disgust, "Well, if I have to."

Sadie stayed in the kitchen to work on something she was making for tomorrow's dessert, and the dishes were nearly finished before she left. When Tamra was finally left alone with Jess, she hurried to open the subject while he finished loading the dishwasher and she wiped off the counters. "I was looking through your family's genealogical records today."

"A hobby of yours, I believe."

"In a way, I suppose, but . . . there's something that doesn't make sense. I was hoping you could explain it so I wouldn't have to go to your parents to appease my curiosity."

"Another of your hobbies," Jess said with a little chuckle.

"What?"

"Curiosity," he said, tossing her a crooked smile.

"Yes, I suppose it is," she admitted.

"So what doesn't make sense?" he asked as he closed the dishwasher and turned it on.

Tamra rinsed out the dishrag and hung it over the tap before she leaned against the counter and said, "I can find no evidence of your parents being sealed."

The look of astonishment in Jess's eyes bordered on panic. "It has to be there," he said with a little laugh that didn't dispel the obvious concern in his eyes. He hurried to the library with Tamra directly behind him and went straight to the book she had been looking at earlier, where they both knew all of the family records relating to temple work and ordinances were kept.

"Here's the marriage certificate," Tamra said, pointing it out, "but there's no sealing certificate, and no sealing date on any of the records."

"But . . ." Jess uttered the one syllable, then frantically glanced through the pages. He finally stated the obvious. "My father has always been meticulous with these records. How can there not be . . . ?" His question remained unfinished as he closed the book and left the library as quickly as he'd entered.

They found Michael and Emily in the lounge room. They both glanced up briefly from their reading and smiled, Emily saying, "Sadie took Evelyn upstairs to—"

"I have a question," Jess said in a tone of voice that made Michael and Emily both turn toward him with startled eyes.

"Yes?" Michael drawled, setting his book aside.

"I can't help wondering why there's no evidence in our family records of the two of you being sealed together."

Tamra's hope for some simple explanation was dashed when Michael and Emily exchanged a long, anxious gaze. Emily's eyes remained focused on Michael as he turned to face Jess and said firmly, "Sit down, Jess."

"I'm fine," he insisted and remained standing, but Tamra opted to sit on one of the sofas.

Michael cleared his throat and said, "There can be no records for something that never happened, Jess. Your mother and I are *not* sealed together."

Jess sat down. He stared into his father's eyes, as if he could find the answers just by looking there. For a long moment everything he believed in, everything he had known to be true and firm, suddenly felt like it was sliding into quicksand. He couldn't even begin to fathom what could justify such an obvious oversight. A harsh silence settled over the room until Jess managed to sputter, "But how . . ."

His mother's voice startled him and he snapped his head toward her. "I can't believe you don't know about this. We've had family discussions about this, Jess. Where were you? I mean . . . I know you were there physically. Were you so detached from the family through those rebellious years that you didn't hear what was being talked about?"

"Maybe I was," Jess admitted, "because I sure don't remember *anything* ever being said about *this.* How can a Latter-day Saint family with access to a temple have such an important piece missing? It makes no sense."

Michael sighed and once again shared a long gaze with Emily. "Okay, well," he said, "I guess we'd better start at the beginning." He shook his head and briefly rubbed a hand over his face. "I really hate this story," he added, reaching for Emily's hand. Jess reached for Tamra's in the same moment, squeezing so hard that it hurt. She knew that whatever they were about to hear would not be well received. She uttered a quick, silent prayer that Jess's heart would be receptive, then she leaned back and waited to hear what Michael had to say.

Chapter Eleven

Michael cleared his throat again, then took a deep breath. "When I met your mother, Jess, I was not a member of the Church. The more I learned about it, the more I respected and admired your mother's beliefs, but I was not willing to embrace them for myself. I was quite adamant that my life had been good and I saw no reason to change it. I felt quite confident that she would be willing to marry me anyway. But in the end her convictions on marrying in the temple overruled."

Michael let out a heavy sigh and leaned his forearms on his thighs. "There are no words to describe the devastation I experienced when she left me. I went through many stages of grief, anger, resentment . . . and ten years later, I still hadn't completely gotten over it. That's when our paths crossed again and I learned that your mother's temple marriage was not necessarily good. Ryan had become inactive in the Church and didn't treat her very well. All those feelings of anger and resentment magnified immensely. I asked your mother to leave him and marry me. I was willing to take her daughters on as my own and we could begin a new life together. But she chose to stay and honor those covenants she had made with him. Ryan made some positive changes before he was killed, and I joined the Church—of my own will. Mostly it was because I had been left so in awe of your mother's convictions and commitment, even in the face of such obvious challenges."

Jess tried not to sound frustrated as he said, "I knew most of that already. But what has it got to do with—"

"I'm getting to that," Michael said. "Your mother married Ryan in the temple, Jess. She is sealed to *him,* and he is dead, and she cannot be sealed to another man in this life."

Tamra gasped, then pressed a hand over her mouth. She was keenly aware of Jess struggling to breathe, and the way he leaned heavily against her. He abruptly sat up straighter as if a thought had occurred to him. A moment later he blurted, "So, who am *I* sealed to?"

Michael's tone was even as he stated, "Your mother. You were born under the covenant."

"And who are *you* sealed to?"

"My parents, my grandparents, my—"

"So, let me get this straight. *You,* my father, are sealed to a long line of ancestors. But my mother is sealed to a *different* man, a *different* family, and there is a huge crack down the middle of *this* family. My half-sisters are sealed to their blood father, but Emma and I have no eternal connection to *you*. And James and Tyson, who are already on the other side; who are *they* sealed to? A man that none of us even knew! Do I have that straight?"

"Technically, yes," Michael said and Jess groaned. "But let me explain some things that took me a long time to figure out. First of all, you have to understand that the sealing ordinance is a wonderful and mandatory part of the plan. Secondly, there are certain limitations in this life, where rules must be established in black and white for the sake of order. But on the other side, everything will be made right according to how we live for those blessings."

"I'm lost," Jess said, his voice strained.

"So, I'll give you an example. Your great-great-grandmother, Alexandra Byrnehouse-Davies, had a similar situation. She was married to Richard Wilhite. He died and she married Jess Davies. When we did her temple work, she was sealed to both men, even though she can only be married to one on the other side of the veil. But the choice will be made there as to which one she will be with throughout eternity. But sealing a woman to more than one man can only be done following death. We all feel strongly that it will be Jess Davies, because he was the father of her children, and she was only married to Richard for a brief time, whereas she spent the bulk of her life married to Jess. Reading their journals you can feel the intensity of the love they had for each other, as if it had been foreordained. Your mother and I have similar feelings about each other. We know that the Lord is in charge, and He will know what is just and right for this family."

"So, what are you saying?" Jess asked in a voice that expressed how deeply this was troubling him. "That there's a chance you won't end up married to my mother on the other side?" He shot to his feet and added, "How can you just . . . sit back and accept something . . . so completely *ludicrous?*"

Michael shot to his feet as well, and Tamra couldn't recall ever seeing him so intense. "Now, you listen to me, son, and you listen well." He lifted a finger and leaned closer to Jess. "Don't go assuming that this has *ever* been easy for me to accept. But just because it's been one of the greatest difficulties of my life, don't think for a moment that any part of God's plan is *ludicrous*. He knows what He's doing, even if *you* don't understand it. You have no idea of the internal grief I have suffered over this issue, and the grief I brought to my family because I was so hesitant to accept it. When I finally came to my senses, and humbled myself enough to *ask* God for the answers, instead of just assuming that I had it all figured out, He let me know beyond any doubt that I would be blessed for how I lived in this life. I have committed my life, my heart, my soul, *everything* to loving your mother, caring for her, and for our children. And I know beyond any doubt that the Lord will take care of us—now and forever."

"How can you believe that when your wife is sealed to another man?"

The ensuing silence made it evident that Emily was crying. Jess and Michael both turned toward her, then back to face each other. Michael's voice was quiet but firm as he stated, "I don't believe, Jess. I *know* it. There are aspects to this situation that cannot be explained with any degree of logic. It's a spiritual matter, with many complexities I still don't fully understand. You have to get your own answers, and there's only one place you can get them. But you'll never get answers when you're angry. Trust me on that one. I learned it the hard way. And until you get those answers, trust me when I tell you that everything will work out for the best, and we will be happy. Our main concern now should just be to live in a way that allows us to return to our Heavenly Father and to accept His will in whatever happens to this family. We don't know exactly how it will all work out, but if we are worthy to live with God again, how could it be anything but fair and happy?"

Jess blew out a long breath and looked at the floor. Half a minute later he said, "I'm sorry if I upset you, Mother. I need some time." He turned and left the room.

Michael sat down abruptly, as if his strength had left him suddenly. He eased closer to Emily and took her into his arms where she cried harder. Tamra wasn't sure if she should stay or go after Jess, but she couldn't come up with the motivation to stand up and leave the room. Her mind became absorbed with the conversation she'd just been privy to, until Michael's voice startled her. "Sorry about the drama, my dear. We seem to have rather a lot of it around here."

Tamra smiled toward him. "Only now and again."

Michael gave a humorless chuckle. "Yes, but when we have it, we *really* have it."

Sadie came into the room with Evelyn. "I went ahead and gave her a bath," Sadie said. "If it's all right with you, I'll just go ahead and read to her and tuck her in."

"That would be great," Tamra said. "Thank you."

Evelyn shared hugs with everyone before she went back upstairs with Sadie. Quiet settled over the room again until Tamra felt she had to say, "I'm afraid I may have opened this can of worms."

Emily, who had calmed down now, turned toward her and said, "How is that?"

"Well," Tamra looked down at her wringing hands, "Jess mentioned how grateful he was to know that the two of you were sealed for eternity. But . . . something nagged at me about that, so I looked through the records and . . . when I couldn't find anything, I just . . . asked him about it, and . . ." Tamra's voice became lost in a surge of regret.

"There's no good in blaming yourself," Emily said. "I had every reason to believe that he knew. He *needs* to know. Better that it come up now when Michael can talk to him about it."

Tamra swallowed hard at the implication. If it had come up after Michael was gone, would it have been even more difficult for Jess to accept?

Michael sighed and said, "I know just how he feels. I only wish he could trust me when I tell him it's going to be all right. I don't want him to go through what I went through before I had the sense to get the answers the right way. But . . . you can't blame him for being upset. He's right, you know. The reality is that . . . in a way, it seems like his family is divided." Michael sighed again then came abruptly to his feet.

"Where are you going?" Emily asked.

"I'm going to talk to my son." His voice broke as he added, "I know *exactly* how he feels, and he needs to know that."

* * *

Jess found himself in the carriage house, instinctively drawn by a memory of his youth when he'd sit in the trap to think whenever he felt lonely or down. He'd felt an abstract comfort curled up on the seat of the historical vehicle, and then his life had gone down many wrong paths and that kind of comfort had left him. He'd realized years later that the choices he'd made had driven many good things out of his life, and he'd also learned that his great-great-grandmother had often sat in the very same spot when she'd needed time to think. It was recorded in her journals. Jess had once believed that this great woman had been his guardian angel; perhaps that's why he had found comfort in the same place where she had once gone for the same reason. Whether there was any truth to such a theory or not, he felt drawn there this evening.

The aging wheels of the trap creaked when he stepped in and sat on the worn leather seat. He contemplated all he had learned in the last hour and his heart filled with a grief akin to learning that his father would die of cancer. The prospect of being together in the next life was the only thing that had given him any peace at all. And now that prospect seemed to be torn away and replaced with an abstract idea that seemed too difficult to swallow.

Growing steadily more angry and upset, Jess closed his eyes and tried to force the anger away. He clenched his fists while he prayed intently to be free of these negative feelings in order to gain some level of understanding. He was startled to hear the door open and turned to see his father standing in the dim glow of a single light bulb burning near the door. Not certain if more conversation between them would help or hinder his feelings, he simply said, "I wasn't planning on being found."

"The light in the carriage house gave you away," Michael said, sauntering toward him, his hands deep in the pockets of his jeans. He stopped beside the trap and added, "Did you know your great-great-grandmother used to sit here when she wanted to be alone and think?"

Jess sighed deeply. "Yes, actually, I knew that. Only because my sweet wife told me." He sighed and leaned his elbows on his knees. "I used to sit here when I was a kid; I felt drawn here for some reason."

"And tonight?"

"It just seemed like a good place to go."

"May I join you?" Michael asked.

"Sure." Jess slid over and his father sat beside him.

Following a few minutes of silence, Michael said, "There's been something I've had on my mind; something I'd like to do before I die."

"I hate it when you put it that way."

"Well, I think *everyone* should have a 'things to do before I die' list. Mine's just been narrowed down considerably. Fortunately, I've lived a good life and I have no regrets; no big ones, anyway. The important things are already taken care of, but . . . there are some experiences of this world I would like to have once more."

"Such as?" Jess asked, pleasantly surprised that the conversation had not gone where he'd expected it to.

"Well, I want to race a horse." He chuckled deeply. "I knew once I was twelve that being a jockey was not for me—and a couple of years later I was far too tall—but I always loved the feel of a racing saddle beneath me and the finish line looming ahead." He gave a pleasant sigh. "Reading similar feelings from my ancestors' journals makes me certain it's in the blood somehow. It's probably a good thing I don't believe in gambling."

"Well, it must be in the blood," Jess said. "Racing, not gambling," he clarified quickly. "Because I love that feeling, too." He paused and added, "Do you think you're up to it?"

"What? A race?"

"Yeah."

"And who might I race against? You?"

"Sure," Jess chuckled, "why not? I learned how to ride that way from you. Let's see how well you taught me."

"Okay, you're on," Michael said. "But I'm riding Crazy's Progeny."

"Fine. I'll take Crazy's Spade." He chuckled and added, "Who names these horses, anyway?"

"Oh, we get input from all over the place. But I've lost count of the horses we've had who have a part of the famous Crazy in them."

"And isn't there some great story about the original Crazy? I know there is, but I can't remember."

"Well then, maybe I'd better tell you. It's a story worth repeating."

"I'm listening," Jess said.

"Well, as I understand it, my great-grandfather, Jess Davies, was on the brink of losing this land. He staked everything he owned on a single horse race, and he hired Alexandra Byrnehouse to train the horse to do it, deep inside believing it would never happen."

"I've heard *that* before."

"Well, the horse's name was Crazy. Alexa trained the horse and the jockey, but she ended up riding the race herself when the jockey got sick. She won the race, saved the land, and ended up eventually marrying Jess."

"And she would sit in this trap to think."

"That's right."

"So, Jess Davies *was* a gambler. And what you're telling me is this land would not be in our possession if he hadn't been."

Michael chuckled. "Something like that. However, he taught his children adamantly that gambling was not the way to go. Gambling initially saved the land, but he inherited the bulk of his fortune because he had proven to be a man of good character and integrity, even given his challenges."

"Now that part I knew," Jess said. "I read his journals once, you know. But he didn't talk about that race."

"I believe Alexa recorded that story. You mentioned before that you'd read his journals."

"Oh yes. They helped me get through that rough spell I had before I married Tamra. I found that my great-great-grandfather and I have a lot in common." He smiled. "And he did love to race a good horse."

"So, when shall we set up this grand event?"

"How about tomorrow?" Jess asked and Michael grinned.

"You're on. But no bets."

Jess feigned great disappointment. "Oh, all right. If you insist."

It became quiet again until Jess asked, "What else is on the list?"

"What?"

"The 'things to do before you die' list."

"Oh, well . . . this might sound strange, but . . . I keep thinking about when my father would take me flying in his plane."

"It's not been so long since you've flown the—"

"No, *his* plane. It was built in the early forties."

"Oh, *that* plane. It's still in the hangar, isn't it?"

"Oh yes."

"Is it safe?"

"Well," Michael said, "when it was last put away, it was in perfect condition. I'm sure Murphy could help us check it out and make sure it's air worthy. What do you think?"

"You want me to help you?" Jess asked, feeling a delighted tremor at the idea.

"What fun would it be to do it alone? And your mother would never go up in it with me. She says it nauseates her."

Jess laughed. "I think it sounds great. We'll have Mom on the lawn with the video camera. It'll be a memory worth looking at."

Michael let out a perfectly joyful laugh. "There now, I have *two* things to look forward to. I have to admit that since we got back from vacation, and then the temple trip was over, I've felt some letdown. I need something to look forward to."

Jess couldn't comment. The statement was a clear reminder that his father knew he was going to die. And that thought brought him back to his reasons for coming out to the carriage house in the first place. He felt compelled to say, "I really thought you'd come out here to talk to me about . . . what we'd been talking about in the house."

"I did," Michael said. "But there were other things I'd been meaning to talk to you about, as well. Now seemed as good a time as any."

"So, now that you know we have something to look forward to, why don't you tell me what you came to say?"

"It can wait," Michael said.

"No, I don't think it can." Jess drew a ragged breath. "I'm having a rough time with this, Dad. I don't know what else to say."

"Well, what I wanted to tell you . . . what I *need* to tell you is that . . . I know exactly how you feel. When I asked your mother to marry me—after her husband had died—I just assumed that we would be sealed, even though she had been sealed to her first husband. When I learned how it works, that she could only be sealed to one man, I was devastated. I tried to put it out of my head and enjoy the life we had together, but then her heart stopped when she had a miscarriage and she hemorrhaged. I was struck with the thought that if she had died, I would have lost her to a man I didn't even like. That's where the trouble began, and it didn't end until after that accident where your mother very nearly died because I was out of my mind with anger over that very thing."

Jess gasped and turned toward his father in astonishment. He recalled the accident well from his childhood. And more recently he'd learned that his father had been angry over something when it had happened. But he'd had no idea . . . "That was the reason you were angry?"

"That was it," he said firmly. "Your mother's mother-in-law—Ryan's mother—stopped by for a visit. She came right out and told the girls that they would be with their father forever, and one of them asked her about you and James. She said that the two of you were only half-siblings, and her implication was that we were out of the picture in eternity. I got angry and told her we would all be together forever—as a family. But deep inside I don't think I believed it. It took a lot of prayer, and soul searching, and a number of complicated puzzle pieces coming together for me to finally understand more of the big picture. And a day came when I knew that your mother and I were meant to be together, and as I lived for that blessing, it would be mine."

"But . . . the ordinance isn't there," Jess protested. "Without the sealing, there's no guarantee."

"Even with the sealing there's no guarantee, Jess. Let me tell you something your mother told me she'd learned through her first marriage. Beyond the last few months of Ryan's life, she was terribly unhappy. She'd married him in the temple with the faith that they would be happy together. But he did many things to hurt her. Not physically. But emotionally she became a shadow of the woman I'd once known. She told me that she'd learned temple marriage is a wonderful thing, but it's not a guarantee. The reality of temple marriage comes through the ins and outs of everyday living. It's enduring to the end, committed to someone you love, and living worthy of those eternal vows. I'm not a perfect man, Jess. I have my weaknesses and I'm keenly aware of them. But I can say that from the day I married your mother, I did everything in my power to be a good husband and father. I made mistakes—some big ones. But I did my best to make restitution. I always tried to improve and grow for the sake of making my family better and stronger. My family has always been my top priority, along with living the gospel. The Atonement is there to make up the difference for my shortcomings after all I can do, and because I know I've done my best, I know with all my heart that the Lord is mindful of our circumstances, and He will make everything as it should be—whatever is supposed to happen, *will.* I can't tell you how I know this, Jess. I just know, and I know it beyond any doubt. Through the years that knowledge has settled more deeply into me."

Jess didn't want to keep arguing, but he still felt so uneasy about it. He had to say, "But, it's all so . . . abstract."

"Yes, it is. That's what faith is all about. If the principle of eternity were tangible, we wouldn't need faith to believe it's true."

Jess thought about that for a minute before his father added, "It will likely be many more years before your mother leaves this life, Jess. But when she does . . . when we're both gone . . . I want you and Allison to make certain that we are sealed by proxy. Promise me."

"Of course," Jess said firmly.

"Well then, now I can die in peace."

Jess groaned and Michael chuckled.

"You know, Dad," Jess said, "sometimes your straightforward approach is a little . . . unnerving."

"Sorry," Michael said and seemed to mean it. "For me, I guess I just feel like I have to face it head on. I think a part of me is almost afraid of going into denial otherwise, and then I'll end up feeling unprepared in the end."

A few minutes later Michael said, "You're still upset; I can tell."

"Well . . . yes," Jess admitted.

"That's understandable," Michael said. "But you need to talk about it with the people you love. That's one thing I *didn't* do, and that's why my fears and anger got so out of control. And for heaven's sake, pray about it. You have the gift of the Holy Ghost, Jess. You're entitled to personal revelation. You have the right to know that we'll be together every bit as much as I do. Just be patient and give it some time . . . and faith. Okay?"

"Okay," Jess agreed and impulsively embraced his father. "Thanks for coming to find me, Dad. I do feel better."

"Well, I hope so. Because you're going to need everything you've got if you think you're going to beat me in that race tomorrow."

Jess laughed. "Oh, come now, old man. Spade can outrun Progeny any day of the week."

"We'll just see about that," Michael said and they both laughed.

They walked back into the house together and found Emily and Tamra still sitting in the lounge room. The four of them walked upstairs together and said goodnight in the hall. Jess took Tamra's hand and together they peeked in on Evelyn to find her sleeping soundly. Then they went to their bedroom where Jess sat on the edge of the bed to remove his boots.

"You okay?" Tamra asked.

"For the moment," he said, tossing the boots aside. He repeated the gist of what his father had said, and admitted that he needed to give the matter some time. Tamra agreed and told him she loved him, and he had to believe everything would be all right.

The following morning Tamra, Emily, and Evelyn walked out to the track to watch this race that Michael and Jess had talked about all through breakfast. The stable hands were all gathered, whooping and hollering and pulling out their pocket change to lay bets on which horse might win. Tamra felt a little fluttery inside when she saw Michael and Jess emerge from the stable, leading the saddled horses. They both wore riding breeches tucked into classic riding boots, leather braces over button-up shirts, and low, flat-brimmed hats.

From a distance, with their faces shaded, it was difficult to tell them apart. She felt certain she was married to the most attractive man on earth, but she wasn't surprised when Emily muttered a dreamy, "Oh, my," as her eyes followed her husband walking toward the track.

Anticipation took hold of her as the men approached the starting line and mounted. The cheering and hollering from all the hired hands added to the event and prompted Tamra to laughter more than once. When the race began, she felt breathless to see the picture they made, father and son, each with an obvious skill in their blood, as well as a deep love for the sport that had been in the family for generations. Michael won the race, just barely, and over lunch they exchanged good-natured banter over the whole thing.

"You let me win," Michael said, "because you think I'm old and sick."

"If I had let you win," Jess said, "it wouldn't have been a photo finish, I can assure you. Think what you want, old man, but I plan on challenging you next week. Same time, same place."

"Ooh, I can't wait," Tamra said.

"And why is that?" Jess asked.

"You just look so . . . *dashing* when you ride that way."

"My thoughts exactly," Emily said, winking at her husband, which made him chuckle.

A few days later, Murphy went with Michael and Jess to have a look at the old plane. They worked on it together for several days, fitting it in between the necessary business, checking everything meticulously to be certain that it was safe.

Jess and Michael raced again as Jess had promised. And this time Jess won by a head, but since they'd traded horses, it still seemed somewhat of a draw. It was evident that it didn't really matter who won. They were obviously having a great time.

With business going well at the boys' home and with the horses, Michael declared that he wanted to take advantage of it by spending time with his family. Amidst picnics and trips to town, Jess and Michael worked on the plane. Occasionally they all went riding, taking little Evelyn along nearly everywhere they went.

Jess concentrated on enjoying every minute he could with his father, while each morning and evening his prayers contained a plea that he might be given the knowledge that his family—*all* of his family—would be together forever. He talked often with Tamra about his feelings. She listened, always offering compassion and a new perspective. But as time passed he began to feel frustrated at not receiving any obvious answer. When he expressed his frustration to Tamra, she suggested, "Maybe you're not getting an answer because it's a faith issue. Maybe you just need to have the faith that it will happen and leave it at that."

Jess didn't like that answer, but giving it some time to settle in, he had to agree that she was probably right. He continued to pray for an answer and otherwise tried to force it out of his head, but the very idea that his parents might be separated at death, never to be reunited again, tore a hole in the deepest part of him. He asked God to help him overcome such fears and have the faith to trust that all would work out according to His will, but still it nagged at him.

With Michael doing so well, he seemed very much like himself, and it was easy for Jess to pretend that the cancer would never come back. Life felt relatively normal, except that Jess felt a deep abiding gratitude for all he'd been blessed with. He had an incredible wife and a baby on the way. He had the rare opportunity to share a home with his parents and glean daily from their company and wisdom. And he'd been blessed to grow and live in this beautiful place where a great legacy of generations surrounded him. Having the gospel, with all its many facets that enriched his life, he felt a reverent awe at how thoroughly good his life was. And he couldn't help wondering if it was the very fact of his father's cancer that had given him a deeper awareness of all he had to be grateful for. If he weren't being faced with losing this man who was his hero and his mentor—his guiding light—would he be so keenly aware of the good they had to share in the time that was left for them to be together?

Through the ins and outs of everyday life, Jess found himself absorbing memories at every turn, taking mental snapshots that would be even more precious than the many photographs and videos being recorded with cameras that were kept within easy access. He loved seeing his parents holding hands, talking and laughing together as they'd always done. Or the way they would occasionally share a quick kiss or a lingering gaze. He'd never questioned the love between his parents, but he felt an extra awareness that made him appreciate what a great gift it was to see such an example. And he made a determined commitment to always share that kind of love with his sweet Tamra. He marveled at how she had so naturally become a part of the family. He admired the personal relationships she had come to share with his parents and many of the people hired to work for them. Everyone who knew her loved her, and he couldn't blame them. Tamra was an amazing woman and easy to love. Jess especially appreciated observing the relationship his wife had with his father. He often found the two of them discussing the circumstances of a troubled resident of the boys' home, or sharing their perspectives on some tidbit from the journals of their ancestors. Her love for generations past made it fitting that she would be such a literal part of the family. But Jess couldn't think about the fact that while he and Tamra were sealed together, there was no sealing that connected them to his father and the preceding generations that Michael was sealed to. He continued praying for peace about that issue and tried to force it out of his mind.

Jess focused instead on every opportunity to be together as a family. Michael initiated some kind of activity nearly every day, sometimes just for the two of them, but most often for all of them, including Evelyn. They went riding, had many picnics, and even got into an occasional water fight on the lawn. They continued working with Murphy on the plane, anticipating the day when they could take it up. Jess became absorbed with the almost magical quality of these days spent together, and he told his father more than once, "Thanks for sharing your 'things to do before you die list' with me."

Michael would simply laugh and give Jess a playful hug.

* * *

Michael and Emily impulsively decided to go and visit each of the girls at their homes. They quickly made arrangements, and Jess flew them to Sydney to catch a flight to the States. They spent about a week with each of the families, and even spent some time with Sean and his family while they were in Utah. Jess missed having his parents around, but he took advantage of those weeks to spend more time with Tamra. Since news of his father's illness had come so soon after their marriage, he had to admit that he'd focused more effort on being with his father than most newlywed men would. But Tamra had never complained, and she was always there for him. In turn he did his best to be understanding of her needs and make certain she didn't feel neglected. But while his parents were away, he took Tamra and Evelyn on a three-day trip, just to get away and relax. It was time well spent, deepening his gratitude further for this little family he had gained, when not so long ago he'd felt completely alone and without hope.

Soon after Michael and Emily returned, his father's plane was finally declared airworthy. When they were ready to take it up, Michael brought out some old flight caps and goggles that had belonged to his father. Jess laughed as they each put them on and climbed in. Michael let out a loud whoop as he moved the plane forward over the flat land that had been cleared many years ago as a runway. When the plane finally lifted into the air, he laughed loudly enough for Jess to hear him above the rumble of the engine. They flew low over the side lawn where Tamra was waiting with the video camera rolling. Emily, Sadie, and Evelyn all waved and cheered as they flew over the house and around again. Murphy and his mother, some of the stable hands, the boys from the home, and many of the staff came out to watch the display

The following day they took the plane up again, this time with Jess at the controls. They had a great time, but Jess especially enjoyed sitting in the tall grass afterward, listening to his father talk about the times he'd flown in that plane as a boy. Memories of his parents and grandparents followed, deepening Jess's gratitude for the rich legacy of his life.

On their way back to the house, Michael slapped Jess playfully on the shoulder, saying, "*Now* I can die happy."

Jess scowled at him. "Not just yet, I hope."

"Nah," Michael said. "I feel great."

"Well, good," Jess said. "Let's hope it keeps up."

Michael just smiled. Jess knew in his heart what he felt sure they all knew. It wouldn't be long before the cancer returned, but he felt grateful for the time and experiences they'd shared, and for the opportunity they'd been blessed with to prepare for this separation. While he knew that losing his father would be difficult, somehow everything would be all right.

Chapter Twelve

Michael's cancer returned in October, and chemotherapy treatments began again. This time his hair thinned somewhat, but didn't fall out as it had before. He wasn't as nauseated, but he quickly became exhausted and weak. Each day he got up and showered and dressed himself, but he stuck to the house and the veranda, doing very little beyond interacting with the family and reading voraciously. Jess wondered if the reading was somehow an effort to soak up as much knowledge and good literature as he possibly could before he left this earth. Or perhaps it was a way to escape thinking about the disease that was eating away at his body. Jess suspected it was a little of both. Whenever family members were around, Michael's books were set aside and he seemed to be soaking in the simple togetherness they shared through everyday living. But when others were busy elsewhere, and he wasn't resting, he delved into books.

Jess began overseeing business with the boys' home and the stables, reporting regularly to his father of all that was happening, and continually seeking his advice. Tamra became involved to some degree with the happenings of the boys' home in much the same capacity as when she had worked there before marrying Jess. But she kept her main focus on caring for Evelyn, so that either she or Jess was with Evelyn the majority of the time. As Mr. Hobbs began to experience increasing health problems, Jess and Tamra gradually did more of his work, while Mr. Hobbs cut back his hours with plans for an early retirement.

Michael shared phone conversations and long e-mails regularly with his daughters. Even Amee seemed more prone to talking with

Michael, although he confessed that she would always divert the topic if it came anywhere near to Michael's health issues. Jess had to admit that he couldn't blame Amee; there were times when he didn't like thinking of—let alone talking about—the fact that his father was dying. But deep within he felt an underlying peace, and an inexpressible gratitude for the opportunity to be prepared for what lay ahead.

The girls all made the decision to come home for Christmas, along with their families. Through the holidays Michael was weak but in good spirits, and he said more than once how grateful he was to have the family all together again, when he'd wondered if the vacation, months earlier, would have been the last time. Saying good-bye after the holidays were over was difficult for everyone, but Jess sensed the same peace in his sisters that he had come to feel, except for Amee who seemed happy and content in believing that their father's cancer would once again go into remission.

The day after the family all left to return to their homes, Jess had an early meeting with Mr. Hobbs, then returned to the house to talk to his father. He found his parents in their bedroom, resting together on top of the bedspread.

"Are you asleep?" he whispered, not wanting to disturb them if they were.

"No," they both answered and looked toward him.

"What's up?" Michael asked.

"Hobbs just told me that the hearing for the Sully boy is tomorrow, and there's no way he can handle the trip."

Michael lifted his head slightly and said, "Looks like you'll be flying to Brisbane tomorrow."

"I'll have to leave this afternoon, actually," Jess said, sitting in a chair near the bed, "since I need to be there before ten in the morning."

Following a stretch of silence, Michael asked, "So, is there a problem?"

"Well . . . yes," Jess said. He wanted to tell his father that he felt almost terrified to leave, fearing the end would come in his absence. While little had been said about Michael's condition over the last few weeks, Jess had noticed him growing steadily more pale and weak. His gut instinct told him it was more to do with the disease than the treatment. He knew that his father had been gradually taking more painkillers that often left him groggy, and there could only be one reason for his father to be in pain. Jess had prayed that he would be blessed with the privilege of being with his father when he left this world, and he wanted to believe there was still plenty of time left. But he couldn't deny a growing fear inside of him that the time was drawing closer and that he might be denied that opportunity to be present when it happened. He also had concerns for Tamra, and chose to focus on those instead. "Tamra's not so far from her due date, and you know at her last appointment the doctor said the baby could very well come early. I just don't want to leave and . . . I don't want to miss it. And I don't want her overdoing it, or—"

"We'll take good care of Tamra," Emily promised firmly. "And I really doubt she'll come *this* early. Labors are usually long anyway; especially the first time. We'll call your cell phone if anything happens."

Jess sighed and knew he had to accept that answer. This had to be done and there was no one else to do it. Still, he felt the need for some reassurance from his father.

"I've never done this before, Dad."

"Done what?"

"The hearing. I know it's far from the first time that we've had such things come up. But you or Hobbs always handled it, and I'm just not sure I can do it."

"You *can* do it," Michael said, "because you *have* to do it." Michael leaned up on one elbow and looked at Jess severely. "You have to keep the objective clear. Travis Sully is a nine-year-old boy who endured unspeakable conditions in his home. We cannot let an abusive father with well-paid lawyers undo everything we've done to help that child heal. You know the boy, you know the situation. You have all the information you need, and you'll have our attorney and counselor with you. You know what you have to do and you just have to do it."

Jess took a deep breath and came to his feet. "Okay, I'll do my best."

"Sit down. I'm not finished yet," Michael said.

Jess took his chair again. "Okay, I'm sitting."

Michael chuckled and said, "I want to tell you a story."

"Oh, I love your stories," Emily said, even though her eyes were closed and she appeared completely relaxed. "Who is this one about?"

"Michael Hamilton the first."

"Your grandfather," Jess clarified.

"That's right," Michael said. "He was brought to the boys' home after living on the streets for years, which he had far preferred over living in a home where his father had inflicted horrendous abuse. One day his father showed up with a gun, taking hostages, shooting a stable hand who later died, and demanding that his son be given back to him. Jess Davies happened to have a gun himself, since he'd been out looking for a dingo that had been killing the sheep. I don't think that was a coincidence. As I see it, God has a way of lining up the right elements to make things work out as they should. Anyway, Jess shot and killed the guy in self-defense. Michael didn't learn until years later what had happened, but after he took over as administrator of the home, a similar encounter happened where Michael was faced with a violent situation from a father attempting to get his son back. And again, good triumphed and that boy graduated from the home and went on to lead a successful and happy life. So it goes, from one generation to the next. Beyond raising a good family and living the gospel, there is no work so important as doing everything in your power to keep those boys safe. Travis Sully's father has already tried to convince us that this was purely a misunderstanding, that his son's scars are the result of happenstance. But we've both been privy to that child's counseling sessions. We know the truth and we have to fight for it to be upheld. *You* have to fight for that boy's freedom. We can't do that with a gun like they did in the nineteenth century, but the battle is no less important. Travis Sully's heart and soul, and even his very life are at stake. So, gather your information, pray, and do the best you can. All you can do is the best you can do, and if it doesn't work out as we hope it will, that child will at least know that *somebody* in his life cared enough to fight for him. Okay?"

Jess nodded, too moved to speak, too overcome with the reality of his father's wisdom and strength. He swallowed the knot in his throat and managed to say, "I'll do my very best."

"That's all anyone would expect, son," Michael said. "You'll do just fine. It will only be a few days. And we'll take good care of your family while you're away."

Jess forced a chuckle to lighten the mood. "You're not in a position to take care of anybody but yourself."

"I can still be pretty bossy," Michael said, and Emily chuckled.

"Yes," she said, "I can attest to that."

Jess put a hand on his father's shoulder. "Just take care of yourself. I want you to still be here when I get back."

Michael showed a serene smile. "I will be. I promise."

* * *

After Jess left the room, Michael rolled onto his back and relaxed his head against the pillow. Emily eased closer and laid her head on his shoulder.

"You okay?" he asked, tightening his arm around her, however weakly.

"Yes, I'm okay, Michael."

"I'm not going to be around much longer." He turned slightly and pressed a tender kiss into her hair.

"I know," she said, unable to keep her voice from cracking.

He sighed and shifted slightly. "I think you're a brave woman, Emily Hamilton."

"And why is that?" she asked.

"Because if you were leaving me, I don't think I'd be holding up so well."

"Oh, I'm not so sure. You're a lot braver than you think."

He gave a dubious chuckle. "I've been confronted with losing you before, my love, and if you'll recall, I didn't handle it well in the least."

"Oh, but that was years ago, and . . . we've both learned so much since then." She tightened her embrace. "And we both know this is not the end."

He sighed again. "That's the only thing that makes the separation bearable, Emily. I thank God every hour of every day for His mercy and the comfort of knowing that everything will be for our best good and happiness."

"Yes, it will," she said, threading her fingers between his.

"But it's still hard," he whispered.

"Yes, it's still hard," she said, "but you know what?"

"What?"

"I was thinking earlier about the day after we got married. Do you remember that day?"

"Remind me. I think the drugs are fogging my memory."

"Likely excuse," Emily said, and he chuckled.

"Okay, so I have a lousy memory even without drugs. Remind me."

"Remember how your sister was upset and rode out in that storm and you went after her?"

"Oh, I do remember. And my horse slid out from under me and fell into that ravine. I thought I was dead there for a minute."

"Well, I thought you were dead a lot longer than that. When they came back and said they'd found your horse but they couldn't get to it, and they thought you might be underneath it, well . . . I just wanted to die, but . . ."

"But?" he pressed.

"Something happened to me while we were waiting. I knew that living without you would be torturous, especially when we had only been married less than a day, and we hadn't even had a honeymoon yet, but . . . I felt at peace. I knew that I'd make it somehow, and we *would* be togther again . . . forever."

"You knew that?" he asked. "That it would be all right and we would be together? You were married to Ryan much longer than a day."

"Yes, I knew. But of course . . . you were all right. And now look at all these years we've had together, wonderful years, Michael. We've had some tough times, but we've gotten through them together. And I feel confident that we will keep working together to look out for our family." She lifted up on one elbow and looked down into his eyes. "Stay close to me, Michael. I know there will be rules on the other side, and you have to keep them, but . . . I need you to stay close to me as far as it's possible. Promise me."

Michael reached up a feeble hand to touch her face. "I promise," he muttered and moisture filled his eyes.

Emily relaxed as he made his promise, and rested her head on his shoulder once again. "I love you, J. Michael Hamilton."

"And I love you," he said, running his fingers through her hair.

A few minutes later he asked, "Did you ever feel Ryan close after he died?"

"No, never," she said. "But then . . . I didn't really expect to. It was so . . . different with him. Everything was different. I was meant to be with you."

"I thank God for that," he muttered. "You've made my life so amazing, Emily, so very worth living. Everything I had here meant nothing until you and the children were with me."

Silence settled around them again until Emily said, "I almost envy you."

"You wouldn't like the hairstyle," he said, and she laughed softly.

"No, I don't envy that, but . . . I do envy you."

"How's that?"

"All those people you'll get to meet. Jess and Alexa Davies. Michael and Emma Hamilton. People like that."

"I've already met Michael and Emma."

"True, but it's been so long. Won't it be good to see them again?"

"Yes, it will."

"Can you even imagine the gratitude they must feel toward you for joining the Church and for seeing that their work was done?"

"I hadn't thought about that. Of course, you had a lot to do with that."

"But they're *your* ancestors." Emily sighed. "However, I envy you most because you will be with our sons." Tears flowed as she added, "Embrace them for me, Michael. Tell them how I miss them."

"I promise," he said, his voice betraying his own tears.

Emily tightened her arms around him and felt him gradually drift to sleep, aided by the drugs he was taking. She felt relaxed but not sleepy, just wanting to enjoy every minute that she could be by his side and feel the evidence of his heart beating. She didn't feel ready to lose him, but she felt deeply grateful that he'd not been taken suddenly from her in an accident, as her first husband and son had been. And in her heart she knew this was God's will, and the separation caused by death was only temporary. If not for that, she would lose her mind. As it was, she could relax beside her husband and know that one day all would be well.

* * *

Tamra drove Jess out to the hangar and walked him to the plane. "You okay?" she asked as he tossed his bag inside.

"I just . . . don't want to leave. Maybe I'm just paranoid, but . . ."

"I know," she said, and he knew she did. He'd grown accustomed to sharing his every thought with her, and they had talked deeply of his feelings just the previous evening. He sighed and took her into his arms as much as possible, considering her well-rounded belly.

After holding her tightly for a long minute, he took her shoulders and looked into her eyes. "Now don't be having any babies while I'm gone."

"I can't promise, but I'll certainly try," she said with a little laugh before she kissed his nose. "Everything will be fine, Jess."

"Yes," he blew out a long breath, "I believe it will. I mean . . . I prayed just before we came out here and it's not like I really think anything will happen, I just . . . don't want to go."

"But you have to. So go and get it over with. I'll see you in a couple of days."

Jess drew her into his arms again, kissing her in a way that could only begin to express the love he felt for her. She looked into his eyes and murmured intently, "I love you, Jess Hamilton."

"Yes, I know you do," he said. "And I love you."

She smiled and touched his face. "Then everything's going to be all right."

Jess smiled in return and forced himself to get into the plane. He had to believe that what she said was true. Once in the air he convinced himself that it really wasn't likely Tamra would go into labor in the next forty-eight hours, and his father really didn't seem that bad off. Then he put the matters out of his mind and focused on the impending hearing.

* * *

Five minutes after Jess's plane had taken off, Tamra began to wonder if his uneasiness had been some sort of premonition. She was standing at the kitchen sink when Evelyn came running from the other room and ran directly into the doorjamb. Evelyn began screaming and Tamra turned to see blood spewing from above her eye. It took Tamra a moment to force back her panic and think clearly. She scooped Evelyn into her arms and pressed a dishtowel over the cut with a fair amount of pressure. Evelyn's screaming quickly brought Sadie and Emily to the scene.

"What happened?" Emily demanded, kneeling beside Tamra on the kitchen floor.

"She just . . . ran into the door and . . ." Tamra lifted the towel to briefly display a gash above Evelyn's eyebrow that quickly disappeared beneath a fresh flow of blood.

"My goodness!" Sadie gasped. "What can I do?"

"You go sit with Michael while I drive them into town," Emily said. "That cut's going to need stitches."

Sadie attempted a protest. "But what if he . . . needs something, or . . ."

"He's resting and he's fine," Emily said. "If you have a problem, call Murphy, or call my cell phone."

A few minutes later Emily was driving the Cruiser quickly toward town, with a cloud of dust flying out behind them. Tamra held Evelyn in her arms, keeping a clean towel pressed over the cut. Evelyn's cries had diminished to a soft whimper. Tamra was grateful for Emily's calm demeanor and quiet conversation.

"I remember Amee doing that once," Emily said. "It was after my first husband died, and Amee was two. It was one of those times when *everything* seemed to be going wrong. I was completely out of money, losing the house, and . . . oh, I don't remember the details. I do remember how discouraged I was. And then Amee ran into something and cut her head in almost the same place. That's a vulnerable spot, I think. More than one of my children have had stitches there."

"Apparently everything got better," Tamra said.

"Oh, it certainly did," Emily said then sighed loudly. "The very next day Michael Hamilton showed up on my doorstep. He'd flown in from Australia because he had a feeling I needed him. He had no idea that my husband had been killed, and I found out later that part of his motivation for coming was to tell me that he'd joined the Church." She let out a soft laugh. "Oh, yes, everything got better after that. Not that we didn't have our struggles; we certainly did, but . . . we've had a good life."

A stray tear ran down Emily's cheek and she quickly wiped it away.

"Are you okay?" Tamra asked, wishing she had a free hand to offer some comfort.

"I'm as okay as I possibly can be," she said, lifting her chin in a courageous gesture. "It's just that . . ." She hesitated as she got her feelings under control, and Tamra waited for her to go on. She finally added, "I've felt my way of thinking change, just yesterday."

"How is that?" Tamra asked.

"I've prayed every day since this came up that the Lord's will would be done, and that we would have the faith and courage to accept it—with dignity. And I've always come away from my prayers feeling peace and hope, and a desire to make the most of the time we have. But yesterday . . . Well, the peace is still there, but . . ."

"But?" Tamra pressed.

"He's tired, Tamra," she said and brushed away another tear. "He's fought hard, and he's still fighting. But I know he's tired. I know he's in more pain than he's letting on, and . . ." Her voice broke and the tears increased. "I know in my heart that it's time to let him go."

Emily wiped at her tears again and took a deep breath, as if to suppress her grief. Tamra turned toward the window, not having a hand free to wipe her own tears. She was surprised to feel Emily's hand on her arm, then she touched Tamra's rounded belly. "But I believe he'll hold on until he sees the baby."

Tamra nodded but was unable to comment. Evelyn reached up her little hand and wiped at Tamra's tears. "You crying, Mommy."

"Yes." Tamra laughed through her tears. "Mommy is crying."

"Are you sad, Mommy?" Evelyn asked.

"Yes, Evie," Tamra said. "Mommy is sad that you hurt your head. But we're going to get it fixed, okay?"

Evelyn nodded, apparently accepting the answer, but Tamra wondered if the child had any comprehension of the drama going on in her world.

* * *

Tamra was grateful once again for Emily's calm presence when she offered to stay with Evelyn while she got her stitches. Tamra took one look at the shot needle they were going to use to numb the area and felt queasy. She went to the waiting room and Emily came out a short while later with Evelyn, who had a balloon and a sticky red sucker in her mouth.

"Once that shot was over," Emily said, "she didn't do too badly."

Before heading home, they picked up some prescriptions and bought a sandwich since it was past supper time. They arrived home to find Michael sleeping and Sadie reported that he'd been awake for a short while, eaten some supper and asked for a pain pill, then he'd gone back to sleep.

Jess called at bedtime and Tamra reported Evelyn's drama. "But she's fine now," she assured him. And she didn't bother repeating the conversation she'd had with his mother. He would be home soon enough and know for himself the situation.

The following day Evelyn was cranky with an apparent headache, and Tamra focused on coddling her. Feeling as if her own body would burst from the baby inside, she didn't have the energy to do much else. They laid down together in the afternoon and both slept. Evelyn woke up in better spirits and helped Tamra make tacos for supper, with Sadie's assistance. They took supper up to Michael's room and had what they'd come to call a bedroom picnic. He seemed alert and in good spirits, but Tamra could see the evidence of strain in his face. In her heart she knew that what Emily had said was true.

As soon as Evelyn was put to bed, Tamra went down herself, feeling exhausted. It seemed only minutes later that the light came on in her room and she heard Emily say, "I need you, Tamra. Come quickly."

Tamra grabbed a robe and threw it on as she followed Emily down the hall to the room she shared with Michael. Her heart quickened to a painful beat as she wondered if Michael really would die while Jess was gone—and before he'd had a chance to meet his new grandson. She entered the room to see him sitting against pillows, both hands pressed to his chest, gasping for breath.

Emily reported calmly, "He woke up a short while ago, having trouble breathing. An emergency helicopter is on its way, but I need to go out and wait for them. You sit with him." She held up the cell phone in her hand and pointed to the phone on the bedside table. "Call the cell if it gets worse."

Tamra nodded and scooted a chair close to the edge of the bed. The moment Emily left, Tamra was struck with the enormity of the situation. She prayed that the helicopter would get there quickly, and her mind flitted back to a memory that caught her off guard. How could she ever forget the night she had found Jess just down the hall from here after he'd taken twenty-five sleeping pills? Waiting for that helicopter had been a torturous eternity. He'd turned out fine physically, but the months of emotional healing had been difficult for all of them. The episode was long in the past, and they'd come far. Now they were facing a different kind of crisis, and she turned her attention to Michael. If only to break the silence, she asked, "Is there anything I can do?"

Michael shook his head slightly. Between gasps of breath he managed to say, "Just . . . talk to me. Tell me what you were thinking just now."

Tamra repeated her thoughts and was surprised to hear Michael say, "You saved his life."

She glanced down. "I was just in the right place at the right time." She looked back up and added, "I wish I could save yours."

"It's not as bad as it sounds," he managed to say.

"Well, that's good," Tamra said, realizing her hands were shaky, "because you promised Jess you would be here when he got home."

"I'm not leaving yet," he said and reached a hand out for hers. Tamra took it and felt him squeeze her fingers. She was startled by his obvious lack of strength.

Attempting to lighten the mood, she said, "Has it ever occurred to you that you don't get to choose when you're leaving?"

Michael actually chuckled, as if he appreciated her straightforward approach. "If I got to choose," he said between gasps, "I would be staying another twenty years at least. Still, I'm not leaving yet."

"That's good because there's someone you have yet to meet." She guided his hand to her belly in a way that had become common. Jess and Michael had made a game of seeing which of them could feel the baby kick the most. Michael was ahead, but mostly because he had nothing better to do than sit around and wait for it to happen.

"You've brought a great deal of joy into my life, Tamra Hamilton."

Tamra smiled. "As you have brought into mine."

He retracted his hand back to his chest when it suddenly became even more difficult to breathe, and Tamra's panic increased. She knew he'd taken all the necessary legal measures to insure that he would not be revived or put on life-support equipment. If he stopped breathing now, would this be the end? She wondered how it might actually happen, and this was not how she'd imagined. She was grateful beyond words to hear the helicopter overhead, and a minute later footsteps bounded up the stairs. Emily entered the room with two men who quickly flanked Michael and checked his vital signs. He was given an injection and put on oxygen, and within a few minutes his breathing returned to normal. Emily called Michael's oncologist and together they made the decision that there was no need for him to go to the hospital tonight, as long as he stayed on the oxygen. But the doctor wanted Michael to call the office in the morning.

After the emergency team left, Tamra went reluctantly back to bed, reminding Emily to get her if there were any more problems. She quickly fell back to sleep, exhausted simply from being nearly nine months pregnant.

The following morning she took Evelyn down to the kitchen, surprised to see Michael sitting at the table eating an omelet. He had the portable oxygen unit with him, but seemed to be doing well. And he was in fairly good spirits. After breakfast he rested on the couch in the library through the day, not wanting to go back up the stairs. He was still there when Tamra heard the plane flying low overhead. She left Evelyn in Emily's care and got into the Cruiser to go and meet Jess when he landed. She arrived at the hangar just as it swallowed the plane, and she felt a giddy lurch at the very thought of being with her husband again. It had only been two days, but having been married a year had not lessened his effect on her. She still felt hopelessly in love, and deeply grateful to know that he was hers forever.

Jess emerged from the hangar a minute later, carrying a dozen red roses, each with a little plastic container of water at the base of the stem. She laughed when she saw him and he did the same. His embrace felt like manna from heaven, and his warm chuckle close to her ear let her know that he felt the same way.

"Oh, you are so beautiful," he said, looking into her eyes.

"I can assure you," she said with a little giggle, "that I have never felt *less* beautiful in my life."

"Nonsense," he said, pressing a hand to her belly. "And I'm glad you're still pregnant. I didn't want him getting here without his daddy. Oh," he stepped back and handed her the roses, "these are for you."

"I was hoping they weren't for Murphy," she said, provoking a deep laugh from him. "Thank you." She closed her eyes and inhaled their fragrance. "They're beautiful. Are they for a special occasion, or—"

"Of course they're for a special occasion," he said. "You're testing me." Tamra laughed, and he added, "Happy anniversary, my dear wife. You've actually survived an entire year being a Hamilton."

"The best year of my life, all things considered," she said, and she saw his countenance falter.

"How's my father?" he asked, knowing full well what she meant by *all things considered.*

"He's doing rather well at the moment; in fact he's had a pretty good day, especially considering that he had a rough night."

"What happened?" Jess demanded.

"Get your bag and lock up the hangar. I'll tell you on the way in."

He looked frustrated but did as she asked. While he was driving the Cruiser back toward the house, she told him about last night's events.

"Has he talked to the doctor?" Jess asked.

"He's waiting for him to call back," Tamra said. "And there's something else I need to tell you."

"I'm listening," he said.

"Well, pull over for a minute. I don't want to get home before I'm finished, and I think you need to know."

Jess pulled over and turned to face her. Tamra took a deep breath and repeated the things his mother had said on their way into town for Evelyn's stitches. When she was finished, she waited in silence for some kind of response. She wondered if he would express frustration, or hurt, or even anger. Or perhaps he would need to cry a little and get it out of his system. But he only sighed deeply and took her hand, saying with a subtle quiver in his voice, "Then I guess we'd better go enjoy some time with him, eh?"

Tamra managed a smile and nodded. Jess gave her a quick kiss, and then drove home. Evelyn came running out to meet them with Emily close behind her. They shared embraces and greetings, then went together to the library to find Michael stretched out on the couch, reading the latest *Ensign.* He was without the oxygen but had it close by. He sat up when Jess came in and they shared a firm embrace.

"So, I hear you had quite an adventure, last night," Jess said.

"Hardly an adventure," Michael scoffed. "Tell me how it went."

"Yes, tell us," Tamra encouraged.

"It went great, actually," Jess said. "The judge threw it out. Travis Sully will be in our care for a good, long time."

Michael laughed with perfect joy and relief. "Well, good for Travis Sully," he said, then he slapped Jess on the shoulder. "I'm proud of you, Jess. You did great."

"I did practically nothing," Jess said. "But I did learn enough to be better prepared if this ever comes up again."

"Oh, it *will* come up again," Michael said.

"Now," Emily said, "it's about time the two of you got cleaned up and got out of here."

"Where are we going?" Jess asked, almost sounding panicked.

"Out to dinner, of course," Emily said. "It was your father's idea. He's buying. You both deserve an evening out, and it's your anniversary. So, hurry up. You have reservations."

In response to Jess's hesitant stare, Michael put a hand over his and said, "I'm still going to be here when you get back, Jess. Now go and have a good time, and don't talk about us, don't think about us, just enjoy each other's company."

"Stay out as late as you like," Emily said. "Sadie and I will look out for Evelyn and put her to bed."

"Okay," Jess came to his feet, "it looks like I'm going out with my wife."

He took Tamra's hand and headed toward the door, laughing as Michael added, "And don't be having that baby before you have a chance to finish your dinner."

"I promise," Tamra said and blew her father-in-law a kiss.

Chapter Thirteen

At breakfast the following morning, Emily asked Jess and Tamra, "Did you have a nice, romantic evening?"

"As romantic as you can get when your date is as big and round as I am," Tamra said.

"It was wonderful," Jess said. "And my date was the most beautiful woman in town—in the world, for that matter." He nodded toward his father and added, "Thanks for the dinner, Dad. We had a great time."

"I'm glad," Michael said, and they all turned their attention to Evelyn's usual chatter.

A few minutes later, Tamra said, "Hey, did the doctor ever call back yesterday?"

"Yes," Emily said, her voice expressing hesitance.

"And?" Jess demanded.

"He wants your dad to check in to the hospital this afternoon and stay for a couple of nights so they can do some tests and see where we stand."

"I hate that hospital," Michael growled. "And I already know where we stand."

"You can only guess," Emily said gently.

Jess wanted to ask what his father might be guessing, but Evelyn distracted them with more of her antics, and he was almost relieved.

That afternoon, Jess insisted on driving his parents to the hospital. He had some errands in town, and he assured them he'd be glad to come and get them when they were ready to come home. Emily packed a bag as well, determined to stay at her husband's side.

That evening Jess was struck by the absence of his parents in the house, but he focused his attention on Tamra and Evelyn and they had an enjoyable time, in spite of Tamra's growing discomfort with the baby seeming to consume every inch of space in her body.

The following day Jess called the hospital to see if his parents needed anything. They assured him they were fine, so he got to work catching up on some items of business with Murphy and Mr. Hobbs. That evening he took Tamra and Evelyn into town to visit Michael and Emily. They were in relatively good spirits, and Evelyn spurred a great deal of laughter. Following the visit, they went out for hamburgers and ice cream and returned home just in time to put Evelyn to bed.

Tamra quickly fell asleep, but Jess had trouble relaxing as he wondered what the test results would be. He couldn't deny a definite calm inside of himself, but he wondered if he could ever be fully prepared to face such a thing. He finally prayed himself to sleep and woke up in the dark to hear Tamra gasping loudly.

"Are you all right?" he asked, wondering for a moment if she might be having a bad dream.

"I think my water just broke," she said with a nervous laugh.

"Oh, good heavens!" Jess said and jumped out of bed. "Any pains yet?"

"Nothing obvious," she said, "but we'd better get going."

Within minutes Jess was dressed and had let Sadie know she was in charge of Evelyn. Tamra's anxious laughter became contagious as he helped her out to the Cruiser. "I can't believe it," he said, driving away from the house. "We're going to have a baby."

"Yes, we are," she said, then her laughter merged into a groan.

"What?" he demanded.

"I think that was a contraction."

"Did it hurt?"

"Oh, yeah," she said and took a deep breath.

By the time they arrived at the hospital, Tamra's contractions were only a few minutes apart and extremely intense. They were quick to get her prepped and hooked up to all the monitors, but her response to the pain was beginning to scare Jess by the time the anesthesiologist arrived to give her some relief. With the pain finally buffered, Jess spoke quietly to her, wishing there were words to express all he was feeling.

"Hey," he said, "do you think we should tell my parents we're here?"

"Heavens, no," Tamra insisted, "they're probably sound asleep. Let them rest." She laughed softly. "We'll just have a surprise for them tomorrow." She moaned and added, "I hope he gets here before tomorrow."

"It looks likely," the nurse said who had just checked her. "You're moving along pretty quickly, especially for a first baby."

Less than an hour later, the doctor arrived and announced that this baby was well on his way. The pain medication wore off and took awhile to take effect once it was administered again. Jess felt almost physically ill at the evidence of her pain, and he was deeply grateful for modern medicine that allowed her to get through the bulk of this without such intense pain.

As the nurses coached her through bearing down in order to deliver the baby, Jess held her hand and took every breath in synchronization with her. He felt a memory stirring but it took him several minutes to place it, and then he almost wished that he hadn't. How clearly he recalled sitting in the psych ward after he'd tried to take his own life, and hearing his mother say, *I gave you life, Jess. I felt you moving inside of me. I felt your spirit with me as you prepared to come to this world. And the moment you were born was one of the greatest of my life.* And only minutes later his father had added, *Seeing you come into this world is something I will never forget. It was a miracle. I had never imagined what a woman goes through to bring a child into this world. Her misery and pain and sickness were all for you. Until you see your own child come into this world, son, you will have no comprehension of the true miracle of life.*

Jess recalled well the perspective their words had given him as he'd contemplated what had driven him to try and take his own life. He'd gained a deep appreciation for the gift of life through that experience, but only now did he fully comprehend what they had meant. And when his little son finally emerged into the world and took his first breath, Jess's comprehension and gratitude deepened further. He held Tamra close and wept with her as he was struck with the miracle of life. And he found it soothingly ironic to think of his father soon passing through the same veil of mortality that his son had just come through.

While Tamra recovered, Jess stayed with the baby as he was taken to the nursery, thoroughly checked and declared perfect. He went back to her room to find her sleeping. He dozed off sitting in the recliner near her bed, and woke up just as the sun was peering over the distant horizon. He thought of his new little son and reached for Tamra's hand.

"Good morning," she said.

"I didn't mean to wake you."

"I was already awake," she said and smiled toward him.

"How are you?"

"Sore . . . and tired, but I don't feel too horrible. The doctor said I came through better than the average first birth."

"That's great," he said. "We'll just need to have lots of babies, since you're so good at it."

She groaned. "One at a time, please."

Jess leaned closer and touched her hair, her face, her hair again. He kissed her hand, then her lips. "You were amazing," he whispered and kissed her brow. "I love you so much."

"And I love you," she said, urging his lips to hers again. She smiled at him and added, "I think this is probably the most romantic moment I've ever experienced."

Jess sighed. "I think I'd have to agree."

A few minutes later the baby was brought into the room and Tamra attempted breast-feeding for the first time. With that accomplished successfully, followed by getting a good burp out of the baby, Jess held his son in the crook of his arm, unable to stop looking at his little face.

After they'd eaten some breakfast, a nurse came and guided Jess through changing a diaper.

"Very good," she said when the baby was wrapped back up tightly in his little blanket. "And what's his name going to be? Have you decided yet?"

"Oh, yes," Tamra said. "Jess Michael, after many great men before him."

"A fine name," the nurse said, helping Tamra situate the baby so that she could nurse him again. "And what will you call him?"

"Little Michael, I suppose," Tamra said. "At least for the time being."

"Until he gets too big to be called *little,*" Jess said with a chuckle.

"That could be next week with the way he's eating," Tamra commented, and Jess chuckled again.

When little Michael was sleeping contentedly once again, Tamra said to Jess, "Get me a wheelchair."

"What for?"

"We're going to introduce little Michael to his grandparents before they call home and figure out that we're here."

"Good idea," Jess said and quickly rounded up a wheelchair and a nurse who helped Tamra into it and tucked a blanket around her legs. Jess put the baby into her arms and pushed her into the elevator and then down long halls to his father's room.

Jess knocked lightly at the door, then opened it slowly. He peered in to see his father sitting in a chair near the window, wearing a hospital gown, with a blanket over his legs. Emily was sitting close by. Michael looked drawn; they both looked weary. But their countenances brightened when they saw Jess.

"What are you doing here so early?" Emily asked.

"I've been here all night actually," he said with a little chuckle. "But we didn't want to disturb you, so . . ." With the door left open he stepped back out and returned only a second later, pushing Tamra in the wheelchair. Emily and Michael both gasped when they saw that she was holding a baby, then Michael chuckled and Emily began to cry. "It's a boy," Jess said, and Emily laughed through her tears.

"Good heavens," Emily said, moving toward Tamra to get a better look. "When did you get here? How long was the labor? Did you—"

"Hold on, Mother," Jess chuckled. "One question at a time. We—"

"Oh, he's precious," Emily said, bending over to get a better look. She glanced up at Jess and added, "He looks so much like you when you were born." She turned back to the baby and pressed her fingers over his wispy dark hair. "There are some things a mother never forgets."

Tamra handed the baby to Emily and quickly explained the events leading up to the birth.

"Your labor wasn't very long then, was it?" Emily said.

"No, it wasn't," Jess said with an edge of drama, taking a chair close to Tamra. "Next time we'll have to camp out in the hospital parking lot."

"And how are you feeling, sweetie?" Emily asked Tamra.

"Pretty sore and tired, but beyond that, I feel fine."

"That's great," Emily said and carefully laid the baby in Michael's arms. She urged her chair closer to his before she sat down again. Michael heaved a deep sigh of contentment before he looked up at Jess, showing a serene smile and a glisten of moisture in his eyes. He then turned to Tamra, saying, "You do good work, my dear. He's perfect."

"Yes, he is," Jess said. "I stayed close by while they checked everything out. The doctor said they don't come any healthier than this."

"That's wonderful," Emily said, not moving her eyes away from the sleeping infant. "New life is such a miracle. No matter how many times I hold an infant, I can't help being struck by how perfectly amazing life is."

They chatted and admired the baby only a few more minutes before Michael's doctor came into the room. Dr. Fairfield had been an oncologist for many years, specializing in the treatment of cancer. Jess knew he was one of the best in the area, and his parents had spoken highly of his compassion and bedside manner, as well as his knowledge regarding the disease. Jess had only met him once, but he remembered being impressed.

"Well, we have a family gathering here," the doctor said warmly. His eye drawn to the baby, he added, "And this must be that new grandson you've been expecting."

"This is him," Michael said proudly, his focus more on the baby.

The doctor took a chair and they visited casually for several minutes before Michael said, "You have the results of the tests, don't you?"

"I do," the doctor said. "But if you would prefer that I come back later when—"

"Now is fine," Michael interrupted, exchanging brief glances with Tamra, Jess, and Emily before he returned his gaze to the baby. "I've got a pretty good idea what you've come to tell me, and I think I'd prefer having my family here. It will save me the trouble of having to repeat it."

Jess's heart began to pound the same moment that Tamra reached for his hand. The hope and positive attitude that he'd seen in his parents was completely absent. They looked resigned and weary. How much had they chosen not to share? How bad had it become? While Jess felt his breathing become shallow, he watched, as if in slow motion, his father's gaze move from the baby to face Dr. Fairfield directly. The doctor sat down, set his forearms on his thighs, and leaned close to Michael.

"Okay, Michael," the doctor said, "there's no way to put it delicately, and I know you well enough to know that you don't want me to beat around the bush. Through my years in this business I've had many triumphs over this disease, but I still never get used to having it beat me. And that's the bottom line, Michael. It's out of control. There's simply nothing more we can do."

Jess felt Tamra's hand begin to tremble in his. He pressed his other hand over his mouth and watched his mother reach for his father's hand. Michael looked down at the infant resting in the crook of his arm as he asked in a ragged voice, "How long?"

"It's impossible to tell," the doctor said gently, "but I don't think it will be long."

Jess squeezed his eyes shut, unable to hold back the tears that flowed down his face. He opened his eyes to see that Tamra and his parents all had tears falling. While he felt a deep temptation to be angry and feel cheated, he had to remind himself that they had been blessed with several miracles. They'd had months of his father feeling well enough to do many things together and create countless, precious memories. He'd had many opportunities to glean his father's wisdom and insight. And Michael had lived to see the Hamilton line go on through the child he was holding in his arms. In his heart he knew it was his father's time to go, and no amount of faith would change that. And being angry would only taint whatever they might have left.

Jess turned to Tamra, unable to speak, but knowing beyond any doubt that she shared his grief completely. She understood how he felt, and the very fact that she was a part of his life was a miracle in itself. He squeezed her hand and turned to see his parents exchange a long, poignant gaze before Michael turned to the doctor and spoke in a voice that was quiet and firm. "I want to go home."

The doctor nodded resolutely. "We can have the home care you need arranged within the hour, just as we've discussed." Michael nodded, and he went on to say, "Is there anything else I can do . . . any questions you have for me?"

Michael shook his head and turned to Emily, who did the same. The doctor glanced toward Tamra and Jess, as if to echo the question for them. They both shook their heads. Dr. Fairfield turned back to Michael and Emily and said firmly, "If any questions or concerns arise, any time, day or night, don't hesitate to call me. I want to do everything I can to help you through this."

Michael nodded and turned his gaze to the baby. Emily said in a shaky voice, "Thank you, Doctor. You've been wonderful; you truly have."

With a few more words exchanged, the doctor left the room, promising that a nurse would be in shortly to see that they had everything they needed. In the doctor's absence the room became eerily still beyond an occasional sniffle. There was nothing to say that could begin to express their feelings. Jess felt as if the tension in the room would make him scream, but the baby stretched and moaned, provoking a chuckle from Michael that became contagious. The tension relented as they all watched little Michael come awake and gradually work himself into a healthy cry. Michael held the baby up and looked into his face as he laughed and said, "He looks just like you, Jess."

A nurse came in with some paperwork to arrange for everything they would need at home. Michael introduced her to his new grandson before the baby was given back to Tamra and Jess wheeled them back to the maternity ward. With Tamra settled in her bed and feeding the baby, Jess stood and stared out the window, attempting to comprehend the reality of life and death before him. Deciding it was too much to grasp when he felt numb with the shock of the doctor's news, he sat close to the bed and admired his beautiful wife and son.

"I love you, Tamra Hamilton," he said, taking her hand.

"And I love you," she replied.

"Yes," Jess nodded and pressed a hand over little Michael's head, "I know you do. And for that I am inexplicably grateful."

A few hours later Jess left his wife and son sleeping and drove his parents home from the hospital. When they were almost there, Emily asked Jess, "Have you called your sisters yet to tell them about the baby?"

"No," he said, "I haven't had a chance."

"When you do, would you tell them about your father?" she added.

Jess was less than pleased with the assignment, but he agreed and dropped the subject. As he drove the Cruiser past the boys' home and around the house, Michael commented in a nostalgic voice, "It's so beautiful here."

"Yes, it is," Emily agreed, and Jess couldn't help wondering about his father's thoughts. Was he taking his familiar surroundings in with the realization that he would soon be leaving them?

Jess helped his father out of the Cruiser and into the house. He felt stunned by the reality of his father's weakness, which had worsened drastically since they had done this routine in reverse only a couple of days ago. He couldn't help wondering if just knowing there was nothing more to be done had taken the fight out of Michael, and he'd finally succumbed to the full effect of the disease. Helping Michael up the stairs was slow and difficult, but Jess didn't feel at all impatient. He was only grateful for the opportunity to be there and be able to help him.

At the top of the stairs Michael chuckled and let out an exaggerated sigh of relief before he said, "Well, I'm never doing that again."

Jess felt incapable of commenting. He simply helped him into the bedroom and onto the bed. A minute later Emily appeared, carrying an armload of paraphernalia sent home from the hospital. Evelyn was with her, acting very responsibly as she helped Grandma by carrying a little sack with some medicine bottles in it.

"There's my princess," Jess said, scooping her into his arms. He sat on the edge of the bed and Michael took her little hand, smiling with his eyes closed while Jess told Evelyn about her new baby brother.

When she finally ran out of questions, Michael asked, "Do you want Grandpa to read you a story?"

Evelyn ran to her room to get some storybooks and Jess asked his father, "Do you want to get into some pajamas? Can I help you with—"

"Just pull my boots off," Michael said. "I'm fine otherwise."

Evelyn returned with her books and Michael made himself comfortable with some pillows behind him so that he could read to her. A few minutes later the hired nurse arrived who would be staying in the home for as long as they needed her. June was a divorced woman with grown children, who chattered about how much she loved her work as she settled a variety of equipment and supplies in Michael and Emily's bedroom. She informed them that she would be able to stay for a few days, or possibly more, and another nurse would come to fill in if she needed to leave.

Jess sat with his father while Emily took June to a guest room close by so that she could settle herself in. Michael was sleeping when the women returned to sit with him, and Jess took Evelyn to be with Sadie in the kitchen so that he could go to the office to make some necessary phone calls.

Sitting in the chair his father usually occupied, he forced his mind to the matter at hand and dialed the first number.

"Hello, Emma," he said, surprised to hear her answer. "You're actually there. You're usually out and about when I call."

"Well, you got lucky. I was about to leave."

"Is Allison there?"

"Yes," she drawled, "don't you want to talk to *me?*"

"Yes. I want to talk to *both* of you. Put her on the extension."

Emma hollered for her sister, and a moment later Jess heard a click and then Allison said, "Is that you, little brother?"

"It is," Jess said.

"What's up?"

"I've got some good news and some bad news."

"Oh, no," Emma said, and Jess felt certain they had to suspect what was coming.

He hesitated a moment until Allison said, "Come on, Jess. Let's have it."

"The good news is that I'm a father," Jess said, and they both expressed noises of delight, followed by questions that he answered, feeling the joy of the experience all over again.

When he'd told them everything worth telling, Allison asked, "So what's the bad news?"

Jess sighed and squeezed his eyes shut, almost fearing he couldn't bring himself to say it. He wondered for a moment *how* to say it, then he just forced himself to speak the words that came. "Dad's come home from the hospital." He swallowed and added, "He's not going back."

Following a long moment of silence, Emma asked, "Are you saying what I think you're saying?"

Jess continued to search for the right words until Allison finally said, "Just tell us."

He cleared his throat and forced back his tears. "There's nothing more they can do. They've arranged for some home care to help until . . ."

Following a chorus of sniffles, Allison asked, "How long?"

"They don't know for sure, but . . . I didn't get the impression he had much time left. He could barely get up the stairs when I brought him home."

"Okay, we're getting on the next flight out of here," Allison said with determination. "Do you think Murphy could meet us in Sydney?"

"I would imagine. Under the circumstances, I think he'd do just about anything to help."

"Have you talked to Amee and Alexa yet?" Emma asked.

"No."

"Well, tell them to call us so we can arrange to meet in Sydney."

Jess hurried to finish the call and broke down sobbing the moment he hung up the phone. He cried for several minutes before he forced himself to get a grip and call Alexa. Their conversation went much the same as it had with Allison and Emma. But Jess wasn't the least bit surprised to hear a completely different response from Amee.

"What do you mean?" she demanded as if he'd done something wrong.

"I mean just what I said, Amee. There's nothing more they can do; he doesn't have much time left."

"But . . . but . . . How can that be?" He heard her breathing sharpen through the phone. "It can't possibly be that bad."

"If you had bothered to ask how Dad was doing any time in the last several weeks, you would know how bad it's been."

"I can't believe it," she muttered as if she'd just been told they'd lost their father completely without warning. "I just can't believe it. How can this be happening?"

Rather than pointing out her year-long denial, Jess attempted some compassion. "It's rough, Amee, I know. I think we need to be together. The others are flying out as soon as they can make arrangements. Allie wants you to call her so you can all meet in Sydney and Murphy can pick you up." She said nothing and he asked, "You will come, won't you?" Still, there was no sound and he repeated, "I think we need to be together."

He heard her sob and realized she'd likely been holding a hand over her mouth while she'd been crying. "It's going to be okay, Amee," he said gently.

"How can it be okay?" she cried. "He can't really be dying! He just *can't!*"

Jess blew out a long, slow breath. "What do you want me to say, Amee? We've done our best to keep you informed, but you didn't ever want to talk about it." Following a full minute of silence beyond her sniffling, he finally said, "Maybe you should call Allie. I think you'd be better off talking to another woman. I hope you can make arrangements to come." He said once more, "I think we all need to be together. Mom and Dad need us to be here."

Jess got off the phone and pressed his head into his hands, uttering a lengthy prayer that Amee would be comforted—not to mention everyone else, most especially his mother. He prayed that his siblings would all be able to come home so they could all be together one last time.

Jess finally stirred himself to go check on the rest of the family. Evelyn was happy helping Sadie with some baking. What a blessing Sadie was at such a time! Going upstairs, he found June sitting in a comfortable chair that she'd placed in the hall just outside the bedroom door. She looked up from a book she was reading, smiled at Jess and said softly, "I'll be close by, but I don't want to intrude."

Jess returned the smile and entered the room to find Michael laying on top of the bedspread, still wearing the jeans and T-shirt he'd come home in. Emily was sitting in a chair close to the bed, reading aloud from Second Nephi. She paused and smiled when she saw him enter the room.

"How did it go?" she asked and Michael opened his eyes.

"Just as you'd expect," he said. "They're all thrilled about the baby. I'm not sure what Amee's thinking about . . . Dad; the others are trying to get here as quickly as they can."

"Oh, that'll be nice," Michael said, his eyes closed again. "I was hoping to see all my girls once more."

"And what about Amee?" Emily asked.

"She's pretty upset," Jess said and went on to explain her reaction. They weren't surprised, but definitely concerned.

Emily commented, "You know, I've been praying a great deal about this situation with Amee, and it occurred to me recently that she was barely two when she lost her father." Michael opened his eyes and shot Emily a deep gaze, as if he'd picked up on her implication even before she explained it more fully. "Alexa was only an infant, and wouldn't have been as directly affected, and even though Amee says that she can't remember her father, I believe at some level it must have affected her deeply at such an impressionable age. It's difficult enough to lose one father, but two?"

"Allison lost her father as well," Jess protested. "And she was old enough to remember and understand how difficult it was."

"But she *does* remember," Emily said. "She's been able to talk about it and work it through. However, if Amee was affected emotionally without consciously remembering, it may be affecting her perception of what's happening now."

"I think it makes perfect sense," Michael said, his eyes closed again. "It will give the two of you something to talk about . . . after I'm gone."

Jess and Emily exchanged an anxious glance in response to the comment, but neither of them said anything more. Emily returned to her reading for a few minutes, then Allison called to say she'd talked to her sisters and they would all be meeting in Sydney the following day. Jess went to talk with Murphy about flying to Sydney to pick them up. He eagerly agreed, anxious to do anything he could to help. His sorrow over losing Michael was evident, even though he didn't say much.

Jess returned to his parents' bedroom to find it eerily quiet. Michael was resting but not asleep. Emily was looking out the window, lost in thought. She turned to Jess when he sat down. "You should be at the hospital with that new baby."

"I'm going back in a couple of hours and I'll stay until late evening. Right now I want to be here."

Michael tossed a questioning glance toward Jess but he said nothing. Jess made a couple of attempts at some conversation, but his parents seemed either too weary or too lost in thought to want to talk. Fearing the silence would make him scream, he asked, "Do you mind if I put on some music?"

"Oh, that's a good idea," Michael said, and Jess stood to look through the rack of CDs near the bedroom stereo system.

"Any preferences?" Jess asked, not wanting to play something that would detract from the mood or stir memories that they might prefer to avoid.

"You know what I like," Michael said. "Just put something in." As if he'd read Jess's mind, he added, "If I don't want to hear it, I'll let you know."

Jess actually found himself praying for some guidance, and he felt a little surprised when he reached for a Sting CD that he knew his father liked. He was thinking maybe the Mormon Tabernacle Choir might be more appropriate to usher someone toward the other side of the veil, but perhaps they'd save that for tomorrow. Putting the CD into the player, he smiled to himself, recalling that Sting and the Tabernacle Choir had performed together at the Olympics, and he'd heard good things about the experience from both sides. Perhaps it was a good choice, after all.

Jess knew the tracks his father liked and he programmed the machine to play those tracks in random order, then he moved his chair closer to the bed and picked up a *New Era* magazine from the bedside table. A few minutes later he was distracted from his reading when Michael rolled onto his side and reached for Emily's hand. He saw a poignant gaze pass between them the same moment he recognized the song as "Fields of Gold," then he tuned in to the lyrics resonating softly through the room. *Many years have passed since those summer days . . . See the children run as the sun goes down among the fields of gold. You'll remember me when the west wind moves upon the fields of barley.*

An image came to Jess's mind of the vast stretches of land surrounding his home, and the years his parents had spent here, raising a family, laughing and crying and growing together. The reality of what they were facing together now made him want to cry, but he couldn't even force the tears to come. He felt lost in some level of shock, but wondered if that might be a blessing. Perhaps he was somehow being shielded from emotions that he couldn't possibly handle if they struck him all at once.

As the CD moved to another track, Jess returned to his reading, grateful for the distraction. He felt certain his father had fallen asleep until he said, "Oh, I love this song."

Jess barely noted that the song was "When We Dance," before Michael went on to say to Emily, "It reminds me of the time when I came to Utah and you were still married to Ryan. I knew how unhappy you were, and when I asked you to leave him and marry me, I really believed that you would, because I felt so strongly that we were meant to be together."

"We *were* meant to be together," Emily said. "The timing was just off a little."

"Well, we know that now, but at the time . . ."

"Yes, I know," Emily said. "It was one of the most difficult things I've ever done . . . to send you away and recommit myself to my marriage, as difficult as it was."

Michael sighed. "But then, your example in that commitment is what made me reconsider my feelings about joining the Church. It all worked out for the best."

"Yes, it did," Emily said, and they exchanged a warm smile.

"Still," Michael said, "this song reminds me of you . . . of that day . . . when I came to your house hoping you would leave him, and instead you told me good-bye."

The song came to an end and Michael lifted his head, saying to Jess, "Play that one again."

Jess rose to restart that track and turned to see his father standing up.

"What are you doing?" Jess asked.

"I'm not so close to death that I can't stand up if I want to," Michael protested lightly. He came to his feet and held out a hand to Emily. "I'm going to dance with my wife."

Emily seemed concerned but didn't protest. As the song began, Michael held her hand close to his shoulder and put his other arm around her waist. They danced slowly, their steps perfectly matched as they gazed into each other's eyes. Jess just watched them, allowing the evidence of their love for each other to completely fill him. While tears still refused to come, he felt deeply emotional, knowing that this moment would always be a meaningful memory for as long as he lived. Watching his parents dancing in bare feet, holding each other close, his emotion deepened when he realized they both had tears streaming down their faces. He could feel a piece of his heart literally breaking as he contemplated the reality that they were both consciously preparing to say good-bye. And while they both had strong convictions about the prospect of being together again, it was as his father had once said, *The problem is separation.*

Jess tuned his ear to the lyrics, contemplating what his father had said about the song. He was grateful for his present inability to cry when the words struck his already tender heart; he felt certain if he started to cry now, he'd bawl like a baby for days. *He won't love you like I love you. He won't care for you this way. He'll mistreat you if you stay. Come and live with me. We'll have children of our own. I would love you more than life, if you'll come and be my wife. When we dance, angels will run and hide their wings.*

While Jess was pondering the meaning of that last line, Michael said softly, "You see, my dear, it's always felt as if the love we share is so incredible . . . so *boundless* . . . that even the angels would be in awe." He sighed and pressed a kiss to her brow. His voice quavered as he added, "I know I am."

When the song ended, Michael and Emily sat close together on the edge of the bed. Michael put his arm around her and kissed the top of her head as she rested it on his shoulder.

"I love you, Emily Hamilton," he murmured.

Emily sighed. "And I love you," she replied, "more than ever."

Chapter Fourteen

Jess was relieved to hear the phone ring, needing a break from the tension. Not wanting to mar the mood for his parents, he hurried out saying, "I'll get it in the other room."

Following a lengthy phone call, Jess returned to find his parents both resting on top of the bedspread, Emily's head on Michael's shoulder. The music was still playing softly and he took a seat with his magazine, not wanting to disturb them. But a moment later his mother asked, "Who was it?"

"It was the Relief Society president. Sister Merryweather, isn't it?"

"That's right."

"She was just wondering if we'd gotten the results of Dad's tests. So . . . I told her what was going on."

"I hope you told her about the baby," Emily said brightly.

"Of course," Jess said. "I did a fair amount of bragging."

"I'm glad to hear it," Michael said without opening his eyes.

"Anyway," Jess said, "the Relief Society will be bringing some food. I told her that really wasn't necessary, that Sadie was here to help and all that stuff, but . . . she insisted that we needed to be putting our focus to other things, and Sadie could certainly find something better to do to help us through—like helping with that baby when it comes home, for example. She also said there were some families who would love to come and get Evelyn to play while we're . . . adjusting. I told her that would be fine . . . to a point. So . . . that's the deal."

"Well, that's very sweet of them," Emily said. "I think people feel helpless and want to do *something*. I've been on the other side of that many times."

Jess contemplated that through the ensuing silence. He'd grown up watching his parents serve others right and left through difficulties and challenges. The hours they'd spent in service were countless. It seemed only right that others would offer some measure of support, and that it would be accepted graciously. In truth, he felt better after talking to Sister Merryweather. Her compassion and willingness to help had lifted his spirits. He had to admit to feeling some trepidation in the reality of him and Tamra adjusting to being new parents, with a four-year-old around, amidst preparing for his father's death. He figured they could use all the help they could get.

Jess went downstairs to find Sadie and June chatting in the kitchen, obviously hitting it off rather well. He made a fuss over the baking that Evelyn had helped with and spent a little time with her before he returned to the hospital, taking some fresh, homemade cookies for Tamra. His gratitude and awe deepened just to see his infant son again, and together he and Tamra admired him and held hands, sharing all they were feeling, and the ironies of life and death surrounding them now. He caught her up on all that had happened since he'd left earlier, and he appreciated her conversation regarding the new baby that added some normalcy to all else that was going on. He was struck with the surreal quality of looking at his little son and trying to imagine how life had felt only hours ago before his arrival. And added upon that was the reality that his father's life was now being measured in hours, as well.

Jess returned home late, grateful that Tamra and the baby were both doing well, other than Tamra being understandably tired and sore. He had promised to return the following morning to take her home, and he drove with the windows rolled down and the radio loud to keep him awake as well as distracted from thinking too hard about what awaited him at home.

Jess went first to Evelyn's room and found her sleeping soundly. He sat and watched her for several minutes, freshly grateful for this precious gift his brother had left behind. He went quietly to his parents' bedroom to find his father sleeping and his mother sitting in a chair near the bed with a lamp on, reading an inspirational book written by one of the Apostles. They talked quietly for a few minutes, leaving him amazed by her courage and faith. He finally went to bed feeling lonely and missing Tamra. Following a lengthy prayer he slept quickly due to the exhaustion from getting so little sleep the night before.

The following morning Jess felt startled when he woke up, even though it was the usual time. Taking a minute to orient himself, he jumped out of bed and grabbed a bathrobe, rushing to his parents' room as he tied it around his waist. He hated the panic he felt in actually having to wonder if his father might have gone in the night, even though he knew it wasn't likely. He found his mother leaning against the headboard, with his father's head in her lap, obviously sleeping. He entered the room and stopped abruptly, feeling as if the atmosphere was somehow different from the last time he'd been here, only hours ago. He credited his train of thought for giving him such an idea, then his mother looked up with moist eyes and a serene smile. She whispered, "Can you feel it?"

"What?" he asked quietly as goose bumps rushed over him just to hear her acknowledge that she too felt something was different.

"The veil is thinning," she said. "On the other side, they're preparing to bring him home."

Jess sucked in his breath as a quickening of his heart and more goose bumps seemed to confirm the truth of what she was saying. He closed his eyes for a moment before he moved closer to the bed, and he couldn't deny feeling a subtle difference in the room. He sat for a few minutes, watching his father sleep, mindful of the rhythm of his breathing, while he simply tried to absorb the tangible peace surrounding them. He finally forced himself to move when his mother whispered, "Why don't you go and get that new baby so we can get to know him a little better?"

"Of course," Jess said, coming to his feet. He bent to kiss his mother's cheek. "I'll hurry."

"Don't worry. We'll be fine. June is wonderful, and she said we still have some time left."

Jess nodded and hurried to take a shower and get dressed. He found Evelyn in the kitchen with Sadie and was able to visit with her while he ate a quick breakfast. Sadie drew his attention to the food the Relief Society had brought in the previous evening while he'd been at the hospital. There was a variety of sandwich fixings, fresh fruits and vegetables, and a couple of salads in the fridge. She also pointed out three different casseroles in the freezer that had been brought to heat up when needed. He couldn't help feeling blessed by the evidence of the caring of others, and he heartily agreed when Sadie commented, "This will free me up to help more with Evelyn so that you can take care of your wife and baby, and be with your parents."

"You're a gem, Sadie," Jess said, kissing her cheek rather loudly.

"However," Sadie said, "Evelyn's going to play with some friends for a while this afternoon, and again tomorrow."

She filled him in on the ward members who were going to help with her, and while he wanted her around as much as possible, he couldn't deny that it might be better for her to be distracted elsewhere, considering that the strain in the home would likely get worse. A quick phone call assured him that the family who had offered to take her hadn't left home yet, and he would save them a trip by dropping her off on his way to the hospital. Through the drive he did his best to explain to Evelyn that Grandpa was going to go live with Heavenly Father, and the easy way she took it for granted with her childlike faith actually made him feel better. He talked to her more about the baby and was pleased with her excitement. He promised her that when her friends brought her home later she would be able to hold her new brother and help take care of him.

Jess thanked the sweet sister who welcomed Evelyn with motherly love, and Evelyn was quickly off to play with the four-year-old boy that she knew from her Primary class. Jess then hurried to the hospital and found Tamra looking almost as good as new, and actually smiling. "Let's take little Michael home to get to know his grandpa, shall we?" she said, and he couldn't help but appreciate her bright outlook. As always, with her by his side, everything seemed easier.

Through the drive home, Jess shared with Tamra more of his feelings about all that was happening with his father and his new son. But still he didn't cry. Emotion burned in his chest and his head, but the tears refused to come.

At home, Tamra and little Michael were received with joy and laughter almost before they made it through the door. Sadie was so thrilled she could hardly stop laughing as she admired the baby, and June fussed as if he were one of her own grandchildren. While Emily carried the baby up the stairs, Jess carried Tamra, since she was still rather sore and slow moving. They went directly to Michael's bedroom and found him awake and even a bit perky. He fussed over the baby in a way that filled Jess with deep pleasure, and while he was still awake, Murphy and his mother came to see the baby and visit with Michael. Their visit was brief but pleasant, then Murphy got his mother settled back at home before Jess drove him out to the hangar so he could fly to Sydney and bring the girls back the following day. He admitted to Jess privately that he was really having a rough time with losing Michael this way.

"He's always treated me like family," he said. "He's always been there and . . ."

Jess felt that burning in his chest tighten as he watched the tough stable master wipe tears from his face. He couldn't even comprehend the number of lives that Michael Hamilton had touched.

With Murphy calmed down and on his way, Jess returned to the house and promptly moved Tamra's rocking chair into his father's bedroom so that she could rock the baby and be close by to visit with Michael when he was awake, and with Emily when he wasn't. Jess found himself hovering in the room as well. He enjoyed every minute his father was awake, even though such minutes became fewer and further between. And when Michael slept, Jess visited quietly with his wife and his mother, while they fussed over the baby and speculated over the life little Michael would lead. Jess enjoyed the tranquility of the room, and just being in his father's presence, even as he slept. When Michael was awake, he insisted on having the baby next to him and settled in the crook of his arm, unless the baby was eating or being burped. And more than once they both drifted to sleep, side by side.

That evening the bishopric came by, bringing along little Evelyn who had been picked up from the home where she'd been visiting. Sadie guided the visitors to Michael's room to find him holding the new baby. After showing Evelyn the baby, Jess gathered some chairs and brought them to the bedroom, glad that it was so spacious. He figured more visitors would be coming, specifically his sisters, and the chairs might as well stay. The bishopric made a fuss over the baby and enjoyed watching Evelyn with him while they all shared a good visit. Before they left, they gave Michael and Emily each a priesthood blessing, and asked Jess to join them in the circle. Jess felt comfort and assurance from the words spoken, but he also felt certain that it wouldn't be long before his father passed on.

Through the night Jess was up three times to help Tamra with the baby, each time checking on his parents to find them both sleeping. The following morning Michael looked dramatically worse, and through the day he went from eating very little to eating nothing at all. June explained the process of the body shutting down, and how his dehydration from not eating or drinking much would actually ease his discomfort and make him naturally lethargic. Between long bouts of sleeping while they all stayed close by, Michael would ask for a little something to drink and exchange bits of conversation. Friends and ward members trickled in and out and Michael would usually exchange a few heartfelt words and quickly drift off to sleep again. Occasionally he woke and asked Jess to help him get to the bathroom. In spite of his obvious weakness, Jess was amazed at how there were moments when he still seemed to manage to get up and move around a bit with some help. He forced memories out of his mind of how his father used to wrestle him to the ground, or chase Evelyn around the lawn and tickle her. Prayers that had once been focused on prolonging his life were now only a plea to keep him free of pain through his final hours.

When Murphy flew the plane over the house, Jess drove out to the hangar to meet them while Emily sat with Michael. Evelyn had once again gone away for the day, and Tamra and the baby were sleeping. After the plane landed, Jess exchanged brief but emotional greetings with his sisters before they hurried to the house. Allison, Alexa, and Emma went directly to their father's room with Jess, while Amee went to her room to unpack and freshen up, as if she wanted to delay the inevitable. Jess finally shed a few tears, barely releasing the growing knots inside of him, as he watched his sisters become emotional when they saw how their father had deteriorated in the short time since they'd been there for the holidays. They all managed to keep their tears quiet, not wanting to disturb Michael's sleep, but their comments clearly expressed the thoughts Jess had trouble putting into words.

When the girls all calmed down somewhat, Emily nudged Michael to wake him, saying in a cheery voice, "Honey, your daughters are here."

"Oh," Michael said and smiled, moving his focus to where Allison, Alexa, and Emma all hovered close to his side. They exchanged greetings and talked quietly for a few minutes before Michael asked, "Where's Amee?"

"She's here," Emily said. "She'll be in a little later." He nodded and drifted back to sleep. The girls left the room to get settled in, and Emily went with them, leaving Jess alone to watch his father sleeping. He turned toward the door when he heard a noise and saw Amee standing in its frame, as if she hardly dared step inside. He stood and moved toward her, noting the obvious shock in her expression as she absorbed Michael's gaunt appearance. When she started gasping for breath with a sudden burst of heaving sobs, Jess quickly guided her out of the room. In the hall he put his arms around her and held her tightly while she muffled her sobs against his chest.

"I know it's hard, Amee," he murmured. "I know." Again he cried a few stray tears, but it didn't begin to release the pressure he felt building inside of him as the reality continued to descend. While Amee was still crying, Emily appeared, coming out of the bathroom. She'd barely put a hand to Amee's shoulder when Jess saw movement and turned to see his father leaning against the doorjamb, breathing heavily.

"Good heavens," Emily said, moving to his side. "What are you doing out of bed when—"

Amee gasped and looked up to see Michael's eyes focused on her. He held up a hand as if to quell Emily's concern, then he feebly reached it toward Amee. She moved into his embrace and Jess moved to his side to offer support that Michael quickly accepted. Jess literally held his father up, feeling his entire weight lean against him. It was evident he had used more strength than he had to respond to Amee's cries and walk as far as he had.

"It's all right," Michael murmured to Amee as he might have when she'd been the two-year-old child he had brought home to Australia. She calmed down, as if she somehow believed him. Then Amee and Jess helped Michael back to bed, where he literally collapsed within Jess's grasp as he guided his head to the pillows and lifted his feet up.

While Amee had stopped crying, Jess couldn't help noticing the shock and horror in her expression as she observed their father's obvious weakness. He was fearing she might erupt all over again when Michael spoke to Jess in a strained voice, "After I have a few minutes to get my strength back, I want to give Amee a blessing . . . if you'll hold me up."

Jess swallowed carefully, in awe of his father's compassion and wisdom. His only concern at the moment seemed to be focused on comforting Amee as he reached out a hand toward her and she took it, sitting carefully on the edge of the bed.

"I'd be happy to," Jess said. "I think I'll get the others," he added, certain they would want to be together for this, but he also needed a minute to collect himself and compose his own emotions. At moments he longed for this pressure inside him to be set free, and at others he feared that if it got started, a dam would burst and a never-ending flood would ensue.

Jess gathered his sisters, then found Tamra awake and burping the baby. He helped her to his father's room, where the mood lightened as the girls all fussed over the baby and passed him around. Michael observed the scene with an expression of perfect serenity, while Emily held his hand and did the same.

With Jess's help, Michael sat on the edge of the bed and Amee knelt on the floor in order to accommodate his reach. Michael placed his hands on Amee's head and gave her a father's blessing of comfort and strength. The room filled with a chorus of sniffles as Michael's words resonated with the peace and strength of his example, and his faith in the power of the priesthood. After the amen was spoken, Amee looked up at her father with a completely different countenance. Peace had replaced her anxiety completely. The room remained completely still, as if no one wanted to break the spell. Little Michael's hiccups finally broke the silence, and there was a string of quiet laughter from everyone in the room.

A moment later Allison said, "I can't help thinking about Lehi in the Book of Mormon, and how he blessed all of his children when he knew he was going to die." With fresh tears rising in her eyes, she took Michael's hand and asked, "Would you give the rest of us a father's blessing too? If you're too tired, it can wait, but—"

"It would be an honor," Michael said with an emotional smile. "But I think I'd better rest awhile first."

"Of course," Allison said. Jess helped Michael lay back down and he drifted to sleep almost immediately. They all remained in the room, visiting quietly and sharing their deepest feelings about all that was happening, intermittently admiring the new baby and passing him around. Emily brought up the issue of her first husband's death, and her speculations regarding how it had affected Amee. They discussed the theory extensively, and Amee admitted tearfully that she believed the theory had some validity. And as difficult as this was, she actually felt better. Still, Jess noticed her crying much more than the others, and he could see that she'd not allowed herself to grieve before today, as the rest of them had done.

They were interrupted only once by Sadie handing Jess the cordless phone. He talked for a few minutes and returned to tell the rest of the group, "That was Sister Merryweather, the Relief Society president," he clarified for those who didn't know. "She's offered to keep Evelyn over night, since they're doing so well. As hard as it is to be without her, I think it's a good idea. She says she got some clothes from another sister who has a child the same age, and they have a spare toothbrush, so I guess they're all set."

"Oh, that's nice," Tamra said. "It would be difficult for her to understand all that's happening."

The conversation returned to the girls' questioning Tamra on her labor experience. Sadie brought sandwiches for everyone on a tray for a bedroom picnic, declaring that she and June had already eaten.

The room was getting dark when Michael woke again and Jess helped him to the bathroom. After he'd returned to bed, he asked Emily if she would offer a family prayer, then he proceeded to give Allison, Alexa, and Emma a blessing. And then Jess. He prayed inwardly that he could recall the words clearly until he could record them in his journal, knowing they would be priceless in his father's absence. Then, to Tamra's obvious surprise, he asked to give her a blessing as well. And finally, he gave a husband's blessing to Emily. While the strength of the Spirit in the room was almost tangible,

Michael drifted back to sleep. Again the family sat in silence, as if they were all soaking in the atmosphere surrounding them, not wanting to mar the feeling. And again little Michael broke the spell with his demands to be fed. They were all tired and decided to get some sleep, taking shifts to sit with Michael. Jess went to bed with Tamra the minute they had the baby to sleep, and two feedings later he took his turn at his father's bedside and sent Allison to get some sleep. He watched dawn filter into the room while he prayed silently and listened to his father's ragged breathing. A short while later June came to check on Michael, then she told Jess and Emily that according to his vital signs, it likely wouldn't be many more hours. After June left the room, Emily took a deep breath then said to Jess, "I'm going to get a little something to eat and tell the girls. You stay with him."

Jess nodded and watched her leave the room. A few minutes later Tamra came in with the baby and set him into Jess's arms before she sat close by in the rocker. Without a word spoken between them, they both turned their focus to little Michael, whose eyes were wide open as if he'd suddenly found a desire to observe his surroundings. Jess watched his little eyes shift as if to follow movement. He felt a rush of goose bumps before he consciously realized the reason. And then he gasped softly.

"What?" Tamra asked in a whisper.

"Look at him," Jess replied in the same hushed tones.

The baby actually turned his head, focusing his eyes intently on something—or someone—that was not visible to Jess and Tamra. But Jess knew beyond any doubt that this child, who had so recently come through the veil, was aware of an unexplainable presence. Jess was about to clarify his feelings aloud when he heard Tamra gasp softly, and he knew she had felt it, too. The veil was indeed thin, and Jess couldn't help wondering who might be close by, waiting to take Michael home.

As Emily and the girls trickled into the room and made themselves comfortable, Jess's attention was drawn elsewhere. But when they were all gathered and the quiet conversation died down, Jess noticed his little son's continued attention to his surroundings. He commented on it and tears rose simultaneously into everyone's eyes, as if they had all felt the evidence for themselves that this precious infant could have had a view through the veil of things that they could only vaguely sense.

June checked on Michael frequently, and when he came awake following hours of deep sleep, she turned to the family and said quietly, "It won't be much longer. You should each say what you want to say."

While the baby slept close to Michael, Jess felt as if he were in a dream as he observed his loved ones exchanging simple words. He had little to say himself, since it had already been said before. But he felt inexplicably grateful for the time they'd had to prepare for this moment. And the peace that he felt was deep and complete, and was shared by everyone in the room.

Michael slipped quietly away in his sleep that afternoon. The mood in the room was more of relief than grieving when it was finally done. They knelt together to share family prayer, then little Michael woke up and rather than fussing, he commenced his silent observances once again. It was Tamra who expressed what Jess felt certain they were all thinking, "Perhaps now he is seeing his grandfather."

"I'm sure you're right," Emily said, still holding tightly to Michael's hand.

* * *

That dreamlike sensation continued to hover over Jess as arrangements were made with a mortuary, and the funeral was planned. Jess was disconcerted to realize that his mother wanted him to speak at the funeral. He protested until she said quietly, "Your father requested it, Jess. Do it for him."

What could Jess say? Allison actually volunteered to speak, so it would be the two of them. At least she could sit by him at the front of the chapel and hold his hand. Family began pouring into the house, including Sean and his family, who had come for the funeral. And Jess was amazed at how they could all talk and laugh in spite of their lingering grief. He thought of what Sean had once told him—that much of the grieving is done prior to the death in such cases. And while Jess still felt a certain amount of shock in relation to his father actually being gone, he could see that what Sean had said was true. It was also evident that the gospel had given this family a great deal of peace. Even his mother, or perhaps *especially* his mother, was completely at peace. Like the rest of the family, her sorrow was evident and tears came easily, but her peace was undeniable. They all knew that Michael lived on, not so very far away. And Jess chose to ignore his nagging concerns as to whether or not his parents would end up married on the other side when all was said and done. They were all in the Lord's hands now—as they always had been.

Throughout the viewing, Jess was continually amazed at the evidence of how far-reaching his father's influence had been. Through the endless line of people who came to pay their respects, he heard over and over of what a fine man Michael Hamilton was, with many specific stories to back up their claims. There were business associates, some who had traveled far. And there were ward members, many who had known him since he had first joined the Church. Jess was in awe, though he figured he shouldn't have been, as he heard one testimonial after another of the service, acceptance, and compassion that Michael had given through his life.

The funeral was perfect, and Jess even felt good about his own words in regard to his father's life, focusing on his own appreciation of the great legacy that Michael had passed to his children, as well as all who knew him. Following the funeral, Michael was laid to rest in the little family cemetery not far from the home where he had lived his life. Jess held Tamra's hand tightly while Evelyn huddled close by, and little Michael slept in the crook of his arm. He glanced around himself at the evidence of generations gone before who had lived and died on this land. And one day, he too would join them here.

"I love you, Dad," he whispered into the air after the crowd had dissipated beyond his own little family. And he could almost be certain that Michael had heard him and answered.

* * *

Jess and Tamra were pleased to realize that most of their immediate family, as well as Sean and his family, would be able to stay a few days following the funeral and attend the sacrament meeting where little Michael would be blessed. Jess marveled at the network of love and support they shared as he stood to bless his little son and looked around him to see his brothers-in-law, and Sean, as well as the bishopric and some friends of the family. Together they had been through much in sharing the death of a loved one, and this seemed an appropriate way to come together and share the beginning of a new life. As they all placed their right hands beneath the baby to support him, and placed their left hands upon shoulders to form a circle, Jess closed his eyes and focused on the words of the prayer. He began with little difficulty, but as he stated the name being given to his son, a name that had been passed down with a great legacy, emotion suddenly overtook him. He heard his own voice crack and hesitated, attempting to gather his composure. And that's when he felt it. *Another* hand on his shoulder. And a presence beside him so incredibly familiar. He sucked in his breath and squeezed his eyes shut more tightly, not wanting his eyes to try and convince him that what he felt wasn't real. Because it *was* real. And he knew it with every fiber of his being. His father was standing beside him, taking his rightful place in assisting with the blessing of this grandson who would carry on his name.

Jess finally found his voice enough to go on, almost as if Michael were encouraging him with feelings rather than words. When the amen was spoken and the circle broke up, Jess froze and hesitated to open his eyes. He felt his father's presence leave, but while he had expected to feel an acute emptiness in its place, he felt instead an incredible peace and gratitude. He opened his eyes and glanced around, startled by the mortality of his surroundings. But as he lifted the baby up for the congregation to see him, a thought appeared in his mind at the same moment a chill rushed over his shoulders. The feeling persisted as he carried the baby back to where he'd been sitting, between his wife and his mother. By the time he sat down, he could barely see through the mist in his eyes. He blinked the tears onto his face and quickly wiped them away before he met his mother's eyes, only to see his own emotion mirrored there. In response to her silent question, he whispered, "He was there, Mother. I felt him."

Emily smiled serenely and replied with the same whisper, "I know."

"And . . ." He hesitated, fighting his feelings. "I know everything is going to be all right. I don't know how I know; I just know it will all work out."

Emily nodded and smiled again, briefly touching his face as she repeated, "I know."

Jess kissed his mother's brow, then turned the other direction to look into the eyes of his sweet wife. He wanted desperately to share his experience with her, as well. But not with any kind of brevity. He looked forward to some subsequent hour when the house would be quiet and he could sit alone with her and their new little son, when he could spill every detail of all he had felt. It had always been that way, since the first time he'd laid eyes on her. She just had a way of making everything seem right, of coaxing his every thought and emotion out of him and into herself. And looking into her eyes in that moment, eternity stretched out before him, with Tamra at his side, surrounded by generations of loved ones. In the same moment that Tamra offered him a serene smile, not unlike the one his mother had just given him, Jess clearly recalled his father once saying, *I know with all my heart that the Lord is mindful of our circumstances, and He will make everything as it should be—whatever is supposed to happen will happen.* Jess couldn't think of anything more joyful than that.

PHOTO BY "PICTURE THIS . . . BY SARA STAKER"

About the Author

Anita Stansfield has been writing for more than twenty years, and her best-selling novels have captivated and moved hundreds of thousands of readers with their deeply romantic stories and focus on important contemporary issues. Her interest in creating romantic fiction began in high school, and her work has appeared in national publications. *Gables of Legacy: The Silver Linings* is her twenty-second novel to be published by Covenant.

Anita lives with her husband, Vince, and their five children and two cats in Alpine, Utah.

SAMPLE CHAPTER FROM A NOVEL BY CAROL WARBURTON:

BEFORE THE DAWN

PROLOGUE

Missouri—1858

The slap of a hand against flesh echoed throughout the tiny kitchen. My fingers flew to my cheek, my eyes staring in disbelief at the man who stood with his hand still raised.

Jacob's angry brown eyes glared back at me, his mouth pulled into an ugly grimace. "That'll teach you to keep your trap shut. I'm tired of your yammering . . . always tellin' me what to do." His words were slurred, and spittle sprayed onto his unshaven chin.

"Don't you ever hit me again," I hissed. Anger and fear trembled through my words. I took a deep breath and fought to hide my fear. "Not ever," I repeated.

For a second I glimpsed Jacob's shame—shame quickly replaced with a sneer. "Then learn to keep your mouth shut. How I spend money is my business . . . not yours."

Jacob turned and stalked across the room, his steps unsteady as he reached for the door. I was glad to see him go, wishing with all my heart I'd never see him again.

"What have I done?" I whispered. It was a question I frequently asked myself, regret at having married Jacob Mueller a daily presence at my table. Then the determination that had helped me weather my three-year marriage to him set in. Sighing, I poured water into a basin to cool my throbbing cheek. I tried not to think of the near-empty flour barrel and the past-due payment on the farm while my lips formed the question again. "What have you done, Clarissa?"

* * *

Tillamook, Oregon—2003

Jessica Taylor followed the old man up the steep stairs to the half-attic, the boards creaking and the musty, closed-up smell of the stairwell filling her nostrils.

"Like I told you when you phoned . . . there's just this old trunk." He opened the door into the cramped room at the top of the stairs. "Think it belonged to my wife's grandmother . . . or maybe it was her great-grandmother." He paused and scratched his grizzled head. "I never paid much attention to things like that. Effie mentioned it a time or two when we were younger, but since we never had any children to pass it on to, the trunk kind of got forgotten." There was another pause and a regretful shake of the head. "Since Effie's passed on, I guess you've got as much right to the trunk as anyone."

The man's name was Bob Whiting, a name that hadn't meant anything to Jessica until three years of research had led her to the yellow-frame home in Tillamook. After the sweet experience in the temple with her ancestor Tamsin Yeager, Jessica had hoped to discover something about Tamsin's elusive sister, Clarissa. She'd almost given up hope, but persistence, bits of information gleaned in genealogical libraries, and the Internet had finally borne fruit.

"Thank you so much, Mr. Whiting," Jessica said.

"Just call me Bob," he responded. "Though you'd probably thank me more if I was to give you some light so you can see better." His blue-veined hand reached for the switch. "There," he said as light turned shadows into a hodgepodge of boxes and cast-off furniture. "The trunk's over by the window."

Jessica's gaze followed his pointing finger to the rounded lid of a brown leather trunk.

"If you need me, I'll be downstairs," Bob said. "There's a couple of old chairs you can sit on, quilts too, if you get cold. Make yourself at home."

Jessica smiled at Bob's attempts at hospitality, but she scarcely heard him when he started down the stairs. By then she'd dropped to her knees by the trunk, not minding the cold of the dusty floor, her fingers exploring the short buckle that fastened into an ornate metal clasp. Was it locked?

She pushed at the fastening. Her impatient fingers found resistance, so she tried a second time with more force. She was rewarded by the click and release of the buckle, rewarded again when the heavy lid lifted and she leaned it back against the attic wall.

An array of items met her eager gaze as she looked into the musty trunk, mementos she hoped would reveal something about Clarissa Yeager, born in Massachusetts in 1839.

Jessica pulled a quilt off a stack of boxes and spread it on the floor next to the trunk. She felt a stirring of excitement when she reached for a pair of gold spectacles, then a cameo locket with an auburn curl tied with a blue ribbon tucked inside. Who had they belonged to, and why had Clarissa kept them?

More questions followed when Jessica took out a worn dog collar with the name "SAM" etched into the old leather. Then a china baby rattle decorated with tiny pink flowers and engraved with the name "Tamsin" and the year 1866 caught her eye. She stared at the name and date. Had Clarissa named one of her children after her sister Tamsin?

Jessica moved her jean-clad legs into a more comfortable position on the quilt, glad she'd worn the thick green sweater to ward off the attic's chill. When she turned back to the trunk, she closed her eyes and invited the past to gather itself around her, the past that had been the present to Clarissa, the time when she had sung or played from the yellowed sheet music lying next to the dog collar, the time when Clarissa had eagerly opened and read the bundled letters before tying them with pink ribbon.

She also found, carefully folded between sheets of tissue paper, a blue dress with sprigs of darker blue flowers covering the full skirt. Her first impulse was to take it out of the paper and hold it up, but caution whispered that something that old should be handled carefully.

Laying the tissue-wrapped dress on the quilt with the rest of Clarissa's treasures, Jessica pushed back a lock of her blunt-cut, dark hair and looked at the three remaining items—an old daguerreotype of a man and woman and baby, a Bible, and a large leather-bound book that looked like a journal.

She took out the picture first. Through the wavy glass in the gold frame she saw a tall, good-looking man standing with his hand on the shoulder of a pretty woman who, though she did not smile, gave the impression of suppressed laughter, as did the child sitting on the woman's lap, her babyish head covered with thick curls.

"What a little angel," Jessica breathed. "And they're so happy. I can see it, feel it." When she looked more closely at the picture, she was able to make out the dark, sprigged flowers on the woman's skirt and realized it was the same dress that had been stored away in the trunk.

Her gaze returned to the daguerreotype, certain the woman must be Clarissa, the man her husband, and the child theirs. If only she could discover the husband's name, and the name of the baby too. Had there been other children?

Something told Jessica that the answers to her questions were in the brown leather book lying in the bottom of the trunk. She picked it up, feeling the smoothness of the leather as she settled it onto her lap. As she opened the cover she saw the swirl of old-fashioned writing. Beginning to read, she forgot about the chill of the attic and the hardness of the wood floor as the flowing script transported her back through the years and into the life of Clarissa Yeager, her great-grandmother's youngest sister.

CHAPTER 1

Oregon Territory—1862

I did not come to love a man, needing him like sun and air and the soft Oregon rain, until I'd been married five years—and the man I loved was not my husband. Lest one might think me wanton, I'd best explain. Wantonness was never in my nature, though I confess there were times in my youth when I was inclined to flirt, knowing others thought me more than comely. I must also confess I was not above studying myself in the mirror to confirm the fact.

Although I was sometimes vain, I was never one who could be untrue to my marriage vows. Yet to understand how I came to love and be loved by another man, I must first explain why I married Jacob Mueller.

When I was thirteen years of age, I moved with my widowed mother and older sister to a farm near the village of Mickelboro, Massachusetts. Deacon Mickelson and his wife, Hester, took us in following the death of my father, letting us live in a cottage on their property. The deacon was inclined to spoil my sister Tamsin and me, his overbearing goodness putting him at odds with his wife, whose resentment of us was but barely concealed. Even so, we were happy. Tamsin and I spent many hours exploring a wooded headland towering over the Atlantic, its protecting height forming a little cove which we came to think of as our own. Our delight in tide pools, shells, and gulls skimming white-capped breakers vied with our enjoyment of evenings in the cottage. I can see us still, the two of us curled up close to Mother—Tamsin dark and angular, me fair and more rounded—listening while she read to us from Shakespeare or sometimes Tennyson. Often we would end the evening with music, me playing the pianoforte and singing while Mother and Tamsin listened, pleasure evident on their faces.

All went well until I approached my sixteenth birthday. Although Tamsin was a year and a half my senior, she was slower to mature, her slender frame still that of a girl, while mine took on the curves of womanhood. More than that, Tamsin was inclined to shyness, while my nature was more open. I dared while Tamsin hung back. I often took the lead, my confidence such that I never doubted I knew best. Perhaps it was my pertness and confidence that first attracted Deacon Mickelson, though my looks were a factor too. It was then that I first noticed him watching me in a manner that made me uncomfortable. For some months it was only looks and knowing glances. I tried without success to explain them away. Amos Mickelson was like a jovial, benevolent uncle. Surely I was mistaken in what I read in his eyes. But deep down I feared I was not.

Some months later, in fulfillment of a terrible premonition, Deacon Mickelson's looks progressed to a touch. A more timid girl might have looked away and pretended it hadn't happened. But I was not timid. To the deacon's surprise, I lifted my head and glared at him, taking satisfaction in the smear of red that came to his fleshy jowls, watching his gaze slide from me to Mother, who was in conversation with his wife.

That glare and my subsequent aloofness bought me time, months actually. Once again the deacon became a paragon of propriety when he came to call, which was frequent, for Mother's health wasn't good and he made it a practice to check on her almost daily. In time I relaxed my guard, laughing with Tamsin and Mother when he made a joke, convincing myself the deacon had learned his lesson and would not try his sly advances with me again. In this I erred.

The day it happened is still vivid in my mind. I had spent the afternoon with my friend Pru Steadman, the two of us giggling about boys and at the antics of her baby sister. My heart was light as I made my way home. I remember the song I hummed, the softness of the evening air, the smell of lilacs. Having stayed longer than planned, I entered the cottage with an apology on my lips. The spicy smell of brown Betty told me Tamsin had spent the afternoon baking. I hung my cloak on a peg by the back door and turned, expecting to see Mother and Tamsin lingering over supper. Instead, I found Amos Mickelson sitting at the kitchen table, his bulky legs stretching the fabric of his trousers, his arms folded across his barrel chest.

"Oh," I gasped, surprise making my voice breathless. "Where are Mother and Tamsin?"

"Gone to Wednesday prayer meeting with my wife and the servants."

"Why aren't you . . .?" I began.

"I told them I had other business to attend to." The deacon smiled and patted his leg while his eyes traveled over me in a hungry manner. "Come sit on my knee like you used to and I'll explain."

I tried to quell my nervousness with a smile. "I'm not a little girl anymore, Deacon Mickelson. Nor do I think it proper for you to be here when my mother and sister aren't present." As I spoke, I reached for the door and jerked it opened.

"Close the door," Amos commanded.

Heart pounding, my mind searched for escape. Could I outrun the bulky man? If only we lived closer to neighbors. If only . . .

The deacon's fist hit the table. "Close the door!" he shouted. He seemed to have read my thoughts, for before I could act, Amos was on his feet, the chair toppled, and the door slammed shut.

"There," he said. His features had lost their genial expression, his heavy jowls and face tightening, his blue eyes narrowing. "Lest you think to play any more tricks, let me inform you there's no one close enough to hear you if you scream." He paused and took a deep, satisfied breath. "I've planned this for days . . . though it took some talking to convince your mother that this evening's prayer meeting was the very thing to make her feel better."

Amos had hold of my arm, his fingers pressing into the tender flesh. "I don't want to hurt you," he went on, his voice softening. "Indeed, I hope this can be pleasurable for us both."

"*This?*" I demanded, striving to make my voice cold and steady. "Just what do you mean by *this*?"

"I think you know," Amos chuckled. "I've seen the way you look at the young men . . . how you smile and flirt. I want no more than what you've probably given to them. Only your company and a sweet kiss or two."

I won't attempt to describe what happened next, the fumbling and attempts to kiss me as he pulled me onto his knee. Instead of fighting off his advances, I sat stiff as a tree with my eyes closed, hoping that just as my glare had stopped his hungry looks before, so would my coldness stop him now. After several unsuccessful attempts to loosen my tight-pressed lips and force my stiff frame to curve against his neck and chest, he swore and pushed me off his lap. Rising to his feet, he glared down at me, his face tight and angry.

"Let me tell you, Miss High and Mighty—"

"Just what are you going to tell me?" Though I pretended bravado, my legs were shaking so hard I feared they'd collapse. *Please, help me . . . oh, please,* I prayed, for to faint or give way to tears would undo any advantage I held over the deacon.

"If you don't do just as I say, I'll stand up in church and denounce both you and your mother as harlots."

"That's a lie!" I cried. "No one will believe you."

"Ah, but they will." Amos waited, the satisfied smirk on his face telling me this had been long planned. "More than one of my friends has joked about the little house I keep right under my wife's nose . . . of my three doxies."

"You . . ." My control vanished and I flew at him, anger overriding fear, blind rage stilling good sense. For an instant my fingers found his face and raked the fleshy skin. Then he pinned me tight against him, his arms pressing so hard I feared he'd break my ribs. I couldn't breathe . . . couldn't think.

Just when I thought I would faint, the deacon's hold on me relaxed slightly. With my arms still pinned to my sides, he forced up my face, his fingers bruising and harsh like his voice when he spoke, "Do exactly as I say."

I closed my eyes and let his greedy mouth cover mine, but when his pudgy fingers began to work at the fastening of my bodice, I tried to twist away. *Please . . . oh, please.*

The barking of a dog broke through the wall of my fear. Amos stiffened and his head jerked up when a male voice called from the direction of his house. "Ho, there, Amos. Where are you?"

There was a moment of startled silence, the heavy pounding of the deacon's heart the only movement until his eyes flitted toward the door. "Meet me at the apple cellar on Friday afternoon. If you don't do exactly as I say, or if you breathe one word of what happened today, I swear I'll talk to the reverend and the two of us will denounce both you and your mother as harlots. Tamsin too."

Amos paused, his breathing ragged as if he'd been running, the scratch on the side of his face oozing blood. My breathing was as ragged as his, my starved lungs acting with a mind of their own. As he forced me to look into his narrowed eyes, I thought only of how much I loathed the man. *Pig eyes,* I thought. And he, like a huge boar who'd gone mad, could wipe out my life as I'd known it—Mother's and Tamsin's too. Unless I did as he said.

"Do you hear me, Clarissa? Do you understand?"

All of the fight had gone out of me. Even so, I had to force the words through my lips. "Yes," I whispered.

"Let me hear you say it again. This time louder."

"Yes."

"Good."Amos released me so suddenly I almost fell. I grabbed onto the table, only dimly aware he had gone to the door, wiping his bleeding face with the palm of his hand.

"I'll make you pay for this," he snarled. Then he closed the door and left.

* * *